A U.S. CHAMPION
AND A BEAUTIFUL RUSSIAN WOMAN
FLEEING THROUGH AN ALIEN CITY
INTO A HOSTILE WORLD....

They met in Helsinki during the Olympic trials. For one week, they shared a tiny room under the eaves of a small hotel. Then they said good-bye—forever.

It seemed a miracle to Elena when Chad appeared at her door in Moscow. A miracle of love. But not even she could know the real mission that had brought him to Russia . . . a mission that would start a time bomb ticking in Moscow and Washington . . . that would trigger a race more harrowing than any Olympic contest . . . a race that Chad would risk everything—his own life, Elena's love—to win.

THE LAST DECATHLON

JOHN REDGATE

A DELL BOOK

Published by
Dell Publishing Co., Inc.
1 Dag Hammarskjold Plaza
New York, New York 10017

Dell ® TM 681510, Dell Publishing Co., Inc.

ISBN: 0-440-14643-7

Reprinted by arrangement with Delacorte Press.

Printed in the United States of America

First Dell printing—May 1980

The author gratefully acknowledges Dan Paulson and the Ziegler-Diskant Agency, without whose cooperation, help, and support *The Last Decathlon* would not have become a reality.

part 1

1.

Chad Norris stood at the window of his fifth-floor hotel room looking out across the wide lawn, the trees and flower beds, across the multiple expressway lanes, to the cubist complex of Kennedy Airport.

It was not a common day. It was, in fact, totally uncommon, nothing at all like a normal or expected New York July day.

At eight in the morning it had begun to be hot. Heavy and overcast, no air moving in the city, a thick shower-cap of inversion holding the air and stench in place, the industrial smoke and exhaust fumes, all along the north and south avenues and in the truck-clogged cross streets of the city.

Brooklyn was the same. And The Bronx and Staten Island. And the streets and neighborhoods of Jackson Heights and Rego Park. In the apartment warrens and two-family dwellings, all the way out to and past Jamaica, the atmosphere was opaque and sweltering.

Then, near the middle of the day, when even higher temperatures would have been expected, some odd and sudden change took place all along the more than one hundred miles from the East River to Montauk.

No breeze came up. There was no break in the smoggy haze, no vents to show the sky or the sun. But an odd and ominous coolness, like an atomizer spray, seemed to mist up from the steaming streets and highways, damp and chilling, smelling of death and sea water.

In twenty minutes, from eleven fifteen to eleven thirty-five, the temperature dropped thirty degrees. Suddenly it was a gray and dangerous, threatening surprise of a day.

Chad missed it all. In the air-conditioned cocoon of his room, not having left it since he'd checked in at four the previous afternoon, he was cut off and protected from everything outside. When his shades were closed even the light stayed constant.

He had eaten in his room. Dinner the night before and breakfast this morning at eight. No lunch. He knew there would be food on the plane. Plenty of food. Steaks and fresh vegetables and good bread. He planned to eat slowly on the plane, to spend a long time with his food. Eating discouraged conversation. And afterwards he could sleep. Or pretend to sleep. And avoid conversation altogether.

2. At the Pan American section of the airport, the freight section, almost a half-mile from their passenger terminal, a special departure area had been set up in a huge 747 hangar. Check-in desks, a baggage facility, two customs and immigration windows, and just at the open end of the hangar, three security stations, all the rest of that end blocked off by sawhorses and shifting lines of airport police.

There were city police too, stationed on the ground by the four waiting 747's, the planes parked a hundred yards out at the landing ramps, their crews at the top of the portable stairs waiting for the boarding process to begin.

There were police on each airplane, too. The planes had been checked and searched by demolition teams at midnight, and there had been guards on board ever since. They would stay there till the planes were fully loaded and would be replaced, just before takeoff, by Treasury Department agents, Executive Security Division, three men on each plane.

Inside the hangar, however, there was no evidence that this elaborate, hard-eyed security was either noticed or needed. In an atmosphere of laughter and triumph, under a series of bright banners that read OLYMPIAD XXII: MOSCOW, more than eight hundred athletes, all sizes and all colors, mingled with their friends and well-wishers, with the members of the United States Olympic Committee and their wives, with the coaches and trainers, doctors and clerks and dieticians, nurses and equipment managers; they mingled and laughed and ate and drank and bounced from one press interview to the next, from one network camera to another, exhilarated, each of them, with their success in the final qualification trials in Oregon, content for the moment to bask in the brilliance of the occasion.

A band was playing at one end of the hangar, barely heard above the voices, the shouts and laughter. When the music stopped, a voice came through the public address system. "Hate to spoil your fun, folks, but the party's almost over. In thirty minutes all the members of our Olympic contingent must be cleared through security and on board his or her designated plane. And in exactly forty-five minutes we take off for . . . tell me where we're going . . ."

A heavy, ragged shout rolled through the hangar. *"Moscow!"*

3. Chad turned away from the window and stood with his hands at his sides, staring into the room. His bed was still unmade and rumpled from the night before; his pants and shirt and shoes and socks were scattered around the floor where he'd dropped them, his breakfast dishes still sitting by the door on a rolling table, his suitcase open on the luggage stand, clothes spilling out over the sides. And the ashtrays were full from yesterday's midnight meeting, the air still tinged with the odor of a sharp, dark tobacco.

Standing there, barefoot in his shorts, back-lighted through the window, his long hair tangled around his face, his eyes and nose prominent above the full, dark beard, his face seemed to have no expression. But when he raised his arms suddenly, held them straight out in front of him, his hands were trembling. When his muscles tensed and knotted at the shoulders, when he tried to control his hands, they shook more than ever.

Dropping forward on the floor then, he caught himself on his extended arms and began to do lightning push-ups, his lean body held stiff and straight, lifting and dropping, over and over, in control, but moving in a lunatic rhythm, self-destructive, faster and faster, sweat glistening on his back, dripping from his face, his cheeks crimson above the beard, his back mottled red and white, the breath gusting, raw and ugly, in and out of his lungs.

At last he stopped, at the top of a final push-up, held himself there, rigid, for a long ten-count. Then he stood up, pulled off his shorts, and went into the bathroom.

Just before he got into the shower, he looked at himself in the mirror over the sink and said, "Get a grip on yourself. You've got a long way to go. You have to fool a lot of people. So concentrate on what you have to do and stay loose. Play the game. Put on the monkey suit and smile a lot. The better you set things up now, the easier they'll be later on."

He frowned at his reflection in the mirror, seemed to challenge it. Then he turned on the water and stepped into the shower stall.

4. In the Pan Am hangar the party was still vibrating, full heat and full volume, the visitors scrambling to take final advantage of the bar before it closed, the bartenders, a bottle in each hand, pouring straight into the extended glasses now. No jiggers. No measuring.

The passport control and security lines had begun to

move steadily, people straggling through and angling across the tarmac toward the planes, waving back to the crowd behind the sawhorses. And the voice on the public address system gave regular time briefings. "Thirty-five minutes till takeoff. Counting down to thirty-four."

Edmund Yost, trim but pale, an elegant-looking man of fifty-three, University of Virginia perhaps, or Duke, a three-term veteran of the Olympic Committee, ill at ease in his official denim blazer, trying to compensate for its tackiness by wearing a thirty-five-dollar white shirt underneath, pushed his way through the crowd and managed at last to get his hand on the sleeve of Homer Barnett.

"Where's Norris?"

"I don't know," Barnett said.

"I've checked with all the officials here and nobody has seen him."

Barnett was a stocky man, sixty-two years old, his skin brown and tough, a thick sprinkle of freckles on his hands and the dome of his forehead underneath a heavy cap of white hair.

"I haven't seen him either," he said.

"Didn't you two fly in from California together?"

"We were planning to. But Chad decided to come early. He flew in yesterday morning."

"Where did he stay last night?"

"I don't know."

"Damn it, Barnett, he's *your* responsibility."

"No, he's not."

"I mean you coached him."

"That's right. But I'm not his chaperone. He knows what time the plane leaves. He'll be here."

"What if he's not?"

"Then you'll have to leave without him, I guess."

"How can I explain that?"

"Just tell the truth. Just say one of the athletes didn't make the plane."

"Then what?" Yost said.

"Then you can either disqualify him or fly him over later on a scheduled flight."

Yost started to say something, then seemed to think better of it. Looking around the crowded hangar, he said, "Maybe Upshaw knows where he is. Have you seen Upshaw?"

Barnett pointed off to his right. "Last time I saw him he was over there doing his act for Curt Gowdy."

5. In a twenty-third-floor studio in midtown New York, Dick Enberg sat behind a bright-lit anchorman's desk with O. J. Simpson beside him, their eyes on the monitor carrying the live report from the airport, at the moment a tight two-shot of Curt Gowdy and Dilly Upshaw, the sprinter from Memphis State, his skin almost blue-black, five feet seven, a hundred thirty-four pounds, and an ear-to-ear grin.

"He's some wild interview," O. J. said. "You don't even have to ask him questions."

"Everybody always asks me about my name," Upshaw was saying. "The *Dilly* part. I mean people say what kind of a sissy name is that for a laid-back macho citizen like me? And I say . . . this is the Lord's truth, Mr. Gowdy . . .

I say . . . the first time my old man ever laid eyes on me he said, 'Now, you talk about *kids, that* is some kid. That boy is really a *dilly*.' So I started out Dilly and I'm *still* Dilly. And when I unload on those Redski sprinters over there, they are going to have a new word in their dictionary. Remember when Papa Khrushchev said he was going to bury us? Well, *I* am going to bury *them*. I ain't gonna be happy with just three gold doodads, for the hundred, the two hundred, and the eight hundred relay. I'm shootin' for three *world records*. And if I don't get 'em I'll come back here and eat this Olympic jacket right in front of your cameras. And after I eat the jacket . . ."

On the talk-back from the booth, Enberg heard the director say, "I can't believe it. Curt can't get a word in edgewise. Stand by, Dick. We're coming back to you. Camera Two."

Enberg turned to Camera Two, watched the floor manager, waited for a hand signal, and said, "Dick Enberg again at Sports Central, along with O. J. Simpson. We've been showing you the bon voyage party for the United States Olympic team, 1980 edition. In less than half an hour they'll be on their way to Moscow for the twenty-second edition of the modern Olympic games."

"And tomorrow about this time," Simpson said, "we'll be making that same trip. Dick Enberg and Curt Gowdy and I will be joining John Brodie, Bruce Jenner, and a whole gang of specialists and experts who are already there. Starting next week, till August the third, NBC will bring you all the action, all the color, all the Olympic drama from Moscow."

Dick Enberg cut in then. "Sorry, O. J., but we're getting a signal from Curt. So let's go back to John F. Kennedy Airport and join Curt Gowdy."

Gowdy's face dissolved through on the studio monitor. "We've got a surprise here at the Olympic departure scene. I just talked with Edmund Yost, the veteran committee member in charge of logistics and personnel, and he tells me that a key member of this year's team is not here. That's right. *Chad Norris*, the decathlon man, is not at the airport to leave with the team. A little more than twenty minutes till takeoff and this dark-horse athlete, the young man who seemed to pop up from nowhere, who not only won his event in the Olympic trials, but also set a new world's record, is nowhere to be found. Chad Norris is *not here*."

6. Earl Chaffee, executive secretary of the Olympic Planning Committee, hurried down the steps of the 747 to join Edmund Yost. They walked a few steps away from the plane.

"What do you mean, you can't find him?"

"Just that. Nobody's seen him or talked with him since before he left California. I've been on the phone for twenty minutes . . ."

"Nobody knows where he was staying here in New York?"

"No."

"How about Barnett?"

"He talked to him night before last. Hasn't heard from him since."

"Jesus . . . great publicity to start things off. Can we keep this quiet?"

"Too late. The television people wormed it out of somebody," Yost said. "So I had to tell the truth when they came to me."

"How about the hotels near the airport?"

"That's the first thing we thought of. No Chad Norris at any of them."

"Have you notified security yet?"

"I had to. If something's happened to him, we can't . . . you know what I mean."

"Yes, you're right," Chaffee said.

"Shall we delay the takeoff?"

"I don't think so. I think that would be a mistake."

"What if he shows up ten minutes after we leave?"

"I don't know. We'll deal with that when it happens. *If* it happens."

The planes steadily filled up. Dilly and Homer Barnett waited as long as possible to board. When they climbed the steps finally, Dilly said, "Man, I'm sick about this. Chad's no dingdong. He's got a stopwatch on himself all the time. He don't miss *nothing*. You mean to tell me he's gonna fool around and miss this plane to Moscow?"

"He hasn't missed it yet," Barnett said.

"The hell he hasn't. This mother will be airborne in about seven minutes and he's no place in sight. He's *missed* it. No question about it."

"Not yet."

"Are you saying you know something I don't know?"

"What do you mean?"

"I mean everybody else is all tensed up and you're as loose as a noodle. So you must know something."

"I just think he'll show up, that's all."

7. The pilot had just instructed the cabin steward to secure the doors when the copilot said, "Hold the phone. I think we've got another passenger." In the mirror system they could see Chad coming out of the security passage and sprinting toward the plane.

"Is that the missing jock?"

"It must be. They said he looks like a Jesus freak."

The captain pressed his intercom button and said, "New instructions to the cabin crew. Unlock and reopen number two forward entrance door. One more passenger boarding. Secure door for takeoff as soon as he's aboard."

"Man, you are the strangest," Dilly said as Chad sat down beside him, slid his bag under the seat, and snapped his seat belt around his hips.

"Lean and mean," Chad said.

"I thought I was the flake in this group."

"You are," Chad said.

"Not me. You're the primo. You had Yost changing colors like the front of a jukebox."

"It'll do him good. I never saw him any color but white."

As the plane taxied to its place in the takeoff line, a stewardess stopped by Chad and said, "Are you Mr. Norris?"

"That's right."

"Is he Mr. Norris?" Dilly said. "You mean to say you've

never seen that ugly face before. I guess you don't sub-
scribe to *Sports Illustrated,* do you?"

"No," the girl said sweetly, "but I read *Hustler* cover
to cover."

"Zing," Chad said.

"She got me," Dilly said.

"*If* you're Mr. Norris," the girl went on, "Mr. Yost
would like to see you up forward as soon as we're
airborne."

"Yeah. Fine."

After the stewardess moved away, Dilly said, "Papa
spank."

"Screw him. I'm too big to spank."

8. An hour later, the plane at forty thousand feet, the
vision clear, a soft floor of cumulus outside the windows,
the upper sky vast and cerulean, Chad came back down
the aisle toward his seat, spotted Homer Barnett, crossed
the cabin, and sat down in the empty seat beside him.

"The phantom," Barnett said.

"That's me. Hope I didn't shake you up."

"You carved it a little thin, didn't you?"

"Better late than sorry. Is that the way it goes?"

"Something like that. Is that what you told Yost?"

"I didn't tell him much of anything. I just blinked my eyes and kissed his ring."

"What did he say?"

"To tell you the truth I didn't pay too much attention. Guys like him give me an earache."

"No threats?"

"Nothing serious. He dragged Chaffee into the act and the two of them told me how Eleanor Holm was shipped home from the Olympics one time because she was naughty. Took too many hot showers or something. I told him I'd never heard of Eleanor Holm, but Yost couldn't stop talking about her. I'll bet he keeps dirty books in the dresser under his shirts."

"So you're in the clear?"

"I guess so. He kept yapping about the Olympic code. Whatever that is. Said if I couldn't obey it, I'd have to go back home and wash out my mouth with soap or something."

"What did you say to that?"

"I said if he was planning to dump me to do it as quick as possible because there's a Bugs Bunny Festival I've been watching on San Jose channel five and I don't want to miss any more of it than I have to."

"Come on, Chad. Save the snow job for Dilly."

"You're right. I didn't tell Yost that. Matter of fact, I was very respectful and apologetic. Told him from now on I'll brush my hair forty strokes a night and change my shorts twice a day. That seemed to make him happy for a minute or so. Then he took off on my hair and beard. Said he thought I'd promised to show up in Moscow with a washrag haircut and a face as smooth as a baby's behind."

"How'd you handle that?"

"Same as before. I told him I've got a chronic scalp

disease and aggravated eczema on my face. Have to protect my skin, the doctor told me. Me and Samson. Can't
make it without the hair."

"You're going to screw around and he *will* send you
home."

"No, he won't, Homer. I won't let that happen. I
promise you. I'm not making this trip just to turn around
and go back to California. You know me well enough to
know that."

"I thought I did."

"You do. I've been counting on this trip for a long
time."

---

9. When Chad was nineteen years old, when his life
had taken an abrupt downhill turn, when all the things
and people he had relied on seemed suddenly unreliable,
he decided one day to write it all down, to examine it
and find, hopefully, some new kind of dependable bed-
rock, something he could build on.

He bought a spiral-bound school notebook, blue lines
on white paper, and two ball-point pens. Then he began
to list the simple facts.

I was born in Lebanon, Indiana, on May 2, 1953. My
father's name was Harlan. He was born in Yankton,
South Dakota, in 1926 and went to engineering
school at the University of Illinois.

When I was born he was working for Jewett Business Systems in Indianapolis, one of the first companies to design and manufacture sophisticated computers.

My mother's name was Stephanie Houk. She came from Winnetka, Illinois, and she and Dad met in college. Mom was healthy and athletic, but she had some physical flaw that made it difficult for her to become pregnant. She had three miscarriages and one stillborn child before me. I was their first and, as things turned out, their *only* child.

In 1960, when I was seven, we moved to Stamford, Connecticut, where my father went to work for Royse-Sheperd, the country's third biggest computer company.

I had pneumonia that first winter in Stamford, and I almost died. But once I got over that I started to grow and fill out and I've never been really sick since.

I had a good childhood. We lived in a comfortable house in a nice neighborhood, there were no money worries, my parents liked each other, and they liked me a lot. We had great times together.

I was a good enough student and a pretty good athlete and I had friends at school. No unpleasant surprises in my life. No drastic changes to adjust to.

So when the big jolt came in 1971, when I was seventeen, in my last year at high school, I couldn't handle it. I couldn't deal with it at all. My mother couldn't either. We fell apart, each of us, in our own way.

He read over what he had written. Then he tried to go on with it. But he couldn't. It was five years later, six perhaps, before he was able to write down the rest of what was building and seething inside him. By then he had solved the problem, all except the biggest and most difficult part.

10.

When Chad came back to his seat, Dilly said, "What did Yost lay on you?"

"Mostly he wanted me to keep an eye on you. He's heard some of those stories that came floating up from Memphis."

"Come on. Cut the crap. Did he give you the treatment?"

"He tried to but I outmaneuvered him."

"How?"

"I killed him with love and humility. I was so humble he didn't have the heart to scold me."

"Humble? You're as humble as *I* am."

"I'm less humble than you are," Chad said. "You are totally humble."

"Where were you?" Dilly said then.

"When?"

"You know when. When they were combing the airport looking for you. Where'd you stay last night?"

"In a hotel. Across the road from the airport."

"Come on. Barnett said that's the first thing they did. Check the airport hotels."

"If they did they asked for the wrong man."

"What does that mean?"

"It means they didn't ask about Lamont Cranston or Jim Thorpe or Henry Longfellow."

"You used a phony name, is that it?"

"Something like that."

"What's the point?" Dilly said.

"You want the truth?"

"If you're capable of it."

"I just wanted to hang out by myself for a few hours. Eat and sleep and look out the window. I also wanted to miss that asshole party with all the cameras and reporters and people spilling drinks on my shoes."

"You're kidding."

"No, I'm not," Chad said.

"You're crazy. You know that? You really blew it. While you were staring out the window and scratching your whiskers, I was being flashed into a few million Amurrican homes, stamping my full-color face and credentials indelibly on the Amurrican consciousness. That's the name of the game, booby. Blow your own horn. Fame is money. When I come back with all those gold medals, perfect strangers will be waiting for me with open bank vaults. Tell 'em you're good and they'll *think* you're good. I mean who knows what the truth is till somebody spreads it around."

"You're spreading *something* around," Chad said. "No question about *that*."

"You don't think my name's Dilly, do you? Nobody ever called me that till I made it up. My name's Raymond. Isn't that a pisser? Raymond Upshaw. Sounds like a biology teacher. But *Dilly* Upshaw, the world's fastest man, that's another thing altogether. Packaging, man. *Display*. Freshen up the label. You'll see. I'm gonna march out of Moscow with all the marbles, all the rubles, all the *gold*. Zap! And you'll be sitting in a corner sucking your thumb and wondering why nobody recognizes you."

"No, I won't. That's the way I like it."

"I give up," Dilly said. "You're a sad specimen from another century. You know that? What you've really got is the mind of an assassin. Hiding behind all that hair. Checking into hotels with made-up names. Someday I'll stroll into the post office and they'll have your picture stuck up on the bulletin board. Chad Norris. Wanted for rape, murder, and arson. Wanted for stealing the crown jewels from the Kremlin."

"Now you've got it," Chad said. "Now you're getting warm."

"You can't snow me. You had some foxy lady staked out in that hotel. One big orgy before the trip. Right?"

"Not me, Dilly. I'm in training. No fooling around."

"My ass. I've seen you come on. Full speed ahead. You went through Helsinki last spring like a snowplow. If you didn't have a little visitor last night I'll push a peanut across Red Square with my nose."

"You win," Chad said. "Matter of fact I did have a little visitor. Two of them."

"I knew it."

"A nice old man and his wife, who live on the Lower East Side in New York. He's about sixty-five years old, and she must be a year or so younger."

"Okay," Dilly said. "Turn off the current. I fold."

"It's the truth, Dilly. Guaranteed straight poop."

"Stop it, will you? You're making me nervous." Dilly tilted his seat back and closed his eyes. "I can *dream* better stories than I get from you."

11. Dilly woke up long enough to eat dinner. Then he went to sleep again. When the movie started, he tried to watch it but he only lasted for twenty minutes. "I'm a serious sleeper," he said. "Did you ever notice that? Man, can I sleep!"

Chad tilted back in his chair, without earphones, watching the silent, graceful shadows slide back and forth across the screen. Finally he fell asleep too.

When he woke up the film was over. The cabin, except for half a dozen firefly reading lights, was totally dark, everyone asleep. The stewardesses were sitting down too. No sound or movement in the cabin.

Since April, in the fuzzy soft moments just before he went to sleep, or in the morning when he was barely awake, Chad had thought constantly of Elena, tried to imagine her face and her body and the sound of her voice, tried to bring her into clear focus, to recreate every word and sound and touch of the last time they had been together, in a tiny top-floor room under the eaves of a hotel, ancient timber and stucco, on a side street in Helsinki.

"We have to get up," he said. "You'll miss your plane."

"I know. But I feel so warm and slow. I want to push back the time as much as I can."

"Don't go at all. We'll defect. Both of us. We'll defect and sleep on a blanket behind somebody's kitchen stove."

"Don't tease me," she said. "What is that other word?"

"*Temptation.*"

"That's it. Don't tempt me. Don't be a temptation." She turned on her side, put her arm around him, and nuzzled her face in his beard. "What are you like when you don't have a beard?"

"I thought you liked it."

"I do. But I was trying to think how you would look without it."

"Naked."

"With short hair and no beard you must look like a little boy."

"A young boy. Not a *little* boy," he said.

"Of course not. Not little at all. But very young like a child in school. Am I right?"

"No. I don't look that young."

"Would I like you with a naked face?" she said. "Would I recognize you in the streets with your face all bare and open with smooth cheeks? I'm serious. Would you look so different to me?"

"I guess I would. I look different to myself."

"How long have you had it then, this beard and the long hair of a poet?"

"Three or four years. I stopped shaving one February. On Lincoln's Birthday. I decided I wanted to look like Lincoln."

"You failed."

"I guess so."

"You look nothing like Lincoln. You look like a terrorist. A man from Milan with a bomb tied to his belt."

"No, I don't."

"That's true," she said. "You don't. There's nothing

cruel about you. You don't look dangerous. What you really look like is a dog of mixed breed who's lived in the streets for a long time. Looking for a good meal and a warm place to sleep."

"I'd rather look like a terrorist," he said.

"Of course. But you have no choice."

She got up and dressed then. He lay in bed, his head propped up on two pillows, and watched her. When she was finally dressed and ready to leave, she sat down on the edge of the bed.

"In America," she said, "what do people say to each other in a situation like this?"

"I don't know. What kind of a situation is it?"

"Classic. De Maupassant. Turgenev. Two young people, strangers in a strange country, meet and fall in love for a little while. They pretend they don't have to go back to wherever they came from. Then suddenly, they *do* have to go back. So they love each other one last time and make a lot of promises they don't believe."

"How about us? Any promises?"

"Never," she said. "We are too clever for that."

"Are we?"

"I think so. We are too intelligent to expect more than we can have." There were tears in her eyes suddenly. "We don't ask each other for things we can't give."

"Maybe you don't," he said. "But *I* do. I don't like the word *impossible*. I don't think *anything's* impossible."

She kissed him, then held his cheek against hers for a long time. Finally she said, "I don't like that word either. Let's promise whatever we feel like. Let's say that I will meet you in . . . some crazy place . . . where shall we meet?"

"Louisville, Kentucky. That's a good place."

"Good. I'll meet you there. In two weeks. Right?"

He nodded. "Two weeks from today."

"And you must keep your beard so I'll know you."

"No question about it. I'll have a beard."

12. A young Ukrainian named Nikolai Kornev, a poet and storyteller, fantasy tales for children, managed in January of 1979 to slip away through Czechoslovakia to Austria, from there to Switzerland, and on to Chicago, where he joined a colony of expatriate Czechs and Poles and began to study English, preparing himself for some future time when he would be able, hopefully, to write down in this new language the folk legends, fantasies, and frustrations he had carried with him from Odessa.

When he was interviewed by a Chicago journalist in May of that year, he said, "I love it to be in this country. I have friends here so soon, new friends who are kind to me, and I am safe. After some time passes I believe I will be able to work, to do my own work, to have a warm place to live and some wine and even some luxury perhaps. I am fond of luxury. Is that a bad thing to say? To me luxury is to not know today what I may decide to do tomorrow. Or where I might decide to go.

"Do I explain myself? I want you to see and print in your journal that I am well here. I have good things in my thoughts and better things tomorrow. But if you ask me do I have a *life,* I do *not.* I have *no* life. It is not a judgment of this place or this country. It is not possible that I could have a life outside of Russia.

"Can you understand this? I miss those people. I need to see those poor meager meals on tiny tables in small rooms. With beds and a stove and chairs all around. I need the warm open touching and contact, mouths and kissing and arms around me and chests laid open with the hearts exposed.

"God pity the Russian people. They have nothing but the most important thing. No decent food, tiny and crowded corners to live in, clothes that are fit only to make a dog bed, fear of tomorrow, total unease and old guilt and insecurity. They are suspicious and mistrustful, angry and rude and without manners. Disastrous.

"That is the word. The Russians are, in almost every way, a disaster. They are surrounded by disaster. They breathe it and live with it. But like all disaster victims they have found ways to survive, tiny homemade skills that can't be taken away from them. Secrets. Private things that can be made in the dark without raw materials, hidden away and fed upon. Things like language and dreams, poetry, fantasy, music, vodka, and love and more dreams.

"The dream is everything to us. That's what it is to be Russian. Work is a waste of life. No Russian will work unless he is forced to. *Unless,* unless he is presented with a task that can't be done, some great challenge, something romantic and unattainable. The Russian leaders know this. They are clever to lead the people into great projects. Next year you will see what I mean. The Olympics was presented as a people's project, something vast and exciting, a total commitment backed with millions of rubles. The people were seduced by an idea, the transformation of Moscow. Great hotels and arenas and stadiums and parks and pools are appearing like modern visions where there was nothing but gray ugliness before. The Moscow that visitors see in 1980 will be a Moscow that no one has ever seen or imagined before."

Chad Norris had never heard of Nikolai Kornev. He had never read the interview that appeared in the *Chicago Tribune* or the excerpt later printed in *Newsweek*. But as he rode through Moscow from Sheremetyevo Airport, along wide clean boulevards, great islands of trees and grass and flowers everywhere, immense glittering buildings, heroic sculpture, and flags of all nations fluttering in endless lines, he saw the results of what Kornev had described. And behind what he saw he sensed an ugly cruelty that Kornev hadn't mentioned at all.

---

13. "Look at all that flash and trash," Dilly said as their bus rolled down Leningradsky Prospekt toward Gorky Ulitsa. "They're not fooling me, these mothergrabbers. This is like going to Disneyland and thinking you discovered America. Ever since I found out I was coming here, I've been reading up on this place. And what I found out is enough to scare the pee right out of you. I mean it. It's a con job. It's all a fraud. The Kremlin lies to the people and the people lie to each other.

"I got this buddy at Memphis State who comes from Nairobi. He was all shot in the ass with the glory of communism till he got here to Moscow. When he starts laying out the facts it makes your gut turn over. First thing he found out is everybody here is crazy about us black folks. But only if we stay in Africa. The government likes to have some of the brothers around all the time, going to school and strolling through the streets and getting their pictures taken. But the regular people don't buy it. They want nothing to do with you if you're black. I mean they don't even pretend. This friend of mine went to a café with a Russian girl for a glass of tea or something, and the next day three big Soviet jocks kicked the shit out of him. They spout off about brotherhood and all that crap, but you find out it's just like everyplace else. We're all equal but some of us are more equal than others.

"They got maybe three hundred million people here. Right? Well, maybe five million of them live pretty good and the rest of them just scrape by. But the real top dogs live like fucking kings. The best of everything. Palaces, servants, limousines, airplanes . . . you name it.

"You think they're eating caviar? Forget it. Two thirds of what the regular people eat is bread and potatoes. And the other third is booze. Vodka, baby. Happy on your back. How does that grab you?"

"Okay," Chad said. "You're an expert on Russia. Thanks for the lecture."

"It's not a lecture. It's an act of kindness. Because I know you're ignorant. A typical athlete. A prototype. Beer and pussy and who stole my jockstrap?"

"Don't start with me, you ignoramus. When was Trotsky born?"

"Who cares?"

"November 7, 1879. What year was the USSR formed?"

"1918."

"Wrong. 1922. When did Lenin die?"

"How the hell do I know?"

"1924. You want to keep going?"

Dilly leaned his head against the seatback and yawned. "There's a certain kind of mind that can't do anything but memorize facts and figures. I'm a conceptual thinker, man. You're a honkie computer."

14. When their bus turned through the security gate, up the curving driveway, and stopped in front of the glass and concrete rambling structures of the Olympic Village, Dilly said, "Man, will you look at that gaggle of newsmen. How you planning to disappear this time?"

"I'm not," Chad said.

"I don't believe it. I've never seen you sit still for an interview yet. Two questions and you're gone."

"Well, I've been holding back. Watching you and trying to learn something. Now I think I'm ready."

"You mean it?"

"Sure I mean it. You're right. It's important for people to see what we look like. Spread the old face around the newspapers. I mean from now on when people hear the name *Chad Norris,* I want them to say, 'Sure. I know him. He's that weird-looking guy with long hair and a beard.'"

At the end of the cordoned-off walkway where the reporters and photographers and television people were clustered, Chad let himself be steered to one side by a tall, deep-chested Englishman. "James Foxworthy," he said. "BBC. Would you be willing to give us a few moments?"

"Glad to," Chad said.

As Foxworthy checked his tape machine and positioned his cameraman, still cameras clicked and flashed around Chad. Carefully following whatever instructions were thrown at him, Chad smiled, waved his hand, looked serious, and looked worried.

Foxworthy shouldered in next to him then, held up his cloth-covered microphone, and said, "This is James Foxworthy at the Olympic Village in Moscow. The American contingent is just arriving and we're here with Chad Norris, their best hope for the decathlon event. You're something of a mystery figure, Mr. Norris. Is there a reason for that?"

"Not that I know of."

"They say you have avoided newsmen in America."

"I guess we just missed connections. Anyway I'm not avoiding you, am I?"

"No. Of course you're not," Foxworthy said. "How does it happen, Mr. Norris, that until the springtime competition in Finland last April, you were practically unknown as a world-class athlete?"

"I wasn't too well known in California either."

"And even in Finland, just four months ago, you were able to finish no higher than eleventh place in your event. How many points exactly did you score in Helsinki?"

"I don't remember."

"As I recall it was something like seven thousand. Not a remarkable showing."

"No, I guess not."

"But then, a little more than two weeks ago, at the Olympic trials, you scored eight thousand six hundred twenty-two points and broke Bruce Jenner's world record."

"Wasn't that something?"

"Yes, it most certainly was. But the question in everyone's mind is this: Was it a flash in the pan? Will Norris give the Soviet man Klemenko a hard contest, or will he fall back to the performance level he showed at Helsinki? How do you answer that?"

"I *can't* answer it. I don't know."

"But you are confident?"

"Oh, sure."

"You are convinced that you'll win the gold medal?"

"I don't see why not. I mean I came all the way over here. It's dumb to make that long trip if I'm not going to win." He turned his face full into the camera and scowled.

At his shoulder, a pale-haired young lady said, "I'm Valerie Poole from the *International Herald Tribune*. Can you tell us something about your childhood and early life?"

"Sure," Chad said. "What do you want to know?"

15. The Olympic Village was a multileveled architectural marvel, landscaped, sprawling, and intricate, with housing for more than twelve thousand athletes from more than one hundred and twenty-five countries, plus recreation rooms, dining rooms, a library with books and magazines in all languages, coffee shops, cafés, exercise areas, television rooms, motion picture theatres, an international telephone center, currency exchange counters, Laundromats, barber and beauty shops, dry cleaners, travel information desks, boutiques, soda fountains, milk bars, and pizza parlors. Also a small but elaborate hospital, a dental clinic, bowling alleys, volleyball courts, a grocery store with foods from around the world, and a lavish sporting-goods shop. And on the perimeter of the walled and closely-guarded complex, just inside the ten-foot walls, were six soft drink nightclubs, each with an orchestra and a floor show.

In the first days the newly-arrived athletes, both sexes, all colors, wandered back and forth in the huge compound, chattering and giggling like high school sophomores on a civics tour of Washington, D.C., staying in groups, ill at ease, many of them outside their own countries for the first time. They seemed uncomfortable in their new clothes, restless, impatient for the moment when they could slip into their competition togs and perform the specialized muscular feats they were trained for.

Chad, on his arrival morning, after almost forty minutes with the press, went to his room and quickly unpacked his bag. Picking up a map of the Village complex from his bedside table, he was heading out again as Dilly came in.

"You weren't kidding, were you?"

Chad stopped in the doorway. "What do you mean?"

"I mean Yost must have put the fear of God into you. You were lollygagging those press guys like a barnyard senator."

"Yost had nothing to do with it. Like I told you, you've been hogging the cameras long enough. I decided to give you a run for your money."

"You gave me a run, all right. You *buried* me." Dilly set his bag down and looked the room over. "Not bad. I'll bet the plaster's still wet, but all in all, for a second-rate country, it's not bad. Where you going?"

"I need some toothpaste. I'll be right back."

Walking along the main promenade of the Village, checking the map as he went, Chad came finally to the building he was looking for, a glass-walled one-story structure with a modified pagoda roof, its identification sign set in blue tiles in the entrance sidewalk: INTER-NATIONAL TELEPHONE CENTER.

Chad went inside to the area's center, gleaming glass-and-chrome phone booths all around the wall, each with an electric sign above it indicating what language its operator would speak. Walking to one of the English-speaking booths, Chad read the sign saying local calls were free, courtesy of the Soviet people.

When he picked up the receiver and the operator came on, speaking clipped Cambridge English, Chad, studying a slip of paper he'd taken from his pocket, said, "I'm calling two-nine-eight–three-nine-oh-four."

"That's a local Moscow number?"

"Yes, it is."

He listened to the clicks and echoes as the operator dialed. There was the sound of sophisticated circuits struggling and switching, a soft silence; then the connection was made and the number began ringing.

Long after he knew there would be no answer, he kept waiting. At last the operator came on again. "No answer, sir. No one at home, I'm afraid."

"I guess not. Thank you." He hung up, stood looking at the telephone for a long moment, then turned away and walked out of the building. He found a drugstore and bought a package of cough drops and a tube of toothpaste. Then he walked farther along the promenade till he came to the exchange bank.

Inside, at the English-speaking teller's window, he took four folded traveler's checks out of his wallet, signed them, and slid them under the grate to the teller, a sallow young man who compared the signatures and said, "You want to change this into rubles?"

"Yes."

"It's a great deal of money . . ."

"That's right. Two thousand dollars."

"If you've read the indoctrination brochure, you'll see that there is not so much to buy here unless you use foreign currency . . ."

"I know that," Chad said. "I don't expect to buy anything. This is bribery money. I need it to bribe the officials. You know . . . they shave a second or two off my running times, give me a few extra inches on the long jumps. That kind of thing. Everybody does it."

The teller, a stunned look on his face, counted out a packet of rubles on the marble counter. Chad picked them up, folded them deliberately, and slid them into his pants pocket.

When he left the bank, he turned left on the promenade and walked back to the telephone center. This time he chose a different booth and a different operator. He asked for the same number as before. Again, there was no answer.

16. For the next five days Chad worked out with lunatic energy. Up at five every morning, he ran seven miles back and forth along the Moskva River. Back at the dormitory, after rubbing his legs with alcohol and taking a shower, he lay down on his bed for fifteen minutes with his eyes closed, not sleeping but isolating each of his muscle areas, one at a time, from his feet to his shoulders, relaxing each one till he was just at the edge of sleep, warm and fluid and loose.

He got up then, put on his track shorts and a sweat suit, hung his tied-together spikes around his neck, and went to breakfast in his sock feet.

After breakfast he read the morning papers for an hour. Then he walked an easy mile to the practice stadium in the Luzhniki Sports Park. He warmed up slowly with stretch exercises and calisthenics, jogged two miles, ran a fast quarter-mile and some short full-speed sprints.

Warm and loose then, just short of a full sweat, he went through each of the decathlon events. He did the full program every day. First the hundred meters, then the one-hundred-ten-meter high hurdles. Then he spent half an hour or forty minutes in the long-jump pit, the same for the high jump, and ended the morning with the four-hundred-meter run on the watch.

After lunch, a half-hour nap, and a slow, thorough

warm-up again, he did all the field events, the shot put, the discus, the javelin, and ten tries at the pole vault, starting at thirteen feet and edging higher till he missed three times. Last of all, he ran the fifteen-hundred-meter.

Homer Barnett was with him all the time he worked out, a Polaroid camera around his neck, a stopwatch in his hand, watching, analyzing, low-key and quiet, and jogging back to the Village with Chad at the end of the day.

"You're coming good. Just right. Just stay loose and don't push. You're ten days away from your first competition. Let's not leave it out here on the practice field. And remember, you'll win it with your smarts as much as your legs. When the chips are down, it's what's in your head that counts."

Except for these long training sessions and the technical coaching talk that went with them, Chad stayed away from Barnett. He was prepared to do what had to be done, to have no second thoughts about anything or anybody, and that included Barnett. It had to. But Chad couldn't feel good about it. So he worked himself like a machine, avoided Barnett as much as he could, and kept his mind on other things.

He continued to submit to interviews. He welcomed, in a way, the distraction. He was questioned daily, probed, challenged, photographed, dissected, and recorded. He answered all the inane questions that were thrown at him. And sometimes he told the truth. But when they asked about his childhood or where he had been those years before he showed up at San Jose City College in 1976, when the reporters nudged and niggled into those areas, he felt free to tell them whatever fanciful story came into his head.

17. ▪ Edmund Yost did not laugh well or easily. He had no skill for it. He laughed, in fact, very seldom. But now, sitting at his desk in the administration building at the Olympic Village, making an odd, painful sound like stifled hiccups or a death rattle in the throat, he was laughing.

"It's the damnedest cock-and-bull story I've ever seen in print. I've read it three times and I still can't believe it. How were those people taken in? Did you see it?"

"No, I didn't," Barnett said. He was sitting in a chair beside Yost's desk.

"Page four." Yost handed over a folded copy of the *International Herald Tribune.* "My secretary circled it in red."

Barnett turned to the article. Centered at the top of the page was a scowling picture of Chad, two columns wide, his face barely visible through the beard and hair. The headline said, OLYMPIC ATHLETE RAISED BY GORILLAS. Barnett adjusted his glasses, pushed them higher on his nose, and read the article.

> Chad Norris, one of the United States athletes here in Moscow for the Olympic games, is the current world record-holder for the decathlon and is one of the favorites to win the event. He is also a young

man who has had a fascinating life. He spent his childhood in the jungles of Zaire in Central Africa.

"My parents were travel writers and photographers. They flew their own plane all over the world. And they always took my sister Lucy and me along with them. Lucy was five years older than me."

By the time he was two years old, Norris had been all over Central and South America, in Mongolia and Tibet, and in all the states of his own country.

"Just before I was three, my folks got an assignment to do a wildlife feature in Central Africa. So away we went, all four of us. We were in Kenya and Tanzania and Uganda having a big time. Lucy and I got a kick out of seeing all those animals.

"Then we flew from Uganda heading for Kinshasa in Zaire. But we ran into an electrical storm, lightning hit our plane, and we went down.

"I was strapped in a small bed in the back of the cabin. I guess that's what saved me. But I did get a bad bump on the head that knocked me unconscious. I found out later that the plane had burned up, so I guess I was thrown clear. Anyway, when I woke up, I was lying in a little clearing outside of a cave, still strapped in my portable bed. And a whole family of gorillas were squatted around looking at me. I started crying and an old female came over and picked me up out of the basket. She held me in her arms and started feeding me grapes and another kind of fruit that tasted like sweet mangoes."

Mr. Norris told us that he stayed with the gorillas till he was eleven years old and that they fed him and protected him as if he were a member of the family.

"I guess I would have been there yet if they hadn't decided to mate me up with one of the females of the family. She was nice enough, I guess, and pretty for a gorilla, but she was only three years old and she wasn't my type. And in case you don't know it, there are no divorces in gorilla families. I mean when you're hooked, you're hooked."

So Mr. Norris slipped out of the cave one night and ran away. He made it to a river town called Kisangani. He met some Baptist missionaries there. "And they helped me to get out of Africa and back to the United States."

"Isn't that something" Yost said when Barnett looked up from the newspaper.

"Doesn't sound much like Chad."

"Neither does this. I ran into him here in the Village a day or so ago and he spent five minutes apologizing to me. Told me how sorry he was that he was late getting to the plane in New York."

"Nothing wrong with that I guess."

"Not if he meant it," Yost said. "But he didn't mean it. Not at all. He was playing some kind of game with me. I could see it in his face. Chad Norris is a strange duck."

18. John Brodie and Bruce Jenner, each of them sun-tanned and wearing his NBC blazer, strolled slowly across the infield of Lenin Stadium, a network camera and sound crew crab-walking just ahead of them.

"As you can see," Brodie said, talking into the camera, "it's a perfect day here in Moscow. And that's the way it's been since we arrived last week. Clear and warm and dry. Just right for all these Olympic athletes to get themselves settled down, loosened up, and ready to compete. Right, Bruce Jenner?"

"Right you are, John. The world is watching, we're here, and on Saturday, July nineteenth, at three in the afternoon, Moscow time, the opening-day ceremonies will take place."

"Followed by fourteen straight days of nonstop competition," Brodie said. "Everything from archery to water polo. And you'll see it all, through our NBC cameras, wherever you're watching from. Bruce, you're an old hand at this action. How do these games look to you? What can we look forward to?"

"So far it's too good to be true, John. Perfect weather, as you said. All the political problems seem to have been worked out, and we have a really outstanding field of competitors."

"And how about these facilities here in Moscow?"

"Dynamite. The best I've ever seen."

"What's going on behind the scenes, Bruce? Which countries would you guess will make the best showing overall?"

"It's hard to say. So many stand-out performers. But teamwise, East Germany looks tough again. Poland also has a fine team. Russia is strong in spots, weak in others, and the United States, especially in track and field and swimming, could make the best showing they've made in years."

"What about your old event? What about the decathlon? What can we look for there?"

"That's a tough one. Six weeks ago I would have called it for you one-two-three. Klemenko of the Soviet

Union was everybody's favorite. With second and third a struggle between Mittag of East Germany and the Cuban, Valderrama."

"Then came Chad Norris with a new world record in the trials at Oregon."

"That's right. The wild man from Cal State San Jose."

"It's hard to miss him," Brodie said. "With all that hair and the bushy beard, he looks like a guy who was just arrested for vagrancy."

"There seems to be at least one eccentric at every Olympics. This time Norris is the one. He prowls the grounds half the night, the guards say. They find him outside doing push-ups at three in the morning. And one morning he ran twenty laps around Red Square."

"And at the same time his coach, Homer Barnett, says he's the hardest working athlete he's ever coached."

"He never lets up, John. That's what has attracted the most attention here these first few days. If hard work can bring in a gold medal, Norris should be a cinch. He drives himself harder, runs farther, practices longer, than anybody here."

"So as of now it looks as though the man to watch in the decathlon is Chad Norris."

"No question about it."

19.

Chad Norris was christened in the Presbyterian church on a street bordered with elm trees in Lebanon, Indiana, but his parents had no church-going habits. He was never sent to Sunday school. He received no formal religious training at all. He was scarcely a Christian, he felt. But neither was he an atheist or an agnostic. Religion was simply foreign to him, another country, truly outside his life pattern.

Nonetheless, on a cool late afternoon three days before the games were scheduled to begin, the first gray and ominous-looking day since he'd arrived in Moscow, he sat in a dark pew in an empty alcove of St. Basil's Cathedral seeking, not heavenly guidance, but isolation, trying to stay calm, trying to sift through his alternatives and reconstruct a plan of action that was steadily coming apart.

He had planned carefully. But some of his assumptions had been incorrect. He saw that now. Most important, he had counted on the fact that when he called Elena he would reach her. Although they had exchanged telephone numbers almost as a joke that last afternoon in Helsinki, knowing, each of them, that the other one would not call, *could* not call, it had never occurred to him that the number might be incorrect, that it might be changed or out of order, or that she simply might not be at home when he called.

As cynical and realistic as he had been in making all his preparations, he had never allowed himself to suspect that Elena might be the flawed link, that everything could founder before it started because of her.

He knew the type of telephone directory he was familiar with in America was not available in Moscow. There was no simple alphabetical listing of subscribers, the telephone number clearly beside the name, the home address just under that. Still, if he had allowed himself to think that when he called she might not answer, he would surely have planned differently, would have found some other way to contact her.

Since his arrival in Moscow he had continued to call her at all hours. Each time, after listening to the endless ringing, he hung up and called the operator. Over and over he tried to locate some sympathetic bilingual supervisor who would respond to whatever wild story he had chosen to tell and give him, contrary to all the regulations, the home address of Elena Baklanova, telephone number 298–3904. No one, as it turned out, responded. From countless different voices, male and female, he heard only, "Nyet."

Earlier that afternoon, he had called the central Intourist office, using the ugliest American tourist accent and attitude he could manage. He asked for a supervisor who "knows how to talk some English."

When a woman's voice came on, cool and precise, he told her he had been on a tour of the Kremlin that morning, that he had lost his Minolta automatic camera, which was worth a lot of money, and that somebody at his hotel had said the lady who had been the guide on his tour would be able to tell him if it had been found or turned in.

"Her name was Elena Baklanova," he said, pronouncing it as crudely as he could and still be understood. "My wife copied it down. She writes down everything."

"If you tell me your hotel, we will check with Miss Baklanova and call you back."

"No good. I don't have time for that. We're flying out of here to Copenhagen in three or four hours' time. I want to look her up myself. I got no time for horsing around."

"What is your name, please? *And* your hotel."

"I told you before. I don't have enough time to . . ."

"There is no possibility that we can give you the home address of any Intourist employee."

"In that case I'd like *your* name," Chad said. "And the name of your superior . . ." The line went dead.

Leaving the telephone kiosk, trying to stay calm, he had taken a city bus to Manezhnaya Square just to the north of Red Square. He found the central Intourist building and went inside.

The ground-floor public information area was crowded, long lines at all the counters. Walking around the area, trying to be inconspicuous, he stopped in front of an elaborate schedule board, all the city tours listed on it, the itineraries, the cost in rubles, time of departure and return. There was no listing of tour guide names.

He got into a long line then at a desk marked INFORMATION: ENGLISH. With no clear idea of what question he would ask, he considered the lost camera routine. Perhaps by being there in person he could bull it through. But even if he succeeded there was an obvious danger. A connection could have been made in someone's mind. Elena's name and his face.

When his turn came at the counter, a soft fat girl

standing there, her cheeks bright pink, her hair tawny and frizzy, he said, "I need some city tour information."

"Here is the folder. All tours are listed inside."

"Good. Thank you. Where do they leave from?"

"All departures at Rossiya Hotel. Just below Red Square." Before he could turn away, the girl, her face a deeper pink suddenly, said, "You are one of the American runners. I remember your beard. I saw you on the television."

There was a sharp metallic taste in his mouth as he maneuvered through the crowd toward the front entrance, an odd emptiness at the bottom of his stomach, a looseness in his legs. "Use your head," he said under his breath. "You're right at the edge of blowing everything."

Walking fast, shaking it off, trying to clear his head, he had found himself in front of St. Basil's and had gone inside, had sat there in the dark for more than an hour. When he went outside again, heading back to the Olympic Village, he stopped at the main entrance of the Hotel Rossiya.

The doorman was a Georgian, tall and dark-skinned, with a gray moustache and strong white teeth.

"In answer of your query, each Intourist coach tour departing always from this place each day. Twenty and four tours all days but Sunday. Thirty-six tours the Sunday."

"What time do they leave in the morning?"

"All tours to depart in the space between eight hours and ten hours in the morning. All tours return to here in the space between midday noon and fourteen hours the *après-midi*."

"There is no other place they leave from?"

"Only from Hotel Rossiya. Most large and luxe hotel in the world, including all of America, north and south."

That night after dinner Chad went looking for Homer Barnett. He found him in the billiard room of the coaches' lounge. "How do you feel about my knocking off tomorrow?"

"It's up to you," Barnett said. "You feeling all right?"

"I feel great. A little tight maybe. I'd just like to cool it for a day, walk around town, get my mind on other things."

"Makes sense to me."

"I'll get in some running before breakfast. The rest of the day I'll hang loose and watch the pigeons."

---

20. The next morning, at twenty minutes before eight, Chad stood outside the main entrance of the Hotel Rossiya watching the tour buses load up, watching the guides, eighty percent of them young girls, arriving by bus or subway, some alone, others in groups of two or three. Their eyes still puffy from sleep, they hurried inside to the Intourist briefing desk, just opposite the hall-porter's station, their briefcases under their arms.

As soon as he detected the arrival pattern, all crews reporting inside to the lobby, Chad also went inside, found a chair half-hidden by a stone column and a thick potted plant, and studied each girl as she came to the desk, picked up her passenger list, checked it over, and hurried outside to her designated bus.

It was three minutes before eight when Elena spun through the revolving door, a light coat over her shoulders, her guide's badge pinned to the lapel. She picked up her list at the desk in a flurry of laughing, teasing Russian and was outside again almost at once.

Chad walked quickly to the plate glass window facing the entrance area, held the curtains open, and watched Elena dodging through the boarding lines and the maze of parked buses.

She stepped on board a long, double-section, glass-domed bus painted red and blue. As it pulled out, Chad saw a white card at the bottom inside corner of the windshield. TOUR 19. He turned away from the window and went back to the Intourist desk.

"Tour number nineteen," he said. "Can you tell me where that's going?"

Without checking the list in front of her, the girl behind the desk said, "Kremlin Gardens and Revolutionary museums."

"What time will it return here?"

"Midday. Twelve o'clock. Exact."

Chad left the hotel then and began walking. Slowly. Deliberately. Four hours to kill. Through Red Square, the golden towers and domes of the Kremlin on his left, past the bright-painted child's colors of the St. Basil's facade, past Spassky Gate on the left, GUM's unending department store on the right, and the blocky mass of the Lenin Mausoleum.

Leaving Red Square, he walked across the Fiftieth Anniversary of the October Revolution Square, turned right on Marxa Prospekt, and angled into Gorky Street, a hundred yards wide, choked with fast traffic. Passenger buses and trolley cars, military trucks and personnel carriers and private cars, the square-built Fiat Zhigulis, tiny Zaphoroghets darting in and out on forty-three horsepower, a few black Volga H-124's, or Chaikas, driven by uniformed chauffeurs, and fewer still, Lincoln or Mercedes limousines speeding in the center lane reserved for the cars of high officials.

Passing the inner ring at Tverskoi Boulevard, Chad continued north to the Garden Ring and, turning right, followed its great curving length south and east, past Zhdanova Ulitsa, past Mira Prospekt and Kirova Ulitsa, on past Karl Marxa Ulitsa and Ulyanovskaya to the Kremlin embankment running north along the Moskva.

He sat in a garden by the river then, ate a grilled sausage on a stick, and drank a glass of Bulgarian wine. At eleven forty-five he walked north on Kitaisk and angled across to the Rossiya Hotel.

All through the morning, trying to push away from the emotional jolt he'd felt when he saw Elena in the Rossiya lobby, he'd forced himself to concentrate on other things.

In silent recitation, like a litany, he listed the names of all the past decathlon champions he could remember. Loveland, Osborn, Paavo Yrjola, Bausch, Glenn Morris, Mathias, Campbell, Rafer Johnson, Willi Holdorf, Toomey, Avilov, Bruce Jenner.

Then he switched to records, to statistics, filling in Jenner's best times and distances, then Klemenko's, and finally his own at the Oregon trials.

One hundred meters: 10.9. Long jump: twenty-three feet nine inches. Shot put: fifty-one feet. High jump: six feet seven inches. Four-hundred-meter: 47.2. One-hundred-ten-meter hurdles: 14.6. Discus: one hundred sixty-six feet. Pole vault: fifteen feet nine inches. Javelin throw: two hundred twenty-five feet. Fifteen-hundred-meter run: four minutes twelve seconds. Total points: eight thousand six hundred and twenty-two.

Finally, reaching back into months of reading and study, he let his mind wander, picking out random facts and statistics he had learned and filed away, information that could be worthless or critical, facts that could clutter his mind or could in some way save his life . . . one ruble equals a dollar and thirty-three cents. One dollar equals seventy-four kopeks. Toothpaste is scarce. Towels and rugs and shoes are very scarce. Potatoes cost six cents a pound. A hotel room for a Soviet citizen costs a little over a dollar. Farmers still hoe in the fields. And Moscow street lights are blue.

Sitting there on a bench looking out across the river, the disconnected facts and figures bouncing through his head, suddenly nothing made sense to him. And everything made sense.

21.

It was just before twelve when Chad edged around the front corner of the Rossiya, trying to see without being seen, keeping some tree or statue or group of tourists always between himself and the bus arrival area.

He was on chancey ground and he knew it. One foolish move, one careless step, and all the planning would be wasted. If Elena saw him, if anyone *saw* her see him and made the connection, either now or sometime later, then everything would dissolve and trickle away.

He maneuvered himself into a position in the recess of a service door, where he could see without showing himself, and waited for her bus to pull in to the marked-off area beside the hotel entrance.

As he waited, ten minutes past twelve now, two gray-haired American women walked past the doorway where he stood, and a voice floated back to him. "Just wonderful gardens, weren't they? Nothing at all like I would have expected. I don't know *what* I expected exactly, but I sure never expected to see something so nice and pretty at a place like the Kremlin."

Chad reacted suddenly. The bus was already in. It must have arrived early. Before he did. He strained his eyes to see the buses, three of them, that were parked and empty in a chained-off area thirty yards away from the hotel entrance. He left the service doorway and walked toward the buses. A card in the front of the farthest bus read TOUR 19.

His first impulse was to rush into the lobby. She might still be at the Intourist desk. Or she might be coming out of the door as he went in. Buster Keaton. Two people spinning in a revolving door.

He couldn't risk it. All he could do was wait. And hope that she was still inside, that when she came out he could follow her without being seen, follow her home, find a way to isolate her in whatever way he could, and talk to her.

22. It was almost two o'clock when she came out of the hotel. He had given up but was still standing in the doorway, numb with disappointment, trying to persuade himself that if he came to the hotel again tomorrow he would surely see her then.

He heard her voice before he saw her. She came out the door and down the short flight of steps to the sidewalk, a tall red-haired woman on one side of her and a stocky young man in an Aeroflot pilot's uniform on the other. The three of them, laughing and talking together, passed the doorway where Chad stood, his hands cupped in front of his face as if he were lighting a cigarette.

When he eased out of the doorway, they were sixty yards away heading for Ordynka Ulitsa.

He followed behind them, hanging back, staying a good distance away, his head buzzing with excitement, his thoughts turning warm and positive again. Then, suddenly, they disappeared, down the stairwell of the underpass crossing Kotelnicheskaya.

He started to run toward the stairway and down the escalator to the lower level.

The underpass was packed with people, shops and cafés on the perimeter crowded with customers, and a steady parade to and from all four escalator exits—the one he'd come down, the one leading to Red Square at the bottom corner of the Kremlin, and two on the river side, one on either side of Ordynka.

Unable to find Elena in the crowd, with no logic to follow and no time to wonder, he guessed. Hurrying diagonally toward the river exit on the Kremlin side, he saw suddenly, ahead of him on the stairs, a flash of red hair. Moving closer, he saw Elena.

Out of the underpass, walking along the sidewalk, they turned and followed the Moskva along the embankment, the Kremlin walls high and heavy on the right, towers rising behind the walls.

Again Chad hung back. The way was crowded with

people, but he could follow easily now. His eyes had made a target pattern, light and dark, of the three figures together, and he kept them clearly in sight, with the girl's bright hair like a flag to fix on.

They followed the river to Gogolevsk Boulevard, then crossed underground again, angled north almost to Volkhonka Ulitsa, and turned sharp left on Metrostoyevsk. At the first corner they turned right on Smolny Ulitsa and walked two-thirds of the distance along the block. At number 18, not far from the Kropotkinskaya intersection, they stopped.

It seemed to Chad, from where he watched, that the man was saying good-bye to the two girls. But at last all three of them turned together, climbed the stairs, and disappeared inside the house.

Smolny Ulitsa, just one block long, is a street that has survived the sixty years of improvements and destruction that have, since the revolution in 1917, transformed Moscow. It has survived because it has been, for the most part, ignored.

For many years its destruction and projected resurrection as a grander and uglier street were simply postponed. Other priorities. Other areas were larger, richer in possibilities, had more scope and potential as a living site for thousands.

In 1932, however, there was a detailed proposal that on Smolny and three nearby streets all the buildings should be dynamited and hauled away so a bus terminal could be constructed. But those plans too were postponed and eventually misplaced, and once the Great Patriotic War with Germany began, Smolny was absolutely safe again from improvement. And later, during postwar reconstruction, it was again not important enough. The space involved was too small. A while later, early in

Khrushchev's period of influence, a literary historian at Moscow State University, a trivial but ambitious man named Obuchowsky, published a long and tiresome article which theorized that not only Pushkin but also Turgenev and Gogol had, in some period of their lives, spent time and done some work in one or another of the old merchant-home, eighteenth-century buildings on Smolny Ulitsa.

Although Obuchowsky's documentation was sketchy and several of his fellow scholars scoffed at his theory, Khrushchev, for reasons of his own, perhaps his well-known weakness for anything connected with Gogol, put the official stamp of acceptance on Obuchowsky, his article, and Smolny Ulitsa. The beautiful block-long street, a true and authentic relic of an earlier Russia, was declared a State treasure, to be preserved forever in its original state.

Chad walked along the street, opposite from number 18, kept walking to the corner of Kropotkinskaya, stopped there, half-hidden by a government truck parked at the curb, and looked back.

Did Elena live there, or was she visiting with those other people? If he telephoned her now and she didn't answer, would it prove that this address wasn't hers? Maybe it would and maybe it wouldn't.

He couldn't follow her into the building. Even if he managed to locate her in that five-story house, he couldn't speak to her in front of her friends, couldn't risk that, couldn't identify himself to them. If he telephoned her and she *did* answer, he couldn't talk to her if there were people in her apartment listening. But if he called and didn't speak. . . .

He turned quickly and stepped into the telephone kiosk just behind the parked truck. Studying the yellow stone facade of her building, he dropped a two-kopek coin into the phone and dialed her number. The phone rang three times. On the fourth ring she answered. With his hand over the mouthpiece, he listened to her voice and said nothing. He didn't hang up till she did.

23.

At three thirty that afternoon Chad came out of a secondhand clothing store on Borovitzky Square with a bulky package under his arm. He hesitated, looked down Volkhonka Ulitsa to the right, then turned left and almost collided with Dilly Upshaw.

"There he is," Dilly said, "strolling around like he owns the town." He turned to the girl beside him, a slender black girl with beautifully chiseled features, strangely Oriental eyes, and hair cut very short, showing the perfect shape of her head. "What did I tell you? This man is *elusive*. Like trying to put an oyster in a keyhole." Turning back to Chad, he said, "You remember Wanda Buck from Laurel, Mississippi. If I am the world's fastest man, and I *am*, then she has got to be the world's fastest female person."

"Hi, Chad," she said. "What's happening?"

"Not much. Took the day off."

"What have you got in that bundle?" Dilly said. He turned and looked into the store window. "Don't tell me you've been spending good rubles in this tacky joint. In Tennessee our scarecrows wear better clothes than that." He tapped Chad's paper-wrapped bundle with his forefinger. "You buying a trousseau or something?"

Chad had figured the odds were one in five thousand that he'd run into someone he knew before he had a chance to cache the clothes he'd bought. But he'd planned a story just in case. "It's a joke," he said. "I've got an uncle in Minnesota. Stingiest man alive. A retired farmer. Sold his place for a bundle. Must have half a million dollars drawing interest in the Red Wing bank. But he buys all his clothes at the Salvation Army. Everything from the skin out. So I thought I'd send him some of these rags from Russia. He'll probably be wearing them to church next time I see him."

Dilly turned to Wanda. "There you are. You believe that story?"

"Sure. Why not?"

"Why not? I'll tell you why not. Because this man can spread the guano like nobody I've ever seen. He's got three different versions of everything. Ask him what color his eyes are and he thinks it over before he answers. I mean the old molasses just keeps coming. If he was an oil well, we'd all get rich. Just stand around with tin cups and catch the overflow."

"Speaking of guano," Chad said.

"Amen," Wanda said.

"I'm telling you," Dilly went on, "this man is an *event*. You should have seen him in Helsinki. He got a fix on a whole squad of girls the Russians sent along with their team. Intourist girls. Translators and like that. This turkey was zipping from one to the other like a honey bee. Isn't that the truth?"

"Not exactly," Chad said. "I finally picked one I liked."

"*Finally*," Dilly said. "*That* is the operative word. Because you have to admit you took what could be called a circuitous route."

"I don't understand those big words," Chad said.

"I don't either," Wanda said. "I like to stick to four-letter words. Like *food*. You hear that, Upshaw? I'm starving to death. Ask Chad. Maybe he knows where that place is."

"We're looking for a restaurant called Tolstova," Dilly said. "It's on a barge or a houseboat or something. On the river."

"First of all, you locate the river."

"That's what I told him," Wanda said.

"I *did* locate the river, *wiseass*," Dilly said to Chad.

"But he lost it again," Wanda said.

"Go to the next corner, turn left on Gogolevsk Boulevard, and it will take you straight down to the Moskva. Tolstova is right there, down some stairs on the far side of the embankment."

"Come eat with us," Dilly said. "Georgian cooking, somebody told us. We figure that's the Russian equivalent of soul food."

"Can't do it," Chad said. "I have to get to the post office over on Gorky Street before it closes. I want to get rid of this bundle. Send it off to my uncle."

"Well, try to come down later then," Dilly said. "We'll be eating for a couple hours. My last decent meal. Next week I'll be so wired I'll be throwing up all that institutional food they give us in the village."

"I'll come if I can," Chad said. "If I don't show up, you'll know there was a long line at the post office."

Chad walked with them to the corner, watched as they disappeared in the pedestrian throng on Gogolevsk. Then he walked west to the Kiev railroad station.

Inside the huge terminal he prowled through the crowds, dodging baggage carts and soft drink wagons, till he came to the baggage storage room. The attendant, sour-smelling and silent as a mute, tied a claim tag to Chad's package, tore off the stub and handed it over, then held out his hand for twenty kopeks.

24. At nine thirty that night Chad came out of a motion picture theatre near the corner of Arbat Ulitsa and Smolensky Boulevard. He had sat through the film twice, the tender story of a girl in love with a tractor.

It was cool in the blue-lighted streets. He walked to the corner, turned down Smolensky to Kropotkin Ulitsa, then left to Smolny. He went to the corner telephone kiosk and called Elena's number. There was no answer.

He crossed to number 18 and climbed the short flight of steps to the front door. There were no outside doorbells, no list of apartment numbers or tenant names. He pushed the door open and stood in the dim-lit hallway. No directory there either. He walked along the hall to the back.

Behind the doors he passed, he heard low conversations, the rattle of glasses and china, and radio music. There were strong cooking smells in the hallway. And stale cigarette smoke.

At the back, through an open doorway, he found a stair leading down the lower level. Down there the air was close and hot and musty. He passed more apartment doors and a doorless opening with an incinerator burning orange inside a square cement room.

Chad climbed back to the main floor, then paused briefly outside each door, hoping to hear some sound that would tell him Elena was inside. On the next floor up he tried the same thing. No luck. Hearing voices and footsteps in the hall above him, he ran down the stairs as quietly as he could, let himself out the front door, and crossed the street to the telephone kiosk.

As he dialed Elena's number, he watched a man and woman, their arms around each other, hugging and kissing and lurching together, come down the outside steps of number 18. They turned left toward Metrostoyevsk and stumbled, like a bulky four-legged creature, down the street.

As soon as Elena's number began to ring, Chad let the receiver hang down loose from the phone, left the kiosk, and ran back across the street to her house.

Inside, he stood in the first-floor hallway listening. There was a faint ringing sound from a higher floor. He ran up the stairs, stopped to listen, then up again to the third floor. There, at the front of the house, he stood outside a heavy carved door and clearly heard the telephone ringing inside.

Suddenly it stopped. He listened for a voice but heard nothing. Then he turned to the hall window, pulled a heavy curtain aside, and looked down at the kiosk on the far curb under the street light. A young man was standing at the phone. He had hung up the receiver, then taken it off again to place his own call. A girl in a leather coat walked back and forth on the sidewalk waiting for him.

Standing there with his back to the hallway, Chad heard a door open somewhere behind him. He stayed where he was, his back to the hall, his forehead against the glass pane, his eyes on the street. Footsteps, slow and heavy, came closer, finally stopped just behind him. A soft voice slurred something in Russian. Chad stood motionless, didn't turn. There was another soft query, guttural and breathy. Then the footsteps moved away, back down the hallway. There was a muffled conversation; a door closed, and a bolt slid into place.

Chad pulled the curtain back from the window then and let in enough light so he could read the number on Elena's door. Number twenty-four. "Eighteen Smolny Ulitsa. Apartment twenty-four," he said to himself. Then he turned, went down the stairs, and left the building.

25.

"You won't be satisfied till you get your tail in a crack," Dilly said.

"What do you mean?" It was eleven o'clock at night and Chad had just come in. He'd walked all the way from Smolny Ulitsa, ideas exploding in his head, his mind full of tomorrow.

"I mean Yost is just aching to unload on you."

"For what?"

"Who knows for what? For anything. The only guy who burns him more than I do is *you*."

"He's all right. He's just trying to do his job."

"That's just it. What *is* his job?"

"I don't know," Chad said.

"Neither does he. You should have seen him tonight.

Like he was presiding over the Nuremburg trials. He's really shot in the ass with importance."

"What happened?"

"What happened was we had a team meeting. All seven hundred of us. Or eight hundred or ten thousand, whatever it is. They took a roll call and you were the only orphan that turned up missing. Absent and elsewhere."

"I went to a movie. There was this girl and this tractor . . ."

"We had a big election to see who carries the flag in the opening day march."

"Who's the goat?"

"It was almost you. I nominated you and Neal Dockery seconded."

"Jesus, Dilly, I don't want that job."

"Don't worry. You didn't get it. Yost shot you down. He got somebody to nominate Frazier, that chickenshit weight lifter."

"Frazier's a good guy."

"No, he's not. He's dog meat."

"I saw him throw a guy through a plate glass window in San Mateo one night."

"So what? He's a dog meat chickenshit bigot with muscles."

"What happened with the election?"

"Yost said it seemed to him that the flag bearer had been a track and field man almost every Olympic year. He thought it might be a good idea if we honored one of the other teams this time. Like a fan dancer or a folk singer or a weight lifter for instance. So everybody whooped and hollered and gave Frazier all the votes on the first go-round."

"What's the difference? Who cares?"

"*I* care."

"Forget it. Let's get some sleep."

"Another thing," Dilly said. "I thought you were coming back to eat with Wanda and me."

"I said I would if I could. But I couldn't. I got hung up at the post office."

"Bullshit. You *knew* you weren't coming back."

"What's eating you?" Chad said.

"Nothing. I just don't like people to dump on me."

"Who's dumping on you?"

"Forget it."

"I don't want to forget it. You're getting jumpy about the meet, aren't you?"

"No."

"The hell you're not. You're wired like a two-dollar toaster."

"I don't *get* wired. I'm loose, man. I'm *always* loose."

"Good."

"I don't choke. I never choked in my life."

"Good. I'm glad to hear it."

When they were in their beds with the lights off, Dilly said, "You hit it. I'm wired all right. It's starting to get to me."

"It gets to everybody."

"I'm great once the gun goes off. But the waiting really bombs me."

"It bombs everybody."

A few minutes later Dilly said, "You asleep?"

"Not quite."

"I want to ask you something. None of my business maybe, but it's been on my mind so I'm gonna ask you anyway."

"Shoot."

"For fifteen years, since I was six or seven years old, I've been a track nut. I mean I'm a *scholar*. I started collecting every track magazine they printed from the time I was in first grade. You got the picture?"

"Sure."

"After I met you the first time, when we roomed together last spring in Helsinki, I went back to Memphis, sat down with all my old magazines, and began to look you up. And you know what I found? *Nothing.*"

"So . . ."

"So where did you come from? Barnett didn't just hatch you out of an egg up there at San Jose, did he?"

"I told you, I went to City College there for a year. Then I transferred to Cal State."

"I know that. What about before that?"

"Before that I lived all over. My dad was an army man. A year here, a couple years there. We never settled anyplace for very long. I ran a little cross-country once in New Jersey and I fooled around with the hurdles in gym class. But I never ran in a track meet till I came to San Jose. That's why you can't find my name in those magazines of yours."

"You've got to admit it's unusual."

"I'm what you call a late bloomer."

---

26. As Chad and Dilly went to sleep in Moscow, the *Today* show on NBC television in New York was showing a series of taped interviews with Olympic contestants from all nations.

The first interview was with Dilly. Then came athletes from Hungary, Sweden, Cuba, Japan, and East Germany.

And last of all, Curt Gowdy interviewed Chad. They were standing at the top of the Lenin Stadium.

"We've been watching you train out here," Gowdy said. "We've also been watching Klemenko and Mittag and the other decathlon men you'll be going up against, and I have to tell you, the consensus from our people is that you're a shoo-in."

"You'll put a hex on me," Chad said.

"No, we won't. After the way you performed under pressure in the trials and the way you've handled yourself here, nobody expects anything less than a top effort from you."

"Well, we'll see what happens."

"How does it feel now that all the training is behind you? Can you tell me honestly that you're not expecting to fly back to America with a gold medal in your pocket?"

"I can honestly tell you I don't take anything for granted and nobody else should either."

"Let me put it another way. If something happens that you *don't* take the top prize, won't you be surprised? Wouldn't you be surprised and disappointed?"

The camera stayed on Chad's face. After a long pause he said, "This trip to Russia is the most important thing that's ever happened in my life. I have something to do here and I sure don't expect to fail at it."

Smiling, with his hand on Chad's shoulder, Gowdy said, "That's all we wanted to know. That answers my question."

Smiling into the camera, Chad thought, "Like hell it does."

part 2

27. Saturday, July nineteenth, the day the opening ceremonies for the twenty-second modern Olympiad would be held, Chad woke up at four in the morning. He lay on his back in the dark, no sound in the room, only Dilly's regular breathing from the bed on the far wall. And no sound at all from the grounds outside.

The tension he had felt—the buzz in his head, the tightness in his stomach, the feeling that had been with him since the day he flew east from California—was gone now. He felt firm and positive. He had full faith, suddenly, in his judgment and his instincts.

He lay warm and relaxed in his bed, fully rested, impatient to be up but forcing himself to wait, to lie there in the soft dark till five o'clock, the time he usually got up to run. It was critical that this day should seem to be like any other day. Up at the usual time, into his nondescript sweat pants and faded sweat jacket with zipper pockets, out of the dormitory, across the wide lawn, down the promenade, and out through the gate, the same as any other morning.

It was eighteen minutes past five when he jogged through the Village entrance gate between the two guard stations and under the Demitria Ulyanova underpass. He ran the length of Gorky Park, then all the way east along the river till he came to the stairway going up steeply to the Kiev rail terminal.

Inside the terminal, the people who had slept there all night were just waking up, stomping around, drinking glasses of steaming tea from the food carts. The fifteen-year-old whores who had worked the station all night, rouge smeared on their cheeks, their mouths bright like fresh incisions, dark lines penciled around their eyes, were straggling toward the subway or to trolley stops, stunned and exhausted, going home to sleep.

The morning trains began arriving then, one after the other, crates and boxes, packages and canvas sacks of mail being off-loaded, garden produce and naked carcasses of pork and lamb, chickens in wire cages, sluggish rabbits, a small herd of delicate goats following a thin, dark man through the terminal to the street, bells tinkling on their collars.

From the outskirts of Moscow, from the endless slab forests of apartment buildings outside the Garden Ring, from Alexye Evski, from Butwiski and Novo Andronovski, came a flood tide of people. Office workers, tradesmen, shop girls, cooks and waiters, scientists, journalists, functionaries and party workers, briefcases or cloth bags in their hands, dark bread and cheese and salami inside the bags. They came through the terminal in dense, surly waves and surged onto the street, jostling and grumbling, smelling of sweat and frustration and last night's vodka, a relentless parade of heavy shuffling people, thick and slow and solid.

Chad stayed close to the wall away from the surge, slowly edged around the terminal's perimeter to the baggage storage window. He took the thick cardboard stub from his pocket and gave it to the attendant, a woman this time, obese and sullen.

She disappeared in the dark stacks. He heard grunts

and oaths then, objects falling and being kicked. And in a few moments the woman, breathing hard from her efforts, was back with his package. When he gave her ten kopeks she grunted. But her expression didn't change.

Just inside the main terminal entrance, Chad pushed through heavy doors to the first-class waiting room, walked on through to the men's toilet, and past that to a hall-like chamber with private compartments for bathing and changing clothes. He put a twenty-kopek coin in the lock slot, opened the door, and locked it behind him. In the tile-floored room there was a toilet, a shower stall, and a sink against the wall with a shelf and looking glass above it.

Chad untied the paper parcel and took out the second-hand clothes he'd bought at the store on Borovitzky Square. A shapeless wool jacket and wide-legged pants, dark but colorless, a pair of worn work shoes, a wrinkled gray shirt, and a brown, lightweight sweater. Also a stained leather strap belt, heavy socks, and a wool cap with a broken visor.

He dropped these clothes on a bench by the wall. Then he unzipped his sweat-jacket pockets and emptied them on the shelf over the sink. A thick packet of rubles, a razor-comb, a scissors, an injector razor, a tube of shaving soap, and a small cake of hard soap. Stripping down to his shorts and bare feet, he dropped his sweat clothes, shorts, socks, and sneakers on the square of rough paper on the floor. Then he turned to the mirror, picked up the scissors, and began hacking off long locks of his hair. When it was two inches long all over his head, he picked up the razor-comb and began to comb and trim the hair that was left, smoothing it out till it was a neat helmet, a workman's haircut, cut by his wife in the kitchen twice a month.

He scooped up hair from the sink and the floor, brushed

the loose hair from his bare shoulders and the back of his neck, and put it all in the toilet. Then, leaning over the bowl, he began cutting off his beard with the scissors.

When it was short enough for the razor, he ran hot water into the sink, soaked his face, smeared it with shaving soap, and began to shave with slow sure strokes. He took off his shorts then, stepped into the shower stall, washed his hair, and rinsed all the loose hair off his body.

When he came out of the dressing room later and walked through the waiting room toward the terminal, a paper-wrapped package under his arm, wearing the shapeless clothes and rough shoes, the soft cap pulled low, shading his eyes, it was impossible to distinguish him from the lumpy people walking along beside him. There was a sour, mistrustful look on his face, his eyes were downcast, and he walked bent forward from the waist like a man who had spent his life carrying hundred-pound bags of potatoes.

28. When Dilly woke up, early for him, at eight o'clock that morning, when he shaved, took a shower, and tried to stumble his way through the twenty or thirty minutes between opening his eyes and the first cup of coffee he could grab at the closest cafeteria, he had no reason to feel that this day was different from any other day.

Chad wasn't there. He was out running. He was always

out running in the morning. His clothes were draped across the chair where he'd dropped them the night before. His billfold, his passport, and his Olympic identification pass were where he always left them at night, in plain sight on his bedside table. Business as always.

Nonetheless, sitting at breakfast with Wanda half an hour later, Dilly said, "That crazy bastard is gonna give me a guaranteed ulcer."

"Chad?"

"Who do you think?"

"Don't worry about him," Wanda said.

"Too late. I'm already doing it."

"He's got it taped. People like Chad don't ever get rained on."

"Who says so?"

"I do. Guys like him dig a hole to plant a tree and oil squirts up instead. If there's a pearl in the oyster stew, they find it. They miss a plane and the plane crashes."

"What *is* all that? Who gave you a witch's license?"

"I'm telling you. I know a lucky citizen when I see one."

"Then why have I got this creepy feeling about him?" Dilly said. "Why did I wake up this morning and decide that something wasn't screwed on straight?"

"That's got nothing to do with Chad. I've seen you in action before. You'll be spooked from now on till you run your final heat."

"Why are you starting up with me?"

"I'm not. I didn't start anything. *You* did. I was telling what gives with Chad and you won't buy it."

"I just got a bad feeling, that's all. Like he's gonna run in front of a truck. Spike himself in the foot or something."

"Not a chance. Guys like him, when they're born, their mothers don't even have labor pains."

29. It was nearly nine in the morning when Chad walked up the outside steps of Elena's apartment building. He opened the front door and walked straight to the back stairs, down to the basement, along the hall, and down the five steps to the incinerator room. He lifted the metal bar-lock out of its slot, swung the fire door open, and shoved his paper-wrapped package, running shoes and sweat suit inside, into the flames.

On the main floor again, a door opened behind him and someone came out. And on the floor above, and on the stairs, he heard voices and footsteps. He walked deliberately to the entrance door, opened it, went outside and down the steps to the sidewalk.

It was too early. He realized he'd come to the house too early, at the wrong time of the morning. Too much activity. People going to work. Women with string bags going out to buy food. Too soon. An hour later would be better.

Crossing the street, he found a crumpled copy of *Izvestia* in a litter basket and sat down on a bench, up the block and across the street from number 18.

Sitting slumped and rumpled at one end of the bench, he stared at the newspaper till someone approached on the sidewalk. Then, testing his new identity, he looked up and scowled.

Most people looked away. When someone greeted him in Russian he growled, guttural and unintelligible, staring, trying to see if they saw him as anything other than the sullen peasant he pretended to be. He saw no indication that anyone did. It gave him confidence. His feet began to feel at home in the stiff shoes, and he settled into the rough, wrinkled clothes.

At a quarter past ten he crossed the street again, entered the house, and went up to the third floor, then down the hall to Elena's door. He knocked firmly. He expected no answer and there was none.

As deliberate as a neighborhood locksmith, he took a long-bladed kitchen knife from his jacket pocket and slid it behind the molding just where he guessed the latch would be. It slipped all the way through. Next time the same thing. The third time, he hit metal, angled the knife blade for leverage, and carefully exerted pressure. He heard the lock click softly and felt the door swing open. He stepped inside and closed the door behind him.

---

30. Dilly waited till two in the afternoon, till just before the busloads of athletes were due to leave for Lenin Stadium. Then he went to the coaches' quarters and up the stairs to Homer Barnett's room.

Barnett was tying his necktie in front of a mirror,

making an awkward job of it, when Dilly knocked. He opened the door and said, "Come in."

"I can't. I mean I can't stay long. I just got a few minutes if I want to make the stadium bus. I just wanted to find out if you've seen Chad."

"Not today. Why?"

"Because he's not around. He went out early this morning like he always does, and I haven't seen him since."

"He didn't come back to change clothes?"

Dilly shook his head. "I've been hanging around all day. Ever since breakfast. All his clothes are in the closet, and his billfold and I.D. are right by the bed where he left them."

"I know he wasn't there at the meeting last night. He came home, didn't he?"

"Sure. He was home all night. But he's not there now."

"Well, I don't think we have to worry. He'll turn up. Remember New York? He'll show up when he's ready."

"What if he doesn't?" Dilly said. "What's the penalty for missing the opening ceremonies?"

"You got me. I guess it's whatever the committee decides it is. We'll find out. If Chad doesn't show up, we'll *all* find out. Yost will be out on the promenade with a bullhorn."

31. Elena's apartment retained some flavor of what those rooms had been like, what Moscow life had been like, two hundred years before, when the building was new.

It was a square room, once a parlor perhaps, with sixteen-foot ceilings and a wide window looking out across Smolny Ulitsa.

On the floor were old patterned rugs from Tashkent and Bukhara, worn thin but still glowing with rich colors. In one corner, away from the window, was a low, wide bed covered with a bright spread, orange and mauve and brilliant blue, woven in Thilisi in 1890. Just above the bed was a wall lamp with a parchment shade.

A table and two straight chairs stood in front of the curtained window, a heavy carved desk in the corner opposite the bed. There was also a settee covered with worn velvet, and two great lounge chairs, deep and soft, on either side of the desk.

The ceiling, festooned with plaster flowers and trailing plaster ribbons and vines, was painted bone white, the four walls a warm gray. One wall, opposite the bed, was hung floor to ceiling with travel posters, ink drawings and watercolors, concert and ballet programs, announcements of art expositions, and signed photographs, all simply framed under glass.

Over the desk was a picture of Lenin; over the bed just one framed poster, a glowing color photograph of an ancient street in Helsinki.

In the front corner, to the left of the window and behind a painted screen, a tiny kitchen had been installed: a sink, a low refrigerator, and a two-burner gas stove with an oven underneath. Two wall cabinets painted white and a squat chest of drawers just beside the sink.

Down a short hall at the back of the room, there was a tile-floored surprise of a bathroom with an eight-foot porcelain tub sitting high on cast iron legs.

Sitting in one of the deep chairs taking in the details of the room, Chad felt at ease. Warmly at home. If he had questioned himself beforehand, tried to imagine what kind of place Elena would be living in, he would have invented, he felt now, an apartment very much like this one. Old things and new things, bright colors, and empty spaces here and there to give your eyes a rest, soft places to sit, and a magnificent bed.

Only one thing disturbed him. On an upholstered bench just beside the armoire a suitcase lay open, filled with clothing neatly arranged and folded, the bag just waiting to be closed, picked up, and carried off to some airport or railway station.

32.
Just after four in the afternoon, in the deep oblong saucer of Lenin Stadium, more than a hundred thousand people cheering, more than twelve thousand athletes standing in the infield, each group behind its country's flag, President Brezhnev rose slowly from his central seat on the Tribune of Honor, moved to a cluster of microphones, and said, "I declare open the Olympic Games of 1980, celebrating the twenty-second Olympiad of the modern era."

A rumbling roar went up from the crowd, long and sustained, as they stood, all of them, waving tiny national flags, as the Olympic anthem played, as the Olympic flag was slowly hoisted.

When the flag reached the top of its pole, as a great swarm of pigeons was released from the floor of the stadium, another sustained roar came from the crowd and over it then, shattering the air, a thunderous salute of cannons.

In the NBC booth on the lip of the stadium, Dick Enberg, headphones in place, surrounded by monitors and telephones, Curt Gowdy and O. J. Simpson on one side of him, John Brodie and Bruce Jenner on the other, said, full into the camera, "You have just heard the traditional words, you are watching the traditional ceremony, and it all means just one thing . . . the 1980

Olympics have officially begun. The twenty-second Olympiad of the modern era is now underway. And there it comes . . . you hear the crowd . . . there comes the Olympic flame. The final runner in that long relay that began weeks ago in Greece has just entered this jam-packed stadium. He will circle the track, mount those steps just opposite us, and light the sacred Olympic fire. Now . . . as our cameras give you a picture of everything that's happening in Lenin Stadium today, here's John Brodie with some information about how it all began, all those centuries ago in ancient Greece."

"When we talk about the modern Olympic Games," Brodie said, "we're talking about a tradition that's only eighty-four years old. The first meeting of these modern games took place in Athens in 1896 . . ."

Curt Gowdy, his microphone switched off, leaned over to Enberg. "Did you pick up that call from the truck?"

"No."

"Klauser called up from the field. He says Norris didn't march in with the team."

"Is he sure of that?"

"Sounds like he is. He and Dave have been picking up single shots of everybody. Not a sign of Norris."

"I'll check with the truck." Enberg picked up a phone from the table in front of him.

"The fact is," Brodie was saying, "the very first Olympic games that we know about took place in 776 B.C., in the sacred valley of Olympia near the west coast of Greece. But those first games consisted of just one race. A two-hundred-yard sprint. Then little by little, through the years, they added other events. In 680 B.C. they even had a four-horse chariot race . . ."

Enberg hung up the phone and said to Gowdy, "Madigan talked to Klauser. He's on top of it."

"What's he say?"

"He thinks we should cool it for now. After the ceremony's over we'll see what's going on."

"It's hard to imagine it now," Brodie went on, "but the thing that finally destroyed the ancient games was professionalism. By 200 B.C. the Macedonians and the Romans simply hired the best athletes, wherever they could find them, and the whole idea of amateur competition was wrecked. So in A.D. 393 the Emperor Theodosius did away with the games altogether. They'd lasted for twelve hundred years through nearly three hundred Olympiads. But it was more than fifteen hundred years before they started up again in pretty much the form we see now."

The crowd was on its feet again, cheering and waving flags, as the fire runner reached the top of the stadium. He dipped his torch inside the huge ornamental fuel-lamp, and the flame shot high into the air.

The athletes on the floor of the stadium all turned to face the rostrum then, like a great army in semicircle. A Russian official, tall with a bald head, took the stage at the platform's center, held a corner of the Olympic flag in his left hand, raised his right hand, and said, "In the name of all competitors I promise that we will take part in these Olympic games, respecting and abiding by the rules which govern them, in the true spirit of sportsmanship, for the glory of sport and the honor of our teams."

Chad sat in Elena's apartment, slumped deep in one of the soft chairs, watching the ceremony on a small black and white television set, hearing the oath, the crowd, the Russian national anthem, watching the columns of athletes, like an eight-pointed star, as they marched quickly out of the stadium by eight separate exits.

He sat motionless for a long time, his eyes shadowed

and opaque, no expression on his face. At last he got up and switched off the set, walked to the window, and stared down at the street, his hands deep in his pockets.

33.

In a long silver trailer, the red and blue NBC emblem bright on either side, Art Madigan sat in his paneled office in a leather chair, feet up, a drink in his hand.

Charles Scales, tall and broad, short-cropped gray hair, wearing a somber banker's suit and a blue and red striped tie, sat on a long couch.

"What do you think?" Madigan said.

"I think good," Scales said. "Dynamite stuff. I guarantee you we gave Roone Arledge a migraine."

"It'll get better when we get into the muscle stuff and there's something to shoot. Not much you can do with this pageant baloney. It's like the Rose Bowl Parade sideways."

Madigan took a long drink, got up for a refill, and came back to his chair. "What about the Norris thing? How we going to handle that?"

"We'll have to see. He could be asleep in his bed for all we know."

"Or in somebody else's bed."

"That's right. But wherever he is, you did the right thing, keeping it off this opening show. Everything's sunny and gung-ho at the moment. Even the PLO is keeping quiet. So we don't need any melodrama if we can avoid it."

"I thought we overreacted in New York," Madigan said, "when he almost missed the plane."

"I agree with you. I say we should go very slow on Norris. Look the other way. Let's not report anything till we've got some hard news."

"That was my instinct too. Now I'm not so sure. We have to realize we could get our tails in a crack."

"How's that?"

"Let's pretend for a minute that there *is* a story. This town is crawling with media guys. If somebody from the Kokomo *Bugle* breaks something big on Norris and we haven't even mentioned it, we are really naked in church. I mean we've been blowing our own horns for six months now. *Total* coverage, we've been saying. That means we have to put our money where our mouth is. We sure as hell don't want to see Cosell or Jack Whittaker doing a network news piece about the disappearance of Chad Norris. That could make us look bad even if he *hasn't* disappeared."

"So what do you think?"

"I think we have to protect ourselves. Unless he shows up in the next few hours, we have to assume there's a story there whether we like it or not. If he turns up dead drunk or plain dead or kidnapped or something, we have to be covered. I say we tape some hard-nosed interviews with Yost and Barnett and Dilly Upshaw, *anybody* who knows Norris, and hang on to those tapes. Then if the shit hits the fan, we've got something to throw on the tube. Right quick."

"Makes sense."

"Also," Madigan said, "the more we sit here talking about it the more I think we have to mention it now.

Preempt the story if it turns out there *is* one. We've got the exclusive. We paid a lot of money for it. And we'd better use it or we could get murdered later on."

He picked up a phone from the coffee table, pressed a button, and said, "Who's on camera, Tim? Good. Put me through to Curt." He flipped a switch and three monitors on the far wall buzzed on. Enberg and O. J. Simpson were recapping the opening day ceremonies.

His hand over the telephone mouthpiece, Madigan said to Scales, "We'll let Curt handle it. He'll do a short wrap-up just before Dick signs off." Into the phone then, "Curt? It's Art. You're looking good . . . no, I'm not in the booth. Charlie and I are having a drink . . . don't worry, I already poured you one . . . listen, do me a favor. When you get on camera again, mention the Norris thing . . . I know I did . . . but I changed my mind . . . that's right. Keep it jolly. No menace. Just make it clear that he wasn't in the stadium today. It's probably nothing, but just in case it turns into something we don't want to be caught . . . that's right." He hung up and turned again to Scales. "He'll handle it."

34.
Yost sat behind his desk, paler than usual, Barnett and Dilly on the couch across from him, Earl Chaffee in a chair to his left smoking a long thick cigar.

"The last thing I want anyone to do," Yost said, "is to

panic. I'm not jumping to any conclusions and I don't want you to. There's no reason for us to have a crisis here unless we turn it into one. Does everybody understand that?"

Nobody answered. Chaffee chewed his cigar and looked embarrassed. Dilly looked uncomfortable and Barnett looked angry.

"You didn't see him at all yesterday," Yost said to Barnett. "Is that correct?"

"That's right."

"And the last time you saw him, what did he say?"

"Said he felt a little tight. Said he was going to skip working out for a day."

"And you gave him permission?" Yost said.

"No. He didn't *ask* my permission and I didn't *give* it. It doesn't work that way. He knows what he feels like. *I* don't."

"Then you didn't have the feeling he was up to something?"

"I don't know what that means," Barnett said.

"I mean he didn't say anything about missing the opening ceremonies?"

"No."

Yost turned to Dilly. "And when you saw him last night he didn't say anything about it?"

"No."

"What did he talk about?"

"Nothing. Just personal stuff."

"So you thought nothing about it when he wasn't there this morning?"

"He's never there when I get up," Dilly said. "He's always out running."

Yost looked at Chaffee, then leaned back in his chair and lit a cigarette. "It's a pity," he said, "when one unreliable person can make difficulties for a lot of other people just by being unreliable. What Norris is doing . . . he's making us all look bad." He sat up straight again, carefully flicked his cigarette ash into a glass bowl. "But I suspect he won't be doing it much longer. I'll be meeting with the full committee this evening. And if they feel as strongly as I do . . ."

"What if he's not staying away on purpose?" Barnett said.

"Unless he's very absentminded, I doubt if he's staying away *accidentally*."

"This is Moscow, for Christ's sake. It's not Pasadena. Something could have happened to him."

"That's what we thought in New York, didn't we?" Yost said. "No, I think he'll turn up when he's good and ready. Then we'll deal with the situation in whatever way seems best."

"What about the press?" Chaffee said.

"I'm sure they'll be very curious." Yost turned to Barnett and Dilly. "I'd appreciate it if you two would refuse to answer any questions."

"Why is that?" Barnett said.

"Just refer them to me. Then we won't have to worry about a lot of conflicting stories."

Barnett stood up. Very deliberately. He looked at Chaffee, then at Yost. "Mr. Yost, let me tell you something. This is not a Boy Scout camp, *I* am not a Boy Scout, and you are sure as hell not my scoutmaster. I don't like anything you've been saying and I don't like the way you say it. It's not for you to decide who I talk to and what I say. *I'll* decide that. As a matter of fact, if Chad hasn't turned up by tonight, the reporters won't have to come looking for me. *I'll* go looking for *them*."

35.

Early evening, a streak of yellow light still visible in the west through the Moscow haze, Elena Baklanova came out through the side entrance of a weather-damaged concrete apartment tower on the south edge of Sokolniki Park and walked slowly toward her car.

She stopped then, turned, and looked at the apartment building as if she might go back inside. But she turned after a long moment and walked toward her car again.

It had started to rain. Before she got into the car, she opened the trunk, took out her wiper blades, and fastened them in position on the front windshield of her black Zhigulis sedan, squared-lined and compact, less than two years old, but its paint surface dulled and scarred already by a hard winter on the streets.

She sat behind the wheel with the engine running and watched the wiper blades arc and squeak back and forth, rubber against glass. Suddenly she reached out to the ignition key and turned off the motor. The wipers stopped at the top of their arc.

Elena sat very still, straight and silent, staring ahead, unable to see out through the rain-streaked glass. Her chin quivered then and she started to cry, her hands in her lap, no expression on her face, great slow tears sliding down her cheeks.

Just those silent tears for what seemed a long time until, finally, an ugly moan tore loose in her throat and she began to sob, her face in her hands, her shoulders shaking, her forehead resting against the hard cool surface of the steering wheel.

She stayed like that, hiding her face, long after she stopped sobbing. Finally she straightened up in the seat, took a handkerchief out of her shoulder bag, and dried her eyes. Then she started the car again and pulled out from the curb.

She drove home the long way. Instead of going west on Kirova Ulitsa directly through the center of Moscow, she turned north into the evening traffic on the Garden Ring. Staying right, in the slowest lane, she crawled along behind the clog of buses and trucks, moving slowly north and west, then south again in a great circle till at last she angled off on Smolensky to Kropotkinskaya, drove east, and turned the corner into her street.

Again, parked at the curb half a block past her house, she sat behind the wheel as if she were frozen there. When she got out of the car at last, the rain had stopped. She detached the windshield wipers and locked them in the trunk again. Then she stood at the curb looking across the street at her building. She started to cross, then turned south on Smolny Ulitsa and walked to the corner of Metrostoyevsk.

At a café on the near corner, she found a seat far inside against the back wall and ordered a glass of hot tea with plum jam. She drank the tea slowly and when it was finished she ordered another one. And a hard bun with currants baked in it.

It was almost nine o'clock when she left the café. On her way out, she stopped by the cash desk at a pay phone cubicle, dropped in a coin, and dialed a number. "It's Elena," she said. "How is she? Are you sure you don't want me to come back? All right . . . I'll call again in the morning."

She walked home then, picked up her mail from the table in the downstairs hall, and climbed the two flights of stairs to her floor.

She was inside her apartment, turning to lock the door, when she sensed there was someone in the room. She jerked the door open, trying to get outside to the hall, but two hands grabbed her and pulled her back inside, one arm tight around her shoulders, one hand over her mouth. As the door slammed shut, she struggled and kicked to get free. Then a voice behind her said, "Don't make any noise. It's *me*. It's *Chad*."

36.

"I can't believe it," Elena said. "I still can't believe it."

It was almost midnight. They were sitting up in bed, a great platter of olives and cheese and salami and black bread between them, an almost empty liter of wine on a stool by the bed.

"*You* can't believe it? What about me? I thought I'd never find you. You keep wild hours."

"No, I don't. I told you. I was with a tour down in Tashkent and Samarkand. When you saw me and followed me here from Hotel Rossiya, that was my first day back in Moscow."

He glanced toward her open suitcase. "And now you're getting ready to leave again."

"I *was* getting ready to leave," she said. "But now I have a sweet man in my bed. Now I have other things to do."

"Can you just cancel a trip and stay home if you want to?"

"*Never.* Not if it's work. But this was not a work trip. I have a two-week summer holiday. Starting today. Free time for myself. I planned to leave tomorrow and come back August third."

"That's the day the Olympics end. That's when I go home."

"I know that."

"Was that the only time you could take a vacation? During the two weeks I'm in Moscow?"

"I chose that time. That's when I *wanted* to be away."

"Why?"

"Why do you think?"

"So you wouldn't have to see me?"

"So I wouldn't be able to see you. So I wouldn't be tempted."

"You mean I've been breaking my bones to find you and you were trying *not* to see me?"

"Does that surprise you?" she said. "Did you think I would be waiting to meet you when you got off the airplane?"

"No."

"Yes, you did. I see it in your face."

"I didn't expect you to be at the airport, but I thought . . ."

"Because they sent me with the Russian team to Helsinki you thought I would be with the Olympic people too?"

"It makes sense, doesn't it?"

She nodded her head. "I could have had the assignment."

"And you turned it down?"

"Yes," she said. "But it's not the way it sounds. You don't know how things work here. I knew how it would be if I saw you. How I would feel. But here I am not allowed to have you in my bed no matter how I feel. I am not permitted to have a foreign person in my apartment for even one night. The rules are very specific. Everyone with a stranger's passport has an assigned room and an assigned bed. If the police come at three in the morning, they expect to find you in that bed."

"What if they don't?" he said. "What if they find me here?"

"They could frighten you or fine you or keep you all night in jail. Or they could ask you to leave the country. For me it would be more serious. It would go in my record. I could lose my job, my car, my apartment. I would certainly lose privileges."

"Like what?"

"Everything good. It's what we all work for. The chance to be upgraded, to go to the better stores, to buy better food, permission to live alone in an apartment, to own a car."

"Is that why you didn't want to see me?"

"No, I didn't say that. I could never measure you that way. You know we took chances in Helsinki. I would have taken chances here."

"Then why?"

"I was afraid. Afraid to start wanting something I knew I couldn't have. I was miserable after I left you in Helsinki. I felt desperate and it frightened me. There was no way I could handle my feelings. So finally I told myself that it had been a beautiful gift, that time we spent together. But just for once. It was something that couldn't be continued or repeated."

"You're crazy."

"No, I'm not. I had to choose between hurting for the rest of my life or making a clean end to it in my mind."

"Didn't you know I was coming here for the Olympics?"

"Later I did. After Helsinki I read all the sports stories in *Pravda* and *Izvestia*. They wrote a lot that you would be contesting against Yury Klemenko." She slid down under the sheet and put her wine glass on the stool beside the bottle. "It made me ache when I knew you'd be coming here. But it didn't change the things I'd decided in my head. It made me all the stronger in my thoughts that I must not see you."

He picked up the plate of food and put it on the floor beside the bed. Then he lay back on the pillow and pulled her close to him. "But here I am."

"Yes, here you are," she said. "Thank God."

"You didn't want to see me but you're glad I'm here."

"What could be more logical than that?"

"I don't like to feel like a trespasser," he said then.

"I don't know that word."

"Trespass. It means to go where you're not supposed to. Someplace where you're not wanted."

"You're teasing me, aren't you?"

"Not necessarily."

"Yes, you are." She raised up on one elbow and looked down at him. She touched his cheek with her fingertips. "I liked your beard before. I *loved* your beard. Now I like your naked face."

"I like *your* naked face." He pulled her close to him and kissed her, felt the length of her body warm against his.

"It's true you are where you are not supposed to be," she said then. "So that means you are a trespasser. But I can't believe you if you say you don't feel wanted."

"It's true. I don't feel wanted."

She eased her leg across his and slowly slid herself on top of him. "Is that better?" she whispered.

"Getting better."

"Better now?" she said.

"Yes."

---

37. ■ In April, when she'd returned to Moscow from Helsinki, Elena had been sent, almost immediately, on a seventeen-day tour of Hungary and Romania. One night in Bucharest, alone in her eighth-floor room in the Hotel Dorobanti, she sat down in her nightgown and robe and wrote a long letter to Chad.

> I know you are back in California now. I am in Bucharest. So we are far away from each other. But all the pictures are still clear in my head. So the time and distance don't seem true or accurate.
>
> We know each other well now, don't we? I feel that way. But I don't know anything at all *about* you. I just know you in the places I saw you. But that's fine for me. I don't need to know more.
>
> Still, I want you to know about me. Even though I am not special or unusual, I would like you to think I am. So I will tell you something about my family. *They* are more unusual than I am.

My grandfather, Gregory Baklanova, was a friend of Trotsky's. He was one of the leaders of the October revolution in 1917. But in 1938 he was arrested, tried as an enemy of the State, and shot. He was a brilliant and important man, but in Moscow I do not speak openly of my relation to him.

My father, Valery Baklanova, became a Soviet hero by publicly renouncing both his father and Trotsky. When he died in 1970, his obituary in *Pravda* said that he had received the Stalin medal, which was true. It also said he was a hero at the Battle of Stalingrad. That was untrue. If I spoke publicly of being Valery Baklanova's daughter, it would be very advantageous for me. But I choose not to. Still my superiors know of the relationship and they defer to me because of it.

My grandmother, who raised me after my mother died, was named Tamara Tsiolkovsky Olenik. I try to pattern myself after her. She was a warm and courageous woman.

Grandmother was the daughter of Kunstantin Tsiolkovsky, one of Russia's first space scientists. He was also a peasant, and I am delighted to be his great-granddaughter. I would claim him proudly even if it were dangerous to do so.

What else can I tell you? I joined the Communist party when I was eighteen. All my friends did. We know it is the only way to have a reasonably solid life.

We do not permit ourselves to think about the truth of things. We remind each other of how much worse things have been in the past and how much worse they could become. We treasure our friendships, enjoy whatever small luxuries we are able to get hold of, and live from day to day.

Before I met you in Helsinki, I honestly never thought of leaving Russia. I never thought of trying to live in some other country. *Since* I met you, I have thought of nothing else. I love you.

Elena

As she finished the letter and read it over, she knew she would never send it. She had no address to send it to. And even if she had an address she could not risk it.

But it gave her a warm and reckless feeling to read the letter out loud, to imagine Chad reading it. She read it through twice before she went to sleep. And the next morning early, before she went down to breakfast, she read it slowly and carefully once more. Then she tore it into tiny, confettilike pieces and flushed it down the toilet.

---

38. At three in the morning Chad and Elena woke up, got out of bed, put on their clothes, and went downstairs into the dark street.

"Is this a wise and brilliant thing to do?"

"No," she said. "It's crazy. But it's no crazier than being together in my apartment. If you are wild enough to dress up in peasant clothes and run away from the Olympic Village, then I am wild enough to walk the streets with you in the middle of the night."

They walked to the corner, down Volkhonka to Gogolevsk and all the way up to Arbatskaya Square.

"In Moscow the best place to hide is outdoors. Especially at night. You can see the city is closed down. There is no life at all after midnight. Even the KGB sleeps at night. At least we pretend they do."

"Do they really put microphones in everybody's home?"

"Only if you are important. Or Jewish. Or if you come from a wicked country like America."

"That means they don't listen to your apartment?"

"If they did, we would both be in some office now, answering a lot of personal questions."

"How about your telephone?" he said.

"That's another matter. No telephone is safe. Did you use my phone before I came home?"

"No."

"Good. You mustn't."

"And what about your neighbors?"

"I know them for a long time. We all help each other. I don't think we have police informers in our house."

"But you can't be sure?"

"Of course not."

At the corner, as they passed under the street light, he said, "Why don't we go off somewhere?"

"What do you mean?"

"Since you have some days off, why don't we drive out in the country?"

"How much time do you have?"

"Three or four days. Five maybe. The decathlon events don't start till the second week of competition."

"But won't they look for you?"

"Sure they will. That's why I shaved my beard and bought these clothes. So I could move around and not be recognized. That Sunday school life was driving me bats. I don't like to eat in a room with five hundred people. I don't need some fool checking my room every night to see if I'm in bed."

"Won't they be angry if you stay away for so many days?"

"I guess so. But they'll get over it."

He felt uncomfortable with what he was saying. He didn't like to deceive her. But he knew he had to feel his way, even with her, had to be sure the ground was solid. If he led her slowly, one step at a time, it would all work. But if he pushed too hard, spoke too soon, he could wreck everything. So he stuck to his timetable, told partial truths, and waited for the moment when he could tell her more.

"So at least I have you for a few days," she said.

"I'll stay as long as I can."

"It won't be long enough."

"Look who's talking. If it was up to you, I wouldn't have seen you at all. You'd be swimming in the Black Sea with some Bulgarian gigolo."

"I told you how I felt. I just thought it was hopeless."

"What do you think now?"

"Ahh . . . I'm *not* thinking. No thinking allowed. I just want to enjoy everything as much as I can for as long as I can, like a child stealing cakes."

"Can we go away for a few days like I said?"

"I'm not sure. Sometimes it's risky to move around. In the country, in a small town, everyone is more visible. But there may be a way. I would like it too. We'll find a way if we can."

"Have you walked enough?" he said then.

"Yes."

"How would you like to go home?"

"I'd like it."

39. Early morning, Alvis Gage, Security Director for the United States contingent, sat in Edmund Yost's guest apartment in an old mansion in Lenin Hills overlooking Moscow.

"Are you absolutely certain?" Yost said.

"No question. We have covered every inch of the Olympic complex, looked every place, and questioned a lot of people. No one has seen him or talked to him since the guard passed him through the gate yesterday morning."

"A man can't just vanish."

"Sure he can. It happens all the time. Seven million people in this city. You could lose a regiment here. The main thing is, he's outside our jurisdiction now. If someone kidnapped him . . ."

"Why do you say that?"

"Because nothing else makes sense. An athlete doesn't work and sweat for years to get to the Olympics, then just walk away from it. Have you ever heard of anybody doing that?"

"No. But there's always a first time." Yost got up and refilled his coffee cup. "The main thing is, I don't want to start a big fuss."

"Nobody does. But when a man's missing, people get nervous. You can't hide it for very long."

"I'm not talking about *hiding* anything. I just don't think we should speculate publicly about what's happened to him. Let's not make any statements about *kidnapping*."

"It's bound to come up whether we say it or not. Meanwhile you have to keep your skirts clean and so do I."

"How do we do that?"

"We have to bring in the Moscow police."

"No, we don't. Not yet. We don't want international headlines on this."

"We can't avoid it. And we're talking about *minutes*. A few hours at most. All anybody knows is that Norris wasn't at the ceremony yesterday. As soon as it leaks that he's been missing for twenty-four hours, that nobody has the slightest idea where he is, all the monkeys are out of the cage. And if it looks like we've been trying to cover up something, we look bad. *You* look bad. The quicker you pass this whole mess along to somebody else, the better off you'll be."

Yost's phone rang then. He picked up the receiver and said, "Edmund Yost speaking . . . Yes, Earl . . . Gage is here now. We've been discussing it . . . What? . . . When? . . . All right, Earl."

He placed the receiver gently in its cradle, sat silent for a moment, then looked at Gage. "Someone solved our problem for us. Chaffee just had a call from Washington. There was a story about Norris on the late news there. They said he's missing and the Olympic Committee is trying to keep it a secret. They quoted Homer Barnett."

Ten minutes later Dick Enberg had a call in his apartment near Lenin Stadium. "This is the communications center, Mr. Enberg. Sorry to call you so early, but we've just had an urgent message from the U.S. Olympic Committee. They've called a press conference for nine o'clock this morning."

40. The heavy drapes in Elena's apartment were drawn tight across the window, shutting out the morning light. She was sleeping soundly, her head on Chad's shoulder, her arm across his chest.

The telephone rang five times before she heard it. When she finally answered it, she said, "Yes . . . yes, Shota . . . I'm sorry. I was dead asleep. I . . . what . . . oh, my God . . . oh, my *God* . . . yes . . . yes, I'll be there . . . yes . . . as fast as I can . . ."

She hung up the phone and slid out from under the sheets. Trying not to wake Chad, she turned on the light in the kitchen corner behind the screen, quickly found the clothes she'd taken off at four that morning, and began to dress. When she came out from behind the screen carrying her shoes and stockings, Chad woke up and switched on the light by the bed.

"Where you going?"

"I'm sorry. I tried not to wake you." She sat down on the edge of the bed beside him and began to pull on her stockings. "I have to go to . . . I mean . . . oh, Chad . . ." She turned suddenly, put her arms around him, and hid her face against his shoulder.

"Hey . . . come on . . . what's the matter?"

"Everything . . . my friend . . . my close friend . . . the red-haired girl you saw me with . . . she's tried to kill herself. That was her brother-in-law who called. She's in the hospital. I mean they're taking her there now and I . . . I have to go there . . ."

She sat up and turned away from him. "Don't touch me or be nice to me. If you do, I'll really fall apart."

She finished putting on her stockings and slipped her feet into her shoes. "I feel so awful. I'm not even awake and I'm crying and I don't know what I'm doing. The poor thing. The poor sweet thing. God help her."

At the door she turned and said, "I'll be back as soon as I . . ." She came back across the room then, knelt down on the bed, and put her arms around him. "I can't stand it for people to be hurt. I *hate* it. I can't stand it when nothing works out right . . ."

She stood up then and crossed the room. She opened the door to the hall and closed it softly behind her. He could hear her quick footsteps in the hall. He got up and went to the window, pulled the drapes open a slit, and watched her cross the street, get into her car, and drive away.

He tried to go back to sleep but he couldn't. Finally he got up and took a bath. Then he went back to bed. He fell asleep immediately but ten minutes later he was wide awake.

He got up and dressed, drank a glass of water, and ate some brown bread and cheese. Then he sat down in front of the television set and switched it on. Edmund Yost's face flickered into focus on the screen. He was being questioned by newsmen in all languages, simultaneous Russian translations flashing on the screen under his picture.

"Of course we were aware that Norris missed the opening ceremonies yesterday; but the Committee was led to believe that he was in the infirmary being treated for a slight cold. As soon as we found out the truth, that he hasn't been seen since yesterday morning, we called this news conference to make the proper announcements."

41. At nine thirty in the morning Viktor Denishev, Second Chief Director, Special Section, First Department of the KGB, walked into his outer office. His assistant, Pavel Lepik, stood up when he came in.

"Is Kuzmin here yet?"

Lepik nodded. "He's waiting in your office."

Valentin Kuzmin, Deputy Director of Internal Affairs, Moscow Police, also stood up when Denishev walked in, Lepik just behind him.

Shaking hands with Denishev, Kuzmin said, "My director asked me to apologize for calling you at home. But since the man in question is an American . . ."

"Of course. He did the proper thing. Now . . . bring me up to the moment. What is the current situation?"

"No change since the director talked with you. Early this morning we had a request from the United States embassy . . ."

"Who contacted you?"

"A woman named Fletemyer in their Public Information Office."

"A routine request?"

Kuzmin nodded. "She simply said one of their Olympic athletes, the one we told you about, Norris is his name, has been missing from the Olympic Village since yesterday morning. Within half an hour they had sent us photographs and information on Norris."

Kuzmin opened his briefcase, took out a folder, and put it on Denishev's desk. Denishev glanced at it, then handed the folder to Lepik. "Check this against our profiles on the Olympic athletes." Lepik left the room.

"What does your director think of all this?"

"He suspects it might be a trick to embarrass the Moscow police."

"That's possible," Denishev said, "but I doubt it." He offered Kuzmin a cigarette, then lighted one for himself. "Let's hope it's something as innocent as that."

42. William Ross Delaney lived in a one-bedroom apartment on Kalinina Prospekt, in a building that American journalists and embassy people called the George Washington Ghetto, an ugly glass-and-concrete tower which Soviet authorities designated in 1950 as a principal dwelling place for American government employees and journalists resident in Moscow.

When Avery Thorp, the *New York Times* man, saw his Moscow home for the first time, he said, "In New

York I finally made it to a two bedroom co-op on Fifth Avenue and Eighty-ninth Street. This joint is like moving back to Queens."

Delaney, young-looking and rugged but only a few years away from retirement, liked to sleep late. Everyone who knew him or worked with him knew that. Usually he arrived at his office in the embassy building at eleven thirty in the morning. Until he was dressed and ready to leave for work, shaken awake by two Gauloise cigarettes and three cups of black coffee, his telephone was turned off.

His second telephone, however, was never turned off. But the number of that phone was known to only two people: Pete Stabler, his associate at the embassy, and Lyman Scruggs, his contact in Langley, Virginia.

At ten thirty, the morning after Chad Norris disappeared, Delaney's phone rang. It was Stabler. "The ambassador's looking for you."

"I thought we had him trained."

"So did I. I told Marie you'd be in between eleven thirty and twelve. But she's all hot and bothered for some reason. Said Sims has to know exactly when he could expect to see you."

"When I get there."

"I told her you'd see him about noon."

"Good."

Delaney had been in Moscow since 1962. Jack Kennedy had sent him. "I need a friend over there," he'd said. "Sooner or later Khrushchev is going to test me. I can smell it. And when he does, I'll need all the firsthand home-grown information I can get."

Delaney had met Kennedy in the spring of 1942. In the Officers' Club in San Diego. Both of them were waiting for ship assignments. They found out they'd been born on the same day, May 29, 1917. When that date came around, they were still in San Diego. So they drank a bottle of Scotch together.

"When the war's over you should move to Boston," Kennedy said. "With a name like Delaney, we'd have you in Congress in no time."

Delaney didn't take that advice. He went home instead to Ottumwa, Iowa. He went to college for a while, worked for a while, drank too much, and ended a cold marriage with a hot divorce.

In 1950 he reenlisted, this time in Naval Intelligence, stationed in Washington, D.C. He kept in touch with Kennedy, and in 1956, taking Kennedy's advice, he left the Navy and joined the Central Intelligence Agency.

In 1961, when Kennedy questioned him about the Cuban invasion, he advised against it. Kennedy didn't listen. Two months later, when they were having dinner together one night, he said, "Okay. You proved your point. You're smarter than I am. I'm better looking but you're smarter. I'd better get you out of town or you'll have my job."

That evening was the first time Moscow was brought up. Delaney said, "I don't think so," but Kennedy persisted. Before the end of the year, Delaney was transferred there.

"Six months if I like it," Delaney said. "Six weeks if I don't." Nineteen years later he was still there, smoothly bilingual and integrated, as Russian as any non-Russian could ever hope or manage to be.

43. "We have a delicate situation here," Ambassador Sims said. "I've had half a dozen calls from Washington this morning. This is something that doesn't involve you, but I felt . . ."

"If it's as delicate as you say it is," Delaney said, "and if it doesn't involve me, I'd just as soon not know about it. I've got a head full of things that *do* involve me."

"I appreciate that. But my orders from the State Department . . ."

"I don't work for the State Department. I take orders from Scruggs and nobody else. I think you and I have discussed this a couple of times before."

Sims smiled and said, "I spoke with Scruggs less than an hour ago. That was one of the Washington calls I mentioned."

Howard Sims had been appointed to his post by Nixon in 1971. Many people in government thought he was an unlikely choice. Even more people thought he was an embarrassing choice.

"Our new ambassador to Russia, Howard Sims, is an outspoken racist, a John Birch supporter, and an advocate of Pentagon control of defense spending," Tom Wicker had written. "These are impressive credentials certainly, but not for the job he's been chosen for."

Senator Javits had said, "If any one man can destroy both the concept and the machinery of detente, that man is certainly Howard Sims. He may never even *meet* Brezhnev."

As it turned out, Javits was mistaken. Fast on his feet, Sims expanded his soft-spoken bigotry to include the Jews in the Soviet Union. He saw no reason why the Kremlin should accede to their demands for emigration or anything else. "A troublemaker is a troublemaker," he had told Mamotov. "It has nothing to do with religion."

Mamotov was pleased. When he told Brezhnev about the conversation, Brezhnev was pleased too. They were also pleased to learn that Ambassador Sims's brother was a director and principal stockholder of International Grains, the third largest wheat export company in the United States.

When President Carter took office in 1977, the Russian ambassador in Washington, through appropriate channels, made it clear that his government was very content with Howard Sims. Carter, through the same channels, said it was customary for a new president to appoint ambassadors who shared his political convictions. For weeks there was lively conjecture about who would succeed Sims. Long lists were made and discussed and public records compared. But when all the conjecture died down, Sims was still in Moscow.

"What did Scruggs have to say?" Delaney asked.

"He said you are to stay out of the Chad Norris situation."

"I'd be happy to. Who's Chad Norris?"

Sims explained what had happened. Then, "My deputy and members of the Olympic Committee met with the Moscow Ministry of Internal Affairs earlier this morning."

"What makes you think I want to get involved in that stuff? I don't look for lost tourists. If I did, I wouldn't get anything else done."

"The KGB seems to think it's important. They've taken over from Internal Affairs."

"That doesn't surprise you, does it? They think everything is their job. They'll send a man to unplug your sink if you make it sound spooky enough."

"One other thing. We've had a request for a group of FBI men to come here and assist in the investigation."

"You're kidding."

"No, I'm not. Eight men left Washington an hour or so ago."

"Requested by whom?"

"The call went straight from the Kremlin to the White House."

"Now I've heard everything," Delaney said.

"That's why you and your people are to stay out of it. The investigation will be coordinated between our FBI people and the Moscow police."

Delaney snuffed out his cigarette and stood up. "I think I'd better have a chat with Scruggs after all."

"*I* talked to Scruggs," Sims said.

"I know you did. But *I* didn't."

44. Delaney's office, behind a door marked PERSON-NEL COORDINATOR, was in a lead-lined subbasement, accessible from the other floors of the embassy by two private elevators, their doors opening only by combination locks, the combinations changed five times every month and known then only to Delaney, Stabler, and Scruggs.

The other four people who worked with Delaney and Stabler—a computer programmer, two secretaries, and an archivist—had been hired and trained at the agency headquarters in Virginia.

When Delaney came into his office, he said to Stabler, "Get Scruggs on the horn."

Stabler looked at the wall clock. "You want to wake him up?"

"He's awake. Call his office."

While he waited for the call, Delaney sat behind his desk and leafed quickly through *Pravda* and *Izvestia*. No mention of Chad Norris.

"Scruggs is on the ghost line," Stabler said.

Delaney picked up the receiver and said, "Hello, Papa. You're up early. What's going on?"

He tilted back in his chair then, smoking and listening. Finally he said, "That's more like it."

45. Chad sat in Elena's apartment, no lamps on, a soft blur of light bleeding through the draperies. The room was half dark, and still. No radio on. No television. No sound of water in the pipes, no faucets dripping. He felt isolated, immobilized, entombed.

Since the day he had returned to California from Helsinki, his hours had been packed with motion and concentration. Running, training, jumping, vaulting. Pressure always. Inside and outside. Straining for some optimum, some peak performance, then straining for a higher peak. A longer jump, a faster time, an unbeatable throw. Up at dawn. Struggle and strain and run all day, scheme and read and study all evening, then sleep like a drugged animal till the alarm went off and he was outside again, running.

After Oregon, after his victory in the trials, more pressure. Training harder, straining to do it better, to stretch himself.

But most pressing, now that he'd brought off the miracle, now that he was going to Moscow, was the weight of his secret.

The details of it exploded in his head like star shells, the uncertainties, the imponderables, the unpredictable days and nights ahead, the shadows and blank spaces.

Still his forward motion had been constant during those final weeks in California, no hesitation or slippage permitted. He had simply told himself that nothing could stop him or sidetrack him.

That unswerving frame of mind had stayed with him. Even when it looked as though Elena was out of reach, he would not allow himself to flag or change rhythm.

But now, silent and by himself, in the soft center of an unquiet city, he began for the first time to have second thoughts. Telling himself over and over that confidence and conviction were his best weapons, he began to lose confidence and to question his convictions.

Just being in Moscow, *seeing* it, the distances, the size, the complexities, the sullen faces and watchful eyes, seeing all that, sensing the strangeness, made the simplest move or forward step seem forbidding.

And Elena . . . what about her? With her scent all around him in the room, his skin still sensitized by hers, he had to face the truth now. She was not a known quantity. Not by any means. If he was beginning to be afraid now, how could he expect courage from her? What if she simply looked at him with disbelief, shook her head, and said no?

Sitting alone in the dark, feeling the foundations tremble under him, he answered himself the only way he could. "She won't say that." And he was persuaded. At least he made a strong effort to convince himself that he was persuaded.

46.

At four in the afternoon Stabler came into Delaney's office and said, "Everything's in motion. The Langley computers are working on Norris. We'll know every freckle on his carcass in a few hours, who his high school girl friend was, and what grade he got in algebra."

"Good. What about the men the Bureau is sending over?"

"We've got the list. Milton Goodrich is coming with them. He'll run the operation."

"That's what he thinks. The KGB will run the operation. Denishev will have Goodrich tied in a thousand knots."

"This is a new one on me," Stabler said.

"That's the idea. Denishev thinks he's invented something, asking the FBI to come to Moscow to work on a case. Goodwill. Brotherly love. He wants to attract attention. Steal a few headlines."

"And if things get sticky, he's got somebody to share the flack."

"That's it. If Norris turns up dead, or if some bunch of cuckoo birds is holding him for ransom, Denishev can say, 'Don't blame us. He's an American citizen and even America's top cops can't find him.' It's a cute idea. But he didn't fool Scruggs. He knows that Goodrich will be nailed down so tight he won't be able to burp. Denishev will let them cruise around the Olympic Village till their legs drop off, but they won't be running loose around Moscow. I promise you that."

"Why did Scruggs tell Sims we'd stay out of it?"

"Blowing smoke. Scruggs is hedging his bets, too. But he's not fooling anybody but Sims. And it's a cinch he's not fooling Denishev. He's a shrewd old bastard."

Delaney's secretary buzzed him on the intercom, then brought in an envelope. "This was delivered for you upstairs."

"How long ago?"

"Ten minutes," the girl said.

As the secretary left the room and closed the door behind her, Delaney opened the envelope and read the card inside. He laughed and tossed it across the desk to Stabler. "I told you he was shrewd. Now he's asking me to have dinner with him."

"Denishev?"

Delaney nodded. "He picked a good restaurant, too. Forty miles out of town. But it's worth the trip."

"You going?"

"Wouldn't miss it for anything."

"Do you know him?"

"I've never met him but I *know* him. And he knows *me*. I guarantee you he's got a file on me that would choke a goat. And a nice snapshot stuck up on his bulletin board."

"What do you think he wants?"

"I know exactly what he wants. He'll tell me he knows I'm looking for Norris and he's glad I am. For once we're on the same side. That kind of guff. But mostly he'll be trying to find out what I know that he doesn't. Anytime an American disappears in Russia, they assume he's a plant. You know that. Somebody we're putting underground. So I'll act mysterious and make him nervous."

Delaney stood up and put on his jacket. "I'm going home. I'll probably drink a gallon of vodka tonight, so don't wake me up tomorrow unless war is declared. When do those Bureau guys get in?"

"Sometime this evening, I guess."

"You know any of them?"

"A couple. One of them's Dick Hough. Used to be my brother-in-law about fifteen years ago."

"You think he'd like to have dinner with you?"

"I wouldn't be surprised. He's still sweet on my sister."

"Good. See what you can find out. Maybe they know something we don't know. It's not likely but there's always a first time."

Just before he went out the door, Delaney said, "What about your sister? How does she feel about it?"

"She didn't even like him when she was married to him."

47.

"If you had been listening to the radio today," Elena said, "if you'd seen the afternoon papers, you would know what I mean. All stories about Chad Norris. Where is he? What happened to him? Every policeman in Moscow is looking for you. And special government police are coming from Washington. They're pasting your picture up on walls. By tomorrow everybody in the streets will know what you look like."

"No, they won't. They'll see a picture of some long-haired joker with a beard. *That's* what they'll be looking for. I could stand right beside one of those pictures and no one would know me."

"Don't be so sure. There may be other pictures. Someone will say, 'What would he look like without a beard?' "

"By then I'll be back in my bed at the Olympic Village."

"They're going to a lot of trouble," she said. "Someone will be very angry with you."

"That's all right. It's worth it," he said. "Don't you think it's worth it?"

"It is to me. I'd like to wrap you up and keep you here till you're an old skinny man with blue veins and brown spots on your hands. I don't want you to leave at all. But I don't want you to be in trouble."

"You could be in trouble too."

"I don't think about that."

"Then don't worry about me," he said.

"I can't help it. This is an ugly day for me. I can't get Larisa off my mind."

Elena sat curled up in a chair, rumpled and exhausted, her bare feet tucked up under her, her skin very pale, soft blue smudges under her eyes. She'd been home for more than an hour and she was calmer now.

She had been angry before. Cold and silent. No tears. She'd seemed past that. Past consolation too. Unable to connect, even with Chad. Unwilling to. She had stood at the window, both hands holding a glass of scalding tea, looking out at the street, her back to the room.

Turning away from the window finally, the coldness still there, she'd said, "I've never felt like this before. For the first time I know how it feels to want to kill someone. If I knew a *name*, if I knew which person in what office had put their stamp on Larisa, I could kill them in a second. Without thinking about it or feeling sorry after."

Coming across the room then, sinking down in the chair by the bed, she had been silent again for a long time. At last she'd said, "The thing is, there's never anybody to accuse, no one to complain to or appeal to. Any office I go to, any pitiful functionary with blue ink on his fingers will give me sympathy. But nobody will take the blame. They point a finger in the air and shrug their shoulders. That means the decision came from a higher office, from some stronger authority. It goes all the way like that, all the way to the Kremlin, where no one gets to ask any questions at all. But even there, if you *could* go there, you'd get the same answer. Brezhnev would point his finger at the ceiling. No matter how angry you get you can never find the enemy. Because *every* order, *every* crazy law, finally dead-ends in Lenin's tomb. He's still the final authority. There are words from Lenin to cover every situation. And if they can't *find* the right words, they make some up. *New* words from Lenin. If we ever have another revolution, it would have to start with Lenin's tomb. Somebody would have to drag out that wax doll they pretend is his body, pour gasoline on it, and burn it. But it will never happen. I promise you that. He's the only god we've got. If a banner goes up on the Kremlin wall tonight with the words *Comrade Lenin said that horse manure is more valuable than gold,* tomorrow morning there will be millions of people in the streets with buckets and shovels hoping to get rich."

Finally she began to talk about Larisa. "I've known her since I was a little girl. She lived here in Moscow with her aunt. In the same building where my grandmother lived. She's three years older than me, but she was always very nice to me. She took me along to her dancing classes, went with me to the cinema the first time I was allowed to go, and taught me to sew and do needlepoint. She was my closest friend. My *only* friend, I used to feel.

"When she got married in 1969, it almost killed me. She was only seventeen and that was bad enough. But worse than that, she married Leonid Zhabotinsky. He called himself a poet and now of course I know that he is. He's written some really beautiful things. But *then,* all I could think was that he was too old and too ugly for Larisa. He was forty-two when they got married. He had a deep scar down one cheek, and he'd been in and out of jail since he was eighteen. He had been a school friend of Yevtushenko and had shared a cell with Solzhenitsyn for fifteen months. But eventually he quarreled with everybody.

"In 1971, when Larisa's baby was seven months old,

the government allowed her and Leonid and the child to emigrate to Israel. Leonid didn't want to go, but the government *allowed* him to anyway. I was sixteen that year and I couldn't stop crying when she told me she was leaving. But she wrote me a lot once she got there and sometimes she sent me little gifts with Shota, Leonid's brother. He's an Aeroflot pilot, the man we were with when you followed us here from Rossiya.

"The three of us had been having a farewell lunch that day. Larisa had been allowed to come here for two weeks to visit her aunt, the woman who raised her. She was scheduled to go back to Israel yesterday. But when she went to pick up her ticket, they told her the trip had been canceled and her exit visa recalled. She knew what that meant and so did Shota. The State was getting even with her husband. She knew they would never let her go back to Israel. So she . . . oh, God . . . I feel so awful . . ."

"How is she?"

"She's not dead. But she lost a lot of blood. And she won't open her eyes or talk to anybody. Not even to me or to Shota. I mean she breathes and her heart is still beating, but she's not really alive. She'll lie there in the hospital with all those tubes in her till they send her home. Then she'll either cut her wrists again or she'll sit in a chair by the window and starve herself to death. I know her. I know how she is. Clinically she's not dead. But she'll never be alive again."

Elena stood up then and walked to the window again. It was dark in the streets. She pulled the drapes together. When she turned back to Chad, she said, "I brought home a very big bottle of very good vodka and some cold roast chicken. How would you like to eat and make love and get very drunk with me?"

Much later, in bed, she finally began to cry. "God, I

feel awful. My heart hurts. I hurt all over." He pulled her close to him, held her face against his chest, stroked her back with his hand.

"I hate it when I can't do anything to help," she said. "I hate it when all I can do is stand there and watch somebody suffer. I can't stand that. What kind of a life is that?"

She cried herself to sleep with his arms around her. He lay awake for a long time, staring up into the dark, trying to fit the pieces together, trying to select the exact words and phrases he would use when he told her.

48.

Delaney drove out Leningradsky Prospekt to the Leningrad Expressway, then northwest past Khimki and Kurkino, through Morsichino and Frisanovka. Finally, just past Malino, he turned off the main road and drove a quarter-mile back through a birch forest to the Praga.

It was a popular restaurant with the Moscow residents who could afford it. Officials high in government came there, army officers, film directors, and ballet dancers. The parking area was always packed with limousines from seven in the evening till long past midnight. Tonight, however, Delaney saw only three cars there.

He spoke smooth Russian, guttural and colloquial, to the emaciated white-haired man who met him just inside the entrance, Mikhail Zatec, a Czech, the owner of Praga. In a climate of fear and subservience, Zatec was independent and egocentric. He remembered no one's name and recognized very few faces. It was part of his legend that he had once made Molotov wait forty-five minutes for a table. When his tables were filled, he simply closed the front door and locked it. Authority and power did not impress him. "What can they do to me? If I am dead or in jail, where will they eat?"

Tonight, however, Praga was empty. At eight thirty all but two of the waiters had been sent home. When Delaney arrived, the heavy front doors had to be unlocked to let him in.

Denishev was waiting at a round table in a private dining room, a heavy brocade cloth on the table, crystal and silver, wine in ice buckets, a decanter of vodka beside each of the two dinner plates, and the waiters standing by.

Denishev, when he stood up, was taller than Delaney had imagined, not so broad, not as bulky. But his hand was rough as a workman's and his wrists were corded and thick. His hair was steel gray, parted carefully on one side and plastered across the high brown dome of his head.

He greeted Delaney in Russian. "You are kind to join me for a meal. I am delighted to meet you."

"The honor is mine," Delaney replied in Russian. "I have looked forward to meeting you."

After Zatec left the room, Denishev said, "Do you know this restaurant?"

"Very well. I have been a customer for almost twenty years."

"Does Mr. Zatec recognize you at last?"

"Not yet. And you?"

"When friends intercede sometimes he can be stimulated to remember. But normally he knows neither my name nor my face."

"Tonight I think he remembered. We have the restaurant all to ourselves."

Denishev smiled and made a small gesture with his hands. "As I said . . . when friends intercede . . ."

The waiters poured vodka and two kinds of wine, put out silver platters of caviar, sour cream, chopped onions, cheese, olives, and smoked salmon at either side of the table, bowed, and quietly left the room.

"I took the liberty of ordering," Denishev said. "I hope you have a good appetite. Zatec has promised to bury us in food."

"Good."

"I congratulate you on your skill with the Russian language," Denishev said then. "I've been listening carefully. No one would guess you were not born in Moscow."

"I've had a long time to practice. And at one time I had a good teacher."

"Mira Diomidov," Denishev said. "No one has ever understood the Chekhov heroines the way she did. She was our most brilliant actress. We miss her very much."

"So do I."

"You put us in a difficult position, you two. Awkward. I'm sure you realized that. Diomidov was a national artist, and she had chosen to share her home with a . . . what shall we call you . . . a government employee . . ."

"A worker," Delaney said.

". . . in the Embassy of the United States."

"But only in the basement."

"Yes, of course. A basement worker."

They smiled and drank from their vodka glasses.

"We expected you to order me home," Delaney said then.

"That was our intention. But Diomidov outmaneuvered us. She took her case to Khrushchev, one of her most adoring admirers. She said she realized that she had been naughty and she understood perfectly that we would have to send you back to America. But all the same, she said, your leaving would make her so sad that she would have no choice but to retire from the theatre. She convinced the premier that on the day you left Russia she would leave the National Theatre and never appear on the stage again. She gave us no alternative. We were forced to look the other way."

"I hope you didn't regret it."

"We had no reason to. Diomidov was a patriot, of course, as well as a great artist." He smiled and poured some vodka into his glass. "But if I told you that I like to be outmaneuvered, I would not be telling the truth. When I was a schoolboy in Minsk, I was a wrestler. I was strong but clumsy. Many of my opponents were better wrestlers than I was, but I usually beat them. Because I hated to lose."

"Everybody hates to lose," Delaney said.

"That's true. But some of us hate it more than others."

They ate slowly and sumptuously. Trout and roast duckling stuffed with apples, venison steak with a Dijon mustard sauce, cheese and tomatoes and mashed eggplant, cauliflower and asparagus and endive salad. Peaches in wine and a tray of pastries with ice cream. Brandy with the coffee and vodka with everything. And long dark Cuban cigars.

When the table had been cleared and the waiters had gone, Denishev said, "As much as I have enjoyed having dinner with you . . ."

"I understand. There are matters that must be discussed."

"I think *must* is too strong a word. There is nothing

official about this meeting. I discussed it with none of my associates. It was strictly my own notion. I thought perhaps you and I could practice a bit of . . . let's call it preventive medicine."

"How do you mean?"

"The Olympic Games. The Soviet people are trying very hard to make an impression on the world. We make no secret of that. We have planned for years, worked hard, and spent millions of rubles. You've been here. You've seen all this happen. We've transformed the city, made it look different. Newer and cleaner and better than it has ever looked before."

"No question about it."

"So you will understand when I say that we don't want to undo what has been done. We want no incidents. We've taken every precaution against terrorists and troublemakers. Our security system is foolproof. Or so we thought."

"You're talking about Chad Norris."

"That's right. He's a citizen of your country and a guest of mine. I can think of no situation in the past where your objectives and mine were identical. But this could be that kind of situation. *If* it is, if we could be candid with each other . . ."

"Why not?" Delaney said. "Let's start with a candid question. I was told that you asked for my people to be kept out of this operation. True or false?"

"True."

"Why?"

"Protecting ourselves. Implying that you may have arranged for his disappearance. Trying to give the impression that we know something we don't actually know."

"Why the invitation to the FBI?"

"Self-protection again. Someone to share the blame if a bad situation develops."

"Like Munich?"

"Anything bad."

"All right," Delaney said. "You say you've taken precautions against terrorists. What about your own dissident groups? Is there any chance they could be holding Norris, planning some kind of power move, using him as bait?"

"I challenge you to find *one* Soviet dissident, either known or suspected, in Moscow. They have all left the city."

"How did you manage that?"

"We have an elaborate resort on the Black Sea near Sochi. Normally it is used by our agents and their families. At the moment we are using it as an expense-paid vacation site for all the people we don't want to see in Moscow for the next two weeks."

"Are you sure Norris isn't in jail somewhere? You're not the only police organization in Russia."

"That's the first thing we investigated. Nobody by that name is in custody. Nobody with that face. We have the best computer system in the world."

"I know. We sold it to you."

"Only the first one. Now we've copied it."

"And improved it?"

"Of course." Denishev smiled.

"And next year you're going to invent the telephone."

"*This* year." Then, "Are you satisfied with my answers?"

"So far. Now I'm waiting for the questions."

"Your government is as complex as mine. You may not know the answers."

"In that case I'll give you an educated opinion."

"Is there any chance that your government would

create an incident to discredit the Soviet Union? Would they instigate a crisis at the Olympic Games to embarrass us before the world?"

"It's possible," Delaney said, "but not very probable. In the first place, our government has nothing to do with our Olympic team."

"I have read that but I've never believed it."

"It's true. They furnish no money, no facilities. *Nothing.* So if we wanted to embarrass your government, chances are we wouldn't use the Olympics to do it. We have no control over the situation and that makes it too risky. The payoff wouldn't be worth the effort. Next question."

"It's not a question. Because I know you wouldn't give me a true answer."

"You never know. I might."

"Some of my associates believe that Norris is a plant, that you plan to lose him here in Russia where he can function as an operative for one of your intelligence units."

"That's not impossible, I guess. But who would be idiotic enough to start a clandestine operation with all the publicity Norris is getting? Why do it? What's the point? We don't want people who get their pictures in the paper a lot. We have the same problems you do. Would you try to plant a well-known athlete in the United States?"

"No."

"That's your answer. We wouldn't either."

Denishev walked with Delaney to his car, two body-guards following a few steps behind. "It was a good dinner," Delaney said. "Thank you."

"My pleasure. I hope you agree that we are not in conflict in this Norris business."

"With a full stomach, I'll agree to anything."

"I'll remember that."

"But if it turns out you've got him locked up in Lubyanka Prison, then we'll be in conflict. I promise you that. For now, I just want to find him."

"So do we," Denishev said. He stood in the parking lot watching Delaney's car pull out. As his bodyguards stepped up on either side of him, he said, "Did you call it in?"

"Yes, sir. Twenty-four-hour surveillance. A follow car will pick him up as he drives through Malino."

On his way home, as soon as the car turned into the road behind him, Delaney spotted it. "There we are. Right on schedule," he said. "Denishev, you're a real lollypop."

49.

It was one fifteen in the morning when Delaney pulled into the underground garage of his apartment building, locked his car, and went upstairs. At the precise moment he opened his door, six hours earlier New York time, Frank Reynolds interrupted the *ABC Evening News* for a special report from Howard Cosell.

Grim-faced but looking somehow triumphant, Cosell said, "Disturbing news, ladies and gentlemen, from the Olympic Games in Moscow. Potential havoc as this reporter sees it. Tragedy in the making. And . . . alarming evidence of government interference and obfuscation.

Our government as well as that of the Soviets. The threat, it seems to me, of an Olympic Watergate aborning.

"Follow these details if you will. Item: Chad Norris, the bearded world record-holder in the decathlon, one of the U.S. team's cardinal contenders for the gold in Moscow, *was not present* in Lenin Stadium for the opening day gala ceremonies.

"Item: Upon investigation, it was found that no one, including his coach, the venerable Homer Barnett, and his roommate, Dilly Upshaw, the lightning-bolt sprinter from Memphis State, *no one* was able to say where this hirsute young man might be.

"Item: Left on his bedside table when he disappeared were his wallet, his United States passport, *and* his Olympic Village identification. In *my* view—and I submit this for your consideration—this is not the act of a person who expects to be away from his room for very long, certainly not in a city of the size and character of the Soviet capital.

"Item: Not only is a diligent search going on at this very second, involving the Moscow city police and the notorious, if I may use that appellation, the *notorious* Komitet Gosudarstvennoye Bezopastnosti, better known as the KGB, but *now,* now we have it on indisputable Washington, D.C., authority that a crack squad of agents from our Federal Bureau of Investigation has flown to Moscow to assist in the search.

"A singular development surely. And even more remarkable, we believe, is the fact that almost nothing has been announced or revealed to the American people about this exhaustive manhunt. No official details. No speculation. No conclusions drawn.

"Thus we can only assume that the proper language here is, plainly and simply, *cover-up*. Repellent and ugly as that word has become to all of us, the evidence dictates that in this instance, it is the proper choice.

"Where is Chad Norris? Is he a political prisoner? Is he being held hostage somewhere behind the Iron Curtain? Is he, God forbid, already a victim of some terrorist's gun? And if so, are other fine young athletes, at this very moment, also in danger?

"All these, we feel, are legitimate questions. All deserving prompt and lucid answers. Is Moscow destined to become another bloody Munich? We hope and pray, as all of you certainly do, that such a tragic occurrence could never be repeated. But the circumstances in Moscow, as we see them at this juncture, are, at the very least, disturbing. And I, for one, am frightened. I am, frankly, scared to death."

50. "What if you had a chance to leave Russia," Chad said. "Would you go?"

They were sitting at the table in front of the window, midmorning, cloudy but hot outside, drinking tea and eating black bread with sweet butter and jam.

He had been awake, off and on, all through the night, trying to plan what he would say, trying to select the best moment to say it, stockpiling all his persuasions and reassurances, searching for answers to whatever questions she might ask.

When she woke up they had a cup of tea in bed, propped up on pillows, laughing and talking. Then they took a bath together in the long tub, got dressed, and sat down at last at the breakfast table. Seated across from her so he could see her face, search her eyes, read her expressions, he asked the first question.

"I leave Russia all the time," she said. "I'm one of the lucky ones. I've been to Poland, Hungary, Romania, Bulgaria, Czechoslovakia, and Outer Mongolia. I've even been to *Finland*."

"That's not what I mean. What if you could get out and *stay* out? Leave and never come back?"

"That's an odd question."

"What's odd about it?"

"I don't know. I just don't want to talk about it."

"Why not?"

"I just don't."

"All right," he said. "We won't talk about it. It's your house. You get to make the rules."

"You're angry, aren't you?"

"No."

"Don't be angry."

"I'm not."

"Yes, you are." She got up and walked to the stove. She stood with her back to him and poured boiling water from the kettle into the teapot. "I'm sorry," she said. "I wasn't trying to make rules. I'm not telling you what you can say and what you can't." When she sat down at the table again, she said, "I was just surprised, I guess. Why were you asking me that?"

"No reason. It was just a question. I couldn't sleep very well last night, and I was thinking about you and your friend . . ."

"Larisa."

"I kept thinking about what happened to her and

everything you said. The way you felt about it. So I thought . . ."

"I know," she said. "It's a logical question." She poured more tea into their cups. "And the answer is . . . of course I think about it. We all think about it and talk about it. But it's not the way you may imagine it is. I have many friends who are dissatisfied and frustrated. But that doesn't mean they want to leave the Soviet Union and go to America. We know your sidewalks aren't paved with gold any more than ours are."

"If no one wants to go anywhere, why do you talk about it so much?"

"Complicated," she said. "No simple answer to that."

"Then give me a complicated answer."

"I can't do that either. But I'll give you an illustration. In Czechoslovakia, in 1968, when Dubcek was arrested and the Soviet tanks came into Prague, three young film directors managed to get out without too much trouble. Two of them went to France and one to America. I remember hearing them talk on someone's shortwave radio. They said they left because they could not live or work under an authoritarian government, that they refused to spend their lives as residents of a police state. But three years later two of them were back in Prague. And a year after that the third one came home too.

"They missed their country. It was as simple as that. They needed to work in terms of their own language, with their own people. In a familiar atmosphere. They still hated the government policies, but they were Czechs and they needed to be in Czechoslovakia."

"Is that the way you feel?" Chad said.

"I didn't say that. Let's say I *understand* that feeling."

"That's the trouble. Everybody *understands* everything. I'm sure your friend Larisa is lying there half dead, *understanding* exactly why she's in the hospital. Does everybody just talk and get drunk and *explain* things to each other? Don't they ever get mad? Don't *you* ever get mad? You were mad last night, I'll tell you that. You were mad as hell when you were telling me about Larisa. You said she was as good as dead and it was the government's fault. No question about it, you were mad then."

"Why are you shouting like that? Why are you so angry?"

"Because all of a sudden, you're *not*. You want to have it both ways and you can't. You can't see Larisa in that hospital bed and know what's happened to her and then turn around and start panting about Mother Russia. It won't work. It never has worked and it won't work now. That's what they *want* you to feel. The *land* and the *flag* and let's all have a drink. That's how you're programed to think."

"I'm not programed."

"The hell you're not. What would you call it? When you start to make excuses for this nut-house country, you're either programed or you're crazy. You're not crazy, are you?"

"No. And I'm not . . ."

"Then you're programed. It's a police state, for Christ's sake. *Face* it! A few people live great and a lot of people suffer. Everybody's scared to speak up, scared to talk on the phone, scared to write letters, scared to *think*. What's good about that? Is there *one* good thing about all that? I mean if you're satisfied to go where you're told, *do* what you're told, live where you're told to live, if you're willing to turn your whole life over to a computer, then this is a great place to be. But if you *want* anything, if you *need* anything, if you *are* anything, then you have to try for something better, don't you? Or at least something *different*. Or else you can give up like Larisa did."

"She didn't give up. She didn't have any choice."

"Bullshit. Everybody has a choice. I'd rather be shot in the head trying to cross the border into Turkey than just give up and get into the bathtub with a razor blade. Death is no surprise. Everybody dies. The trick is to die while you're still trying to *live*. Larisa's not doing herself any favors. Or her kid. Or her husband. She's just making life easy for the people she hates most. They'll dump her in a hole in the ground and forget she was ever alive."

"Don't talk like that."

"Why not? It's the truth."

"It's *your* truth. It's the way *you* see it. Other people see it differently. Other people know what the problems are. All of us had friends who are dead now because they talked the way you're talking. They thought it was better to die trying, and that's what they did."

"Wait a minute. First you said nobody wants to get out. Now you're saying they *want* to but they're afraid. Which is it?"

"Both. A *lot* of things are true. Not just *one* thing. It's not enough just to *want* something. It takes courage, too. Most people don't have that courage. They can't go after what they want. They settle for what they can *get*. You know that as well as I do. For every smart hero there are a million dumb cowards."

"What about you?" he said then.

"We're not talking about me."

"Yes, we are. *I* am. That's *all* I'm talking about. Do you have the courage to go after what you want?"

"Sometimes I do. Sometimes I don't. If it's important . . ."

"Let's say it's *very* important. Let's say it's the most important thing in the world. What if you decide you want a different kind of life? And what if it turns out there's no way to have that life as long as you stay here? Would you have the guts to leave, to *try* to leave?"

"What does that mean . . . the *guts* to leave?"

"The *courage*."

She looked down at her teacup, turned it slowly in the saucer. Without looking up she said, "The truth is I don't think I would. I'm like everybody else I know. I'd rather keep what I have than end up with nothing. I don't want to be in jail and I don't want to be dead." She looked up at him then. "Also, it's more than just courage. You can't ignore what your head tells you. It's one thing to decide *what* you want to do. It's another thing to know *how*."

"What does that mean?" he said.

"It means the authorities don't make it easy. They don't pass out handbooks telling people how to run away. All those walls and soldiers and guns are not to keep people *out*. They're to keep people *in*."

"All right," he said then, "let me ask you something else. What if I told you, right here, right now, that I have no intention of going back to the Olympic Village? What if I said I'm going to stay here in Russia? What if I said that I've made up my mind that I want to be with you, no matter what, and if the only way I can do that is to give up my U.S. citizenship and stay in Moscow, then that's what I want to do."

Her voice was very quiet when she answered. "You're *not* saying that. I know you're not."

"How do you know?"

"If you *were* saying it and I believed you meant it, I'd say it was an insane idea. I would never let you do it."

"Why not?"

"Because . . . because there's nothing here for you."

"*You're* here."

"This isn't fair. I don't like this conversation."

"Why not? Are you saying you've never thought of it?"

"Of us?"

"That's right. Are you telling me you've never wondered if there wasn't some way we could stay together?"

"Of course I've thought about that. You know I have. I think about it all the time. Sometimes it seems as if I don't think about anything else."

"What do you think when you think about it?"

"I think it's impossible."

"Of course it is," he said. Then, "But what if I showed you that it wasn't impossible? What if I proved to you that it was very *possible*?"

She sat looking down at her cup for a long, silent time. When she looked up, there were tears in her eyes.

"That's all I wanted to know," he said.

part 3

51.

Delaney sat in Ambassador Sims's office, legs crossed, smoking a cigarette. On his right, in a straight-backed chair beside Sims's desk, sat Milton Goodrich, Deputy Operations Director of the Federal Bureau of Investigation, based in Washington.

A bland-looking man in rimless glasses, wearing a conservative brown suit and expensive black shoes, Goodrich looked ill at ease. Sims also looked ill at ease. Only Delaney, the smoke curling lazily out of his nostrils, seemed well-nourished and content.

Sims resettled himself in the soft leather chair he'd had shipped to Moscow from his Chicago office, cleared his throat, and tried to take command.

"Mr. Delaney, this is a branch of the United States Department of State. You are a senior employee here, that's true, but I am in charge. Whatever your feelings about me, I expect you to have respect for this office."

"No problem there," Delaney said. "You're the fifth ambassador I've seen sitting here. And I had no problems at all with the first four. Because they realized that I don't work for the State Department."

"Technically, that's true."

"Not just technically," Delaney said. *"Totally."*

Trying to regain some stature in front of Goodrich, Sims squirmed in his chair, popped a mint into his mouth, and said, "These are unusual circumstances. I think you'll agree with that. When the Soviet officials requested the assistance of our federal investigators, they made it very clear that there should be no Central Intelligence involvement. Wasn't that your understanding, Mr. Goodrich?"

"That's the way it was passed along to us. No KGB. No CIA. Just the Moscow Internal Affairs Police and our people."

"Nobody in Washington took that seriously, did they?" Delaney said.

"We had no reason not to," Goodrich said.

"You have *every* reason not to. Who do you think dreamed up those rules? Who do you think that request came from?"

"It came to me through diplomatic channels," Sims said.

"Maybe it did. But first it came from Viktor Denishev. If that name doesn't mean anything to you, I'll tell you what he does. He's in charge of the First Department, Special Section, of the KGB. First Department means he watchdogs all foreign nationals coming into Russia. Special Section means he can get involved in anything else that comes along. He's the original thousand-pound gorilla joke. He sleeps wherever he wants to."

"Who gave you this information?" Sims said.

"Denishev."

"Why would he do that?" Goodrich said.

"Because he knew I'd guess it anyway. We've been bumping heads for fifteen years. We both know what we can get by with and what we can't."

"All I know is that my office promised the Kremlin and you promised me that your people would stay out of the Chad Norris investigation."

"I didn't promise anything," Delaney said. "And if *you* did, you shouldn't have. Let's not kid ourselves. Mr. Goodrich and his people are window dressing. They won't be able to take a leak without Denishev's men looking over their shoulders. I'll tell you the truth. I have no idea where Norris is. But if anybody can locate him, my people can. They know the terrain and they're free to move around. So that's the way it is. I'm cleared with Scruggs and I won't back off till he tells me to."

"You're making it very awkward for me," Sims said.

"No, I'm not. Nobody expects the ambassador to know what's going on. Just play innocent."

"That's pretty hard to do when Stabler is all over the Olympic Village asking questions. What do I say when they call me on that?"

"They won't."

"And if they do?"

"Tell them it's news to you and pretend to be very shocked. Tell them you're starting a full investigation."

"Then what?"

"Then nothing. Just forget it. The Kremlin will understand *that*. That's the way they operate."

52. "It's eight hundred and forty-eight kilometers from Moscow to Vyborg," Chad said. "Exactly five hundred and twenty-seven miles. From Vyborg to Valdagersk is a little more than twenty miles. So let's say five hundred and fifty miles total.

"At fifty miles per hour that means it will take us eleven hours. Can we average fifty miles an hour?"

"Yes," Elena said. "Those are good roads."

"Good. But I'm estimating *twelve* hours just in case. That means we leave here at three in the afternoon and arrive in Valdagersk between two and three the following morning. So most of the trip will be at night. We'll take turns driving and we won't stop. We'll take food and water in the car and cans of extra gasoline in the backseat.

"In Valdagersk there's a community parking lot in the center of town. We'll leave the car there and walk down to the shore road. Muonio's house is a half-mile outside the village. It sits on pilings fifty yards up from the beach. His dock has a red light on it and his mother's name, Vera, is painted on his boat."

"How does he know . . ." Elena began.

"Let me finish. Then you can ask questions." They were still at the breakfast table. But the room had an electric atmosphere now. "Muonio takes his boat out every morning between three thirty and four. He's kept that same schedule for twenty years. Seven days a week.

"You and I will be lying in the bottom of the boat, covered with canvas and fishing gear. He'll go southwest into the Gulf of Finland, drop anchor, and start putting out his nets. Sometime later a Finnish boat will pull alongside. They do this every morning, Muonio and the Finnish fisherman. They smoke and talk and drink coffee for fifteen or twenty minutes. While they're doing that, we will go from Muonio's boat into the other one. By noon we'll be in Hamina and by the middle of the afternoon we should be at the United States Embassy in Helsinki."

"I understand all the words you're saying," Elena said, "but I still can't believe what I'm hearing. When you describe it, it sounds very easy. Can it be so easy?"

"It may be easy. It may be impossible. It all depends on Muonio. I only know what I've been told about him. He has no connection with any known underground groups. He is a party member and has no black marks on his record. He lives alone and fishes every day and gets drunk with his friends every night. He is a dull man. Even his mother says so. He has no real interests outside of fishing and drinking. No strong political convictions . . ."

"Then why does he take the risk? . . ."

"His mother. She's the radical. She's a die-hard Ukrainian separatist and has been since she was a school girl. She's married to a Finn and they've lived in New York for twenty years. But she's got a permanent hammerlock on Muonio."

"How did you find out about him?"

"I didn't. I found out about her. I got to know some White Russians in San Francisco. I spent a lot of time with them over a period of months. And finally I found one I thought I could trust, an old man with one arm, mean and stubborn and tough as a piece of leather. I told him what I needed and he sent me to Vera and her husband. I called them as soon as I got to New York, and they came to the hotel to see me. I gave them a thousand dollars and they told me about Muonio."

"Do you have to pay him, too?"

"Sure. A thousand rubles."

"And the boat man from Finland?"

"Five hundred rubles."

"Do you have that much money?"

"Yes. That's *all* I've got. But I have enough."

They sat quietly at the table looking at each other. "You started to ask me a question before," Chad said.

"I started to ask you why he does this, why he takes such a big risk. Is it for the money?"

"I asked his mother the same thing. She says he does do it for the money. But she also says it's not as big a risk as it seems to be. Muonio gives a hundred rubles a month to the harbor inspector. And another hundred to the state fishing inspector for the area, the man who decides which boats will be searched."

"You mean they never search his boat?"

"Sure they do. But he always knows in advance when they're going to do it."

"How will he know when you're coming?"

"When *we're* coming."

"Yes. How will he know?"

"He won't. Not exactly. He goes out every morning at the same time no matter what. He gets some signal from his mother by mail. He knows no names or dates. All he knows is that somebody will show up at his door some morning and say 'Tompkins Square.' That's where his mother lives in New York. Money changes hands and the fishing boat goes out as usual. That's it."

She got up then, came around the table, and stood behind him, her hands on his shoulders.

"Can we really do it?"

"You tell me," he said. "If you really want it, we can do it."

"I never wanted it before. I was afraid to want it."

"Are you still afraid?"

"Yes. But not for myself. I'm afraid for you. You're risking so much."

THE LAST DECATHLON   139

"No more than you are."

"But you're giving up so much."

"Are you talking about the Olympics?"

"Yes. That's important to you."

"No, it's not. I'm giving up nothing. Compared to *this,* what you and I are going to do, all that means nothing to me. I've *done* it. I've proved I can do it."

"It's so strange," she said then. "You've had this in your head all these hours we've been together, and I didn't know it. When you said you just wanted to get away from your training for a few days I thought, 'Oh, yes, that makes sense.' But that wasn't it at all. All the time you had this secret. Why did you wait so long to tell me?"

"No guts. I was afraid of what you might say."

"Like what?"

"I don't know."

"Did you think I might say, 'No, thanks. I'm not interested'?"

"Not exactly. But it could have happened. It still could."

She pulled him up and stood facing him, her arms around his neck. "No, it couldn't." She kissed him, then let her head rest against his shoulder. "I wrote you a letter once. After I left you in Helsinki."

"I didn't get it."

"I didn't mail it. But I remember what I wrote, just at the end of the letter. I said that before I met you I'd never thought about leaving Russia. But since I'd met you I couldn't think of anything else."

"You should have sent me the letter," he said.

"No, I shouldn't. It's better to tell you in person. This is much better."

53.

"What about Barnett?" Delaney said. He and Stabler were sitting in Delaney's office, Stabler with a clipboard on his lap.

"Goodrich has two men crawling all over him. I couldn't get close. But we'll shake him loose one way or another."

"How about Yost?"

"Happy to talk but he doesn't know anything. Mostly he's afraid he might get *blamed* for something."

"He has no information about Norris?"

"Nothing. I think he'd pretend he never heard of Norris if he thought he could get away with it."

"No theories about where he might be? No ideas?"

"Zero. Doesn't know and doesn't want to know."

"What about Upshaw?"

"That's something else. He's a good guy. And he really likes Norris. But he doesn't know much either. Said Norris mentioned something about being an army kid. Moving around from one base to another. Said he lived in New Jersey once. We're checking army installations there for anybody named Norris."

"Good."

"Outside of that, Upshaw wasn't much help. He's nervous and scared and he'd help if he could, but Norris didn't give much away. There was something about an uncle in Minnesota, but Upshaw didn't know his name so we're dead on that. He said Norris sent the uncle some clothes."

"From Moscow?"

Stabler nodded. "Secondhand Russian clothes. Norris said his uncle was a thrift-shop nut so he mailed him a bundle of crap from here."

"See what you can get from the post office. They might have a name and address for that parcel. Maybe it's still there on the counter waiting for somebody to lick the stamps."

Stabler made a note on his clipboard. Then he slid a photocopy page out from under the clip and put it on the desk in front of Delaney. "I had a few drinks with my friend from the Bureau last night, and we got a printout from Langley this morning. I had Doak squeeze it all together."

As Delaney read the printed sheet, Stabler looked at an identical copy. "Mostly college records. Infirmary visits, dental charts, Olympic Committee junk."

"Born May 2, 1953," Delaney said, "but no verification. What does that mean?"

"No birth certificate."

"Bullshit. Everybody has a birth certificate."

"Norris doesn't."

"Tell Langley to look again. Look till they find it."

"I already did that."

"Enrolled San Jose City College August 1976. Twenty-three years old. Got a late start, didn't he?"

"Looks like it. Transferred to Cal State San Jose the next year. Been there ever since."

"Did he graduate?"

"Not according to his transcript."

"But he managed to stay eligible for track?" Delaney said.

"That's it."

"Was he in the service?"

"No record of it."

"Did they try *Charles* Norris?"

"No Norris at all with that birthdate in any branch of the service."

Delaney looked up then. He lit a cigarette. "Who put this stuff through?"

"Zwigard."

"They better pension him off. He must have punched this stuff up with his elbow. No high school record. No grade school. No parents' names. No family at all, living or dead. What the hell is happening over there?"

"That's what I asked Zwigard. I called him at home first thing this morning."

"What did he say?"

"He says that's the story. Not a line of background on Norris before August 1976."

"He's crazy. How about the FBI?"

"Same thing. Same information."

"What about a Social Security card?"

"He had one. It's there on page two," Stabler said.

Delaney flipped the page. "October 1976. Here we go again. Are we saying that this guy hatched out full-grown at the age of twenty-three? Was he invisible for the first twenty-three years of his life? No family, no school, no job, no address. He wasn't even *born*. What the hell do they think we're *doing* over here?"

"Zwigard says they'll keep digging."

"I should hope so. Who's this guy Kincaid?"

"George Kincaid. Lumberyard in San Jose. Norris worked there."

"His first job?"

"His *only* job, it looks like. According to the date he didn't get his Social Security card till the week he got the job with Kincaid."

"Driver's license?"

"Didn't have one. No license or application in any state."

"At least he's consistent. If you can't prove you're born they won't let you drive. So tell me this. How did he get a passport? He was in Finland in April. Now he's in Russia. You mean to tell me he doesn't have a passport?"

"The Bureau checked that out. His school got the passport for him. Muscled it through last March before he went to Helsinki. It can be done. Sworn statements. Character witnesses. A little pressure from the district congressman. Immigration's not as nervous as they used to be. You know that."

"You still have to list your parents' names."

"His application said: Orphan. Parents' names unknown."

Delaney's phone flashed on. He picked up the receiver and said, "Yeah . . . Delaney." He held it out to Stabler. "It's for you."

Stabler was only on the phone a moment. When he hung up, he said, "I think we can get a crack at Barnett now. The Bureau guys went off to a tea dance or something. You want me to talk to him?"

"No. I'll do it. I need to get some information that won't dissolve in my hands."

54.

"I don't care who you are," Barnett said. "I've had guys on my neck all day. I'm fed up with questions that I don't have any answers for." He was sitting on the bleachers in the basketball arena, watching the Yugoslav team work out. "And all from a bunch of jaybirds who look like they went to the Richard Nixon Finishing School."

"Are you saying you don't want to talk to me?" Delaney said.

"That's it."

"All right. Suit yourself. But let me tell you something. I'm the only guy around here who's got a shot at finding that decathlon man of yours. I'll get the job done whether you help me or not, but maybe you could have saved me some time." He turned around and walked down the steep bank of bleachers to the floor, then angled toward the exit door. He was halfway there when Barnett caught up with him. "I don't know if I can help you any, but I'll do what I can."

Walking back to the bleachers, they sat on a lower level this time, facing the floor, their feet up, the Yugoslav team sweating and fast-breaking down the court against their green-shirted reserves.

"These guys have a chance?" Delaney said.

"If they keep running they do. They'll beat the East Germans, and I think they can handle the Cubans. And they might even beat us if they race-horse us to death and play their own game."

A wild pass bounced on the bottom bleacher then and straight into Barnett's hands. He tossed it back to the floor. "What about Chad? Any leads at all?"

"Not yet. But we're on it full-time."

"Who's we?"

"We is *me*. I have an office at the embassy here. I've been here for eighteen years."

"I didn't know anybody stayed that long with the government."

"Neither did I."

Barnett repositioned himself on the smooth bleacher plank. "I don't know much about Chad, but I'll tell you what I can."

"We're trying to find out where he comes from. Who his folks are."

"Can't help you on that. He never talked about it."

"Dilly Upshaw got the impression that Chad's father was an army man. But his passport application says he's an orphan. Parents unknown."

"I don't know," Barnett said. "My wife met him a few times, and *she* got the idea he was an orphan. But I don't think it was from anything he said. Far as I can tell, she was just guessing."

"How long have you known him?"

"Three years now. A little more. Since seventy-seven. In the spring. I saw him running the hurdles and long-jumping in a meet at San Jose Junior College, and I thought he had some potential. So I wangled a rinky-dink scholarship for him and that fall he transferred to Cal State. He worked hard that first year but he didn't pan out the way I'd hoped he would. He was versatile, I found out. He could do a lot of things. But we had a hot team. We always do. So there were a couple guys who could beat him in any event he picked. His junior year with us I was about ready to give up on him. Then he got the notion that he should go for the decathlon. I was lukewarm on the idea. I knew he could sprint and jump pretty good, but I didn't think he could handle the heavy stuff. The shot and the discus. But he lifted weights all winter and the next spring he started coming into his own a little bit."

"When did you start to see him as Olympic material?"

"*I* never did. *He* did. He's been talking Olympics for the last year or so. But I didn't think he was hungry enough. Natural ability but not enough push. Always just at the edge but never breaking through. Based on his record he had no business being in Finland last April, but I got him invited. I thought the idea of international competition might shake him loose. But he couldn't get untracked there either.

"After that meet I gave him hell. I told him he was stumbling around out there like he was half asleep. I guess it shook him up. I know *something* did. From the time we flew back to California from Helsinki, he was a changed kid. He'd always trained hard, but now he turned into a fanatic. It was like something finally clicked in his head. That happens with athletes, especially one-on-one guys, like track men and tennis players.

"Anyway, Chad caught fire. Ran away with everything in our conference last spring. No great point totals but always winning. And getting stronger every week. By the time the trials came there was nobody could touch him. He knew it and so did I. The world record surprised me but I knew right along he'd win. I thought he'd win here in Moscow, too. But . . . now I'm not thinking about that. I just hope he's all right."

55.

One o'clock in the afternoon, a warm July day, Elena sat on a stone bench in the sunshine in a park beside the Donskoi Monastery. A young man sat beside her, thin and pale with ruined teeth, his hair slicked back with water, his eyes flat and exhausted, yellow nicotine stains on his fingers.

He wore a dark, threadbare suit, almost worn through at the elbows and knees but carefully sponged and pressed. And his broken boots were polished. The worn collar of his shirt, the button missing, was held together by a stained necktie, meticulously knotted.

His name was Vitaly Lusis. He had graduated from Moscow State University in 1968 with the highest marks in his class.

"How old is he?" he said to Elena.

"In his twenties."

"How big?"

"Eighty kilos maybe. A meter and three quarters. Maybe a bit more. Brown hair. Gray eyes. Clean-shaven."

"You have the photograph?"

"Yes." She handed him two coin-booth portraits of Chad, taken that morning in a department store on Kropotkin Ulitsa. He handed one back to her.

"I only need one," he said.

"I thought if you made a mistake . . ."

"If I only have one picture, then I can't *afford* to make a mistake." He studied the photograph for a moment, then slipped it into his pocket. "I'll do my best," he said.

"How long will I have to wait?"

"Tomorrow morning."

"So soon?"

He smiled awkwardly, trying not to show his teeth. "I'm a serious craftsman," he said. Then, "I'll meet you at seven. Before I go to work."

"Here?"

"No. At the student café behind the Bolshoi."

"I will buy you a fine meal," she said.

"I don't eat so much. We'll have a coffee. Or you can buy me a vodka if you like."

"I'll buy you a dozen vodkas."

"So much the better. I'll go to work happy." He took a crushed brown cigarette out of his pocket and lit it. He inhaled hungrily and coughed behind his hand.

"Have you talked with Shota?"

"No. He's afraid to be seen with me now. But I met Kozomov yesterday. He told me about Larisa."

"I'm sure you're wrong about Shota. You should go to see him. He needs friends now. He is crazy from worry about Larisa."

"Shota's a fool. He's slobbering in love with his brother's wife. I would not like to be a passenger in any plane he is flying."

"It's not the way you think. He and Larisa are friends. That's all."

"Not at the beginning. I was there. They were friends of the skin. Then Shota introduced her to his brother. He wanted his brother's approval. As it turned out, he got more than he asked for. In a week she was in his brother's bed."

"It wasn't that way," Elena said. "It's not that way now."

"Why would I lie? Gossip doesn't interest me. Shota was a fool then and he's a fool now. And Larisa is a bigger fool than he is. She doesn't know what she wants. She cuts her wrists and thinks she did something important."

"You don't hate Larisa. Why do you talk about her as if you hate her?"

"I hate people who deceive themselves. Why did she come back here in the first place? Her aunt is dying. There is nothing Larisa can do for her. She should have stayed in Israel with her husband and child. Did she think the authorities would let her come and go like a visiting Pope?"

"They gave permission. They guaranteed she could return."

"A piece of rat cheese in a rat trap. Who would believe such a guarantee? Only a fool. That's what I'm saying." He stood up suddenly. "I have to go now. I'll see you in the morning."

"If anything happens . . ."

"Nothing will happen. I'll be there and I'll have what you want."

He turned and walked away, his hands deep in his jacket pockets, his thin coat stretched taut across his bony back. His shoulders hunched over and shook as he began to cough again.

56.

"You know what they say about this place," Stabler said.

"What place?" Delaney said. He was behind his desk in his shirt sleeves, holding a glass of bourbon, a stack of folders and computer printouts in front of him.

"Russia. It's a riddle, the man says. A riddle wrapped in a mystery inside an enigma."

"My first wife," Delaney said.

"Everybody's first wife."

"Anything new?" Delaney said then.

"Nothing. The Moscow police are combing the town, and Goodrich's guys are combing their hair. There's a picture of Norris on every wall in town, there's a reward of ten thousand rubles, and we're no further along than we were. Nobody knows him. Nobody's seen him. The guy went up in smoke."

"How often do they check the hospitals?"

"They got half a dozen policewomen doing nothing else."

"How about the morgue?"

"Every hour. Any stiff with a beard gets a full inspection."

"What's the reaction in the States?"

"Panic. It's all over the papers. And television bulletins every twenty minutes. The right-wingers are having a field day. They want to bring the whole American team home. Last night they picketed the United Nations, yesterday morning the White House. And the kicker is, nobody's been able to come up with any information about Norris that we don't have. Except for the cranks. There's a crazy lady somewhere in Connecticut who keeps predicting the end of the world. She says she *knows* Chad Norris and that's not his real name at all."

"What's his real name?"

"I told you she was a crank. She can't seem to remember his real name. The other crank theory—even David Brinkley mentioned this—is that Norris is a Soviet agent, that they planted him in California four years ago and now they've brought him home. It could happen, I suppose."

"No, it couldn't. The KGB's crazy but they're not *that* crazy. I say we're missing something obvious. I don't know what it is but I know it's there."

Delaney sat up straight in his chair, finished his drink, and lit a cigarette. "Let's start over. We can't even be sure he's alive, but let's assume he is. So he's not dead, he's not injured, and as far as we know, he doesn't have any friends in Moscow. But . . . he's missing.

"The obvious conclusion is: somebody grabbed him. The Red Brigade, the PLO, somebody. They want to make a political point so they take a hostage. Norris was outside the grounds a lot, running along the river every morning. Barely daylight, nobody around, an easy target.

"All right, if that's what happened, why the big silence? What's the wienie? Terrorists love an audience. What's the point of kidnapping somebody if you keep it a secret? You have an answer for that?"

"No."

"Neither do I. But even so, it's still the best theory."

"That's what *I* think," Stabler said. "That's what everybody thinks."

"The only other wrinkle is this . . . maybe *nothing* happened to him. It doesn't make sense but it keeps coming back into my head. He disappeared because he *wanted* to disappear."

"It's left field."

"I know it is. But so is everything else. What about those clothes he bought? Did anybody else pick up on that?"

"Not that I know of. Maybe Upshaw didn't tell anybody but us."

"We know he didn't send those clothes to his uncle like he said he was going to."

"We're not sure of that," Stabler said. "We know we couldn't come up with any record of it. But that's no guarantee the package wasn't sent. That post office is like something out of *Oliver Twist*. Even *Izvestia* says they lose almost as many packages as they send."

"All right. Maybe he *did* send it. But until we're sure, until we see some receipt or something, we can assume there's at least an outside chance that he *didn't*."

"Then what?"

"Then we say, What does he need those secondhand clothes for? I say he'd only want them for one reason. If he wanted to pass himself off as somebody he's not."

"As a Russian?"

"It looks that way."

"Why would he do that?"

"I don't know. Why wouldn't he?"

"Because he came to Moscow for a specific purpose. He's a jock. He came to compete in the Olympics. He sure as hell didn't come here with the idea that he *wasn't* going to compete."

"You wouldn't think so."

"Unless maybe he knows somebody here."

"Somebody who lives here," Delaney said.

"Somebody he wants to visit on the sly."

"Why not? He doesn't want publicity. He doesn't want to make trouble for this person, whoever it is, so he leaves all his papers in his room, puts on the Russian clothes he bought, and goes off for a secret visit somewhere. Then he comes back to the Olympic Village and picks up where he left off."

"He wins a gold medal," Stabler said, "and marries Amy Carter."

"You're fired."

"You have to admit we're reaching."

"So we're reaching. That's because we don't know anything. What if his parents are Russian? What if Norris *isn't* his real name? What if he grew up in America with foster parents or something and his real parents have been here in Russia all the time? Is that possible?"

"Sure it is," Stabler said. "When you don't have any facts, when you don't *know* anything, everything's possible. So far all we've been able to do is think up new questions."

"I guarantee you one thing. If I knew where Norris spent the first twenty-three years of his life, I'd have a damned good idea of where he is right now."

"So we're back to square one."

"No, we're not. I'm going to California. Get me on that nine o'clock flight to San Francisco."

"Naked or covered up?"

"FBI papers. The same ones I used last fall."

"Ralph Hermeling?"

"That's it."

"How long will you be gone?"

"Three days. Four at the most. It won't take me long once I get there. What about the military trace on Norris's old man?"

"It's going slow. A lot of those old records aren't computerized. But Perigo's on top of it."

"Good. Stay away from Zwigard. He's been living alone too long. The other thing, when Perigo gets hold of that Social Security application tell him to keep it with him. I'll call him on it tomorrow from California. And let's get hold of every picture anybody ever took of Chad Norris. All the stills and team pictures and track-meet footage we can locate."

Leaving the room, Stabler turned at the door. "Maybe we should lay off the Hermeling cover. Denishev might have a file on that one."

"I know he does. That's one reason I want to use it. Let's make him sweat a little."

57. ■ Late at night, the house still, no sounds at all from the street, Elena, in her nightgown and robe, sat across the table from Chad, two candles guttering low between them, the remains of bread and cheese on plates, and an empty wine bottle. She was laughing.

"You are one surprise after the next. First you have a beard. Then no beard. And now, suddenly, you speak Russian. Since I met you I have never heard you say

one Russian word. And now you recite Pasternak's poetry
like a university scholar."

Chad tilted back in his chair and affected a soft and
husky theatrical voice.

We have a fragile future, you and I . . . pale and evanescent
Without stanchions or pilings or firm holdings
No ring of keys, no deed, no title,
No map to lead us through tomorrow
No surety of anything at all past sunrise
But God, how beautiful tonight is.

"*That* is Gordovkin," she said. "You can't fool me."

"I did fool you," he said. "You thought I was a dumb
American in track shoes who could only speak sign
language."

"You really speak well."

"But not like a Russian."

"But very well all the same. Where did you learn it?"

"In the army. Three years in language school."

"See what I mean? Whenever you open your mouth a
new secret comes out. I didn't even know you were *in*
the army."

"There was no reason to tell you," he said. "It wasn't
important. It's still not important."

"But in Helsinki when I met you . . . when you spoke
to me . . ."

"We got along too well in English. I didn't want to
change my luck."

"You changed *my* luck," she said. "You've made me
very lucky."

"That's right. Just remember that. Keep it in your
head all the time. We're lucky ducks."

Later, when they were lying in bed with the lights out,
she said, "I had my car looked after today. And I bought

two extra cans of gasoline. Then I went to see my supervisor at Intourist. I told him I had delayed my holiday but that now I am ready to leave. In a day or two, I said."

"Did he ask where you were going?"

"Yes. I told him I had decided against the Black Sea. He agreed that it is too crowded this month and next month. I told him I probably would just drive around in my car and visit small villages. Like a gypsy with no real schedule or planning ahead."

"What did he say about that?"

"He thought it was a fine idea. He said he would not expect to hear from me till August fourth. He's a sweet old man. He will retire next year. He kissed me on the cheek and said I was his best work person."

"I'm jealous."

"Of course you are. You should be. I am very fond of him."

"Good. You can send him a postcard from California."

"Did you feel that?" she said then.

"What?"

"My skin got cold. I shivered when you said that about California."

"Nobody shivers in California."

"Is it always so warm?"

"Not always. But it's never really cold. Not like here."

"You like it there?"

"Yeah, I do."

"Were you born there?"

"No, I wasn't."

When he didn't say any more, she said, "Where do you come from? Where does your family live?"

He lay very still in the bed and didn't answer. Finally he said, "I'm like you. I don't have any family. My mother was in a plane crash five years ago . . ."

"Oh, I didn't mean . . . I mean I'm sorry. That's terrible. Was your father . . . was he . . ."

"No. He wasn't with her. I don't know where he is. I haven't seen him for a long time."

"Why is that?"

"I just haven't."

She moved closer to him, then put her arm around him and rested her head on his shoulder. Just before she went to sleep she said, "Can we really do it?"

"With your luck, we can't miss."

"What if something goes wrong?"

"What can go wrong? I told you. We're lucky."

"You know what I mean."

"Nothing will go wrong," he said. "I won't let it."

---

58. Even before he boarded the Aeroflot jet at the Moscow airport, Delaney picked out the man who was following him. He was slender, with gray hair, wearing dark-rimmed spectacles and a trim London-tailored suit. An attractive blond woman, carrying a bouquet of yellow flowers, had come to see him off. She gave him a copy of an American novel as he went off to board the plane, and he carried it under his arm.

As he boarded the plane, Delaney saw the man turn in to the first-class section and take a seat. It was the last time he saw him until they arrived in California.

When Delaney disembarked in San Francisco, it was nearly midnight. Carrying his small leather bag, he walked through the long glass-walled corridors to the car rental desks.

He felt fresh and rested. He had read the Russian newspapers on the plane and had two small glasses of bourbon. Then he'd turned out his reading light and slept for almost eight hours.

As he walked through the terminal and outside to the curb to pick up his car, he made no effort to locate the gray-haired man. But when he was inside the car, adjusting the rearview mirror, he saw him in line waiting for a taxi.

As Delaney pulled away from the curb, he saw a young couple leave the taxi queue—the man with long hair, wearing jeans and a vest, the woman in a cotton dress to her ankles, her hair pulled back straight, falling down her back to her waist. They got onto a gray pickup truck, the bed rigged with side planks and a canvas top to make a crude home-built camper.

Delaney maneuvered through the maze of airport roads and ramps, stop signs, cut-offs, and detours, turned at last onto the Bayshore Freeway, and drove slowly toward the San Francisco city center.

At a filling station outside the community called South San Francisco, he pulled in, went to a phone booth, dialed the operator, and said, "This is a police emergency."

Looking out through the glass he saw the pickup truck pull in at the pumps. The young man got out, careful not to look toward Delaney, took the top off his gas tank, and lifted the nozzle off its rack on the pump.

The police number answered then and Delaney said, "I'm from the Justice Department. Give me the officer in charge."

After a beat a voice said, "Captain Magnuson."

"This is Agent Ralph Hermeling, FBI, Atlanta office. I.D. number three-one-oh–seven-six-four D. as in David. I need your cooperation. I'm on the Bayshore Freeway, three miles north of the airport. You know the Shell station there? Good. I'm in a red Chevrolet Caprice and I'm being tailed by two suspects, one male, one female, both Caucasian, in a gray Dodge pickup, camper on the back, California license six-seven-four–NWT. Please apprehend at once, search for firearms and drugs, and hold them in jail at Burlingame. My office will contact you . . . Don't worry. You'll have a violation. Speeding and reckless driving. I'll stall here for five minutes or so, then head north. Just be sure your men don't pick *me* up. I'll be speeding, too."

He left the phone booth then, strolled across to the station office, and bought a bottle of cola. He drank half of it, standing with his back to the gas pumps; then he took the men's room key off the hook, walked around to the back, and killed another few minutes washing his hands.

When he went back outside and got into his car, he drove slowly across the service station area to the access road, and up the ramp to the freeway entrance. When he spotted the gray truck in his rearview mirror, he angled across three lanes to the fast center lane and jammed his foot down on the accelerator. When the speedometer reached eighty he held it there. In the mirror, he could see no sign of the truck. But a few minutes later, going into a sweeping left-hand curve, he saw it behind him again, holding him in sight, speeding ahead in the second inside lane.

Far behind him then, he heard the police car whine. In his mirror he saw a flash of red. He slowed down, crossed right to the emergency lane, and stopped. As he sat there, the truck raced past him, then the police car.

Delaney pulled out then and followed at normal speed. A mile farther north he saw the two cars pulled off to the side. Driving past them, he saw the young man and woman spread-eagled against the side of the truck, being body-searched by two uniformed policemen.

At the next cloverleaf, he crossed the freeway and headed south toward San Jose.

---

59. Pavel Lepik, a slender young man of thirty with light red hair and a fringe beard, wearing steel-rim glasses, sat in Viktor Denishev's office waiting for a reaction.

At last Denishev said, "We have absolute identification for all those passengers on Delaney's flight?"

Lepik nodded. "The list was triple-checked. We have an up-to-date file on every individual, including the crew members."

"There's no possibility that Norris could have been on board using somebody else's papers?"

"None. I'm sure of it. You think Delaney and Norris are linked in some way?"

"Not *some* way. The obvious way. Norris disappeared because Delaney wanted him to. Because they are linked together in some kind of operation. And if Delaney leaves suddenly for America using false identification, that means only one thing to me. Something went wrong and he's pulling Norris out."

"It's possible. But he wasn't on that plane."

"It doesn't make sense that Delaney would be going to California just now. What information could he need? They must know everything there is to know about Norris."

"If he's working for them, you mean?"

"Whether he is or not," Denishev said. "Why do you think our people in Washington can't find a trace of information on Norris? Only one answer. Central Intelligence has captured his files. Frozen all the information. Additional proof that Norris is working for them. And it must be something important. Delaney doesn't fly halfway across the world just to have lunch. He wouldn't arrange to have two of our people arrested and detained unless there was something at stake. He wouldn't risk the FBI cover he's using."

Lepik referred to the clipboard on his lap. "Another thing . . . we had word from Finland that Delaney's people requested all the official films from the Helsinki games last April."

"Kill that. You know who to talk to there. Have all that material sent to us. Anything else?"

"Something just came in an hour ago. From one of the surveillance teams in New York. They did a routine break-in on East Fifth Street in the Ukrainian community, and when they went through the stuff they'd picked up, they found a slip of paper with the name *Chad Norris* written on it."

"Whose apartment was it?"

"A man named Arvid Wiberg. He's a Finn. Been in America for twenty years. His wife says she's Austrian, but all her friends seem to be Ukrainian. That was the reason for the break-in. They thought there might be some link with that movement. But they didn't find anything important. Just grocery lists and letters from the welfare office and the piece of paper with Norris's name on it."

"Just the name? Nothing else?"

"A couple of scribbles. I gave the microfilm to decoding. Told them to work it out."

"Good. Let me know what they report."

60. Elena arrived fifteen minutes early at the Tambov, a student café on Petrovka Ulitsa behind the Bolshoi. It had rained all night, cold and slashing, nothing of summer about it, filling the gutters and flooding the streets of the city from midnight on. And it was still raining.

Not yet seven in the morning, the café was already crowded with students and young working people, many of them poorly protected from the weather, their hair soaked, their clothes drenched; others, like Elena, in rubber slickers and knee-high boots, all of them gulping down hot tea laced with plum jam, some of them munching on hard black rolls, most of them smoking cigarettes, and a few of them drinking small glasses of vodka.

Elena sat just inside the front window, sipping tea and

looking through the steamy plate glass at the sidewalk, searching the early morning crowds for Vitaly, and waiting.

The rain began to slack off. By seven thirty it had stopped. Elena, concentrating on the steady movement of people into and out of the subway station just opposite the café, examined each new cluster for some sign of Vitaly and tried not to look at her watch or at the wall clock.

By eight o'clock the Tambov was half empty. New customers straggled in, but in small numbers compared to the heavy exodus of workers and students hurrying off to work or to class.

Elena ordered a third glass of tea and persuaded herself that Vitaly was late only because of the weather, that he would surely appear at any moment, slumped over and coughing, with cigarette smoke trailing gray behind him.

When nine o'clock came, she realized he wasn't coming. She called for her check and paid it, stood up and fastened the buckles on her slicker, when she saw him.

Coming from the subway station, he walked quickly across the sidewalk and through the main door of the café. He didn't stop or even slow down. When their eyes made contact, he moved his head slightly, a beckoning gesture, pushed through a line of people waiting at the *caisse*, walked directly to the side door of the café and out into the street again.

Following along behind him, Elena understood that she was not supposed to catch up. Just keeping him in sight was difficult.

He hurried off to his left, all the way around the building that housed the café, came out on Petrovka Ulitsa half a block below the subway station, dodged across the six traffic lanes of the street, and ran down the steps to the subway level.

Pushing through the turnstile, Elena saw him disappear into a subway car. She ran, maneuvered and dodged through the crowd, and squeezed in through the doors just before they closed.

She could see him standing halfway back in the crowded car, just inside the center door. At the first stop he stepped off and walked quickly to the escalator. Elena followed. As soon as he reached the upper level, he crossed to the descending escalator and started down again.

Under her raincoat Elena was perspiring. Her cheeks were flushed and her heart thumped. When she was halfway down on the escalator, she saw him step off it at the bottom, and she heard another train speeding into the station. She sniffed the burnt-toast smell its brakes made as it slowed by the platform.

When she reached the lower level and turned toward the train, she saw Vitaly standing in an open doorway looking at her. Again that slight beckoning gesture with the head.

Running toward him, her breathing harsh in her throat, her legs starting to tremble under her, hearing the blast of the departure horn, she stumbled and half fell through the doorway. As he caught her, he pressed a small envelope into her hand. Then he slipped out through the subway car doors just before they slammed shut.

Vitaly walked slowly now, all the way along the platform to the Kirova Ulitsa escalator. From there he took an electric streetcar to Mytnaya Ulitsa and walked two blocks north to the building where he worked. At the side entrance a guard stopped him and said there was a request for him to appear in the supervisor's office.

He had never been asked to come to the supervisor's office before today. But the request did not surprise him. Each day for the past three years he had expected that invitation.

When he was ushered into the bare and ugly office, when he saw that there were two other men waiting along with the supervisor, two ordinary-looking men in anonymous dark suits, that didn't surprise him either.

---

61. As far as she knew, Elena had never been followed in her life. She had no instinct for hare-and-hounds, had never developed sophisticated evasion skills. Nonetheless, after Vitaly left her on the subway, she continued the same pattern she had followed with him.

Going directly to the women's rest room in the next subway station, she locked herself into one of the cabinets. She tore open the envelope Vitaly had given her and took out a Soviet internal passbook, dark blue, smooth and worn. Opening the front of her shirt, she slipped the small, flat booklet down inside her brassiere.

Flushing the crumpled envelope down the toilet, she went to one of the wall sinks, washed her hands, and dried them deliberately on a rough paper towel, her ears alert for the sound of an approaching train.

When she heard the whistle and the brake squeal, she hurried out of the rest room, crossed the platform, and boarded the train just before it pulled out.

For the next hour she rode the crowded morning subways all over central Moscow. From Kirova to Dubininskaya to Komsomolsky Prospekt to Kutuzovsky. To Pushkinskaya Square, on out to Riga Stadium, and back to the Hotel Leningradskaya.

From there she took a westbound bus, then a taxi, then another bus. It was just after eleven o'clock in the morning when she knocked lightly, then unlocked her apartment door.

"What happened?" Chad said.

"I'm not sure. I'm afraid Vitaly's in trouble." She told him what had happened. "Maybe he was just being cautious, but I don't think so. Vitaly doesn't know about caution. Reckless is all he knows. With everything except his friends. I think he knew he was being watched, and he was being careful not to involve me."

"Why would he meet you at all then?"

"Ahhh . . . that's what he lives for. He would never pass up a chance to outwit the KGB. They've arrested him half a dozen times in the last years. But he continues to buzz around their heads like a wasp, stinging them whenever he can.

"He's very clever, so it always takes them some time to figure out what he's up to. But finally they catch him and he goes to jail for a while. Or to the oil fields or the glass factory in Irkutsk. And the next thing his friends know he's back in view, smoking and coughing and drinking himself to death.

"This time, he's been free for more than three years. He spent eight months in a terrible work camp south of Petropavlovsk, and when they let him come back to Moscow, doing his defeated act, meek and mild with his head hanging down, they put him in the grisliest place they could think of, the Moscow city morgue. And they gave him the worst job there. Receiving the bodies as they're brought in, drunks and suicides and traffic victims. He has to undress them, clean them up, and tie name tags on their toes before they're slid into the refrigerator for a two-day wait before the crematory.

"It's the most awful job anyone can imagine. Like a scary Goya. Or a nightmare out of Dante. All of Vitaly's friends were horrified, but he just laughed and said, 'I'll find a way.' And he did."

She took the passbook out of her brassiere and handed it to Chad. He opened it, turned the limp pages, and studied his photograph, stained and faded, looking as if it had barely survived a number of years in somebody's pocket.

"I don't believe it," he said.

"It looks more authentic than mine," Elena said. Then, "How do you like your new name?"

"Somebody else's old name."

"That's right."

"*Igor Kozyv,*" he said. "Can't miss with a name like that."

"Don't be too optimistic. The advantage is that you have the genuine passbook of a real man. But that can be a problem too. Since nobody knows he's dead, maybe the police are looking for *him.* We don't know anything about the *real* Igor Kozyv. All we know is that he's an unidentified dead man in the Moscow morgue."

"And I have his papers. We know that."

She nodded. "But I'm worried about Vitaly. If someone was following him they could have seen me. They could be watching me too."

"In that case . . ."

"In that case, we'd better change our plans."

"Let's go a day early," he said. "We're ready. Let's go this afternoon."

She walked to the window and looked down at the

street where her car was parked. "We could do that," she said then. "But I'm nervous now about leaving in the daytime. I think it's better if we go at night."

"Tonight?"

"I think so."

part 4

62. The temperature in San Jose was one hundred and two degrees. The grass on the campus was burned brown, and the leaves hung limp from the tree branches.

Inside Dean Slocum's office, however, it was air-conditioned cool. Too cool. Dr. Slocum sat behind his desk stiffly overdressed in jacket, vest, tie, collar pin, cuff links, and a flowered handkerchief in his breast pocket. His face was ruddy and freckled, his brown hair carefully parted and brushed; his fingers were busy with a gold desk medallion encased in plastic, and there was an unpleasant pouty look around his mouth.

"I know you've talked to other investigators about this," Delaney said, "but we still don't have the information we need. I'll be candid with you, Doctor Slocum. A lot of first-rate investigative people are working full-time trying to locate Chad Norris, and so far we've come up cold and dry. We don't have the slightest notion where he went or where he was taken, and we don't know why.

"And our biggest problem, aside from finding him, is simply getting hold of some information about him. We know he's twenty-seven years old, we know he's been a student here at Cal State. Beyond that . . . we don't know a damned thing."

"I showed you his student file. Other than that . . . you see, as long as our students stay out of trouble, we very seldom learn much about their personal lives. By the time they come to us, they're legal adults. We concentrate on instruction rather than supervision."

"Are you saying that Norris's file is a typical one? No parents listed, no home address, no high school or grade school transcripts, no evidence of any previous existence before he showed up here."

"He did have that year at the city college."

"That's right. And they don't have any information either. It's like they invented him."

Slocum smiled weakly and stroked his lower lip with his thumb. "Nothing's typical any longer, Mr. Delaney. We've learned to accept all kinds of things. We're not allowed to send grade reports to the parents now. Violates the student's civil rights. Soon we won't be able to give grades at all. You see, the community college policy in California is strictly open-door. Anyone who *is*, or *seems* to be, eighteen years old, can enroll without proof of *any* prior education.

"At Cal State, of course, we're not quite so permissive. But almost any student with a year of community college behind him is acceptable to us, providing he can pay his fees and maintain an acceptable grade average.

"We are certainly aware of Chad Norris's athletic achievements, and some of us know what kind of scholastic work he's done, but as far as his personal life is concerned . . ." Slocum stroked his lip again, smoothed his hair, and fondled his medallion.

Forty minutes later Delaney was sitting on the front porch of a frame house on San Miguel Street, perched on a wooden railing. The owner of the house, Clara Kellogg, eighty-two years old, thin and wiry and contentious, sat in a porch swing facing him, a glass of iced coffee in her hand, a cigarette with a long ash tucked in the corner of her mouth.

"I'm just sick about it," she said, "but I ain't surprised. I told him before he went off, if you want to get your tail in a crack good and proper, just go over there and screw around in Russia. God knows we got it bad enough here. They'll walk into your house in broad daylight and drag out your TV or anything else that's loose. Or they'll pee on your front steps while you're asleep. I had a rash of that last year.

"And a woman ain't safe anyplace. We all know that. You can get raped or scraped or fricasseed right in your own kitchen. And being an old soup bone like me don't protect you none either. A cousin of mine that lives down on Mariposa, two years older than me, not a tooth in her head, got attacked six weeks ago while she was sitting on the john. Eight thirty in the morning.

"But anyhow, taking all that into consideration, bad as things have got over here, it's still a country mile better than being over there with those crazy assholes in their fur hats, eatin' fish heads and slobberin' vodka all over themselves. That's what I told Chad. I said, 'Tell 'em to put those gold medals where the sun don't shine and you stay home here.' "

"What did he say to that?"

"Just laughed, like he does, and said, 'You're right, Clara. You're *always* right.' That's what he says, anytime I try to tell him where the bear shit in the buckwheat."

"What about his family? Did he ever . . ."

"Never said a word about any family. And I never asked him. I don't pry."

"He never mentioned where he lived? where he was born?"

"Not a squeak."

"What was his schedule like?"

"Worked his tail off. Always up running at sunrise. Went to his classes. Did his homework. And two or three hours a day, track practice. And any free time he had, he put in at Kincaid's lumberyard. Then like as not he'd sit up half the night reading. Books stacked in all the corners. You seen his room. It's neat now, but that's not the way it usually was. Maps and atlases and a bunch of foreign-language crap that would give you a headache just looking at it, let alone reading it."

"What happened to all that stuff?"

"Beats me. Packed it up and hauled it out just before he took off to go over there to Moscow."

"With that schedule you described, I guess he didn't have much time left for social life."

"He didn't smoke dope or get falling-down drunk every Saturday night if that's what you mean. But he sure never suffered for any lack of girl friends. I seen 'em come and go. Three years' worth, each one of them cuter than the last one. Laughing and giggling and trotting up the stairs like a string of show ponies.

"Nice girls, too, all the ones I got to know. And none of them ever had a bad word to say about Chad. So that's worth something, I guess. Funny thing, though, once he came back from Finland last April, he had no time for anything but work. No sweet little pussy cats around here since then."

"You said his room was never very neat. Why do you suppose he left it so neat when he went away this time?"

"One of those detectives that was here before asked the same question. He said it looked like Chad was expecting somebody to go through his stuff. So he didn't leave anything for a person to look at."

"It almost looks as if he'd already moved out. Maybe he wasn't planning to come back here."

"I don't know," she said. "I never thought of that. I just hope he's all right. I hope nothing's happened to him."

63. Vitaly Lusis sat in a comfortable chair in an office on the fifth floor of a drab, monumental building on Zhdanova Ulitsa.

Behind a heavy desk in front of him sat Renart Ornishchenco, an ascetic, almost saintly-looking man, sixty years old, who had served as an interrogation specialist under Beria and who had by some miracle kept his position and his privileges after Beria was tried and shot.

Beside the desk, facing Vitaly, sat Rita Talisheva, a fair-haired, slender girl in her mid-twenties, neatly dressed, a pleasant voice, nothing about her giving any clue to the nature of the work she had chosen.

"We've known each other a few years now," Vitaly said to Ornishchenco. "I've sat in this office at least five or six times. So there's no reason to make all the speeches you make to the beginners."

"It's not a question of speechmaking," Ornishchenco said. "It's a matter of communication. And sometimes that's a slow process. But we have plenty of time and so do you. The key word is *detail*. The details are important."

"Not true. I say the details are insignificant. In my case only one thing matters. I am a Stalinist. Militant. I've been that way since I was sixteen, and I'll be that way when you shoot me."

"No one's talking about shooting anybody. I don't look at this meeting as an adversary situation. You must remember that I was a Stalin supporter myself."

"No, you weren't," Vitaly said. "If you had been, you'd be dead now. You'd have died with Beria. You were a professional opportunist. That's what you still are."

"Why is he permitted to talk this way?" the girl said.

"Because that's the way he talks," Ornishchenco said. "He doesn't ask permission."

The girl turned toward Vitaly. Quietly and firmly, remembering her lessons at the academy, she said, "Comrade Ornishchenco is a senior official. I forbid you to speak to him in a disrespectful way."

"Kiss my ass," Vitaly said.

"What did you say?"

"I said, 'Kiss my ass.' "

Rita Talisheva got very pale suddenly. She turned to Ornishchenco, who gave her no help, then back to Vitaly. "I can't understand it that you are still alive."

"I can't understand it either," Vitaly said. "What's the answer, Ornishchenco?"

Ornishchenco smiled and twined his fingers together. "We allow a reasonable amount of dissent," he said to the girl. "You realize that. And that is the irony of this man's situation. The policies he opposes are the ones that keep him alive. If we returned suddenly to the code of Stalin he would be executed within a week."

"Doesn't he realize that?" the girl said.

"Of course he does. That's what makes him interesting. That's why he requires particular treatment. We are not in business to kill people on demand."

"Is that what you want?" the girl said to Vitaly.

"Of course not. Only saints and fanatics want to die.

But if you put me up against the wall at least I'd know the State had some guts again. So maybe I'd die happy."

"He's crazy," the girl said.

"No, I'm not," Vitaly said. "*You* are. All of you. Everybody spouts the words of Lenin but nobody remembers what he said. He said, 'The *people* don't decide what's good for them. *We* decide. It's *our* revolution, *our* government, *our* country.' Socialism is *not* democracy."

"You're not a dissident," she said. "You're an anarchist."

"No. I'm not. I'm a Socialist. There's no such thing as freedom. And if there *were*, people wouldn't want it. They want security. For a guaranteed future *any* man will sacrifice *anything*."

"Anarchy," the girl said.

"You're in the wrong line of work," Vitaly said. "Girls like you should be whores or house painters."

There was a hollow silence. Then the girl said, "Do you realize that every word you say is being recorded?"

"I hope so. I wouldn't want it to be wasted."

After another long silence Rita Talisheva said to Ornishchenco, "Shall we go on to the specific charges?"

"Yes, I think so."

Turning back to Vitaly, she said, "We will recommend to the people's prosecutor that you be indicted and tried for a treasonous crime against the State. We charge that you stole internal passbooks and altered them so they could be used in an unlawful way by unqualified persons."

"Guilty," Vitaly said.

"We're not in court," Ornishchenco said. "You are not required to make any statements here."

"It's all right. I don't mind. Somebody should have known better than to put me in that morgue job. Drunks and derelicts and traffic victims being hauled in there every day. A lot of them didn't even have papers. But most of them did. I figured out I could pick up two or three passbooks a day without any trouble."

"How many would you estimate . . ."

"All together? I don't know. Several hundred. A thousand maybe. I didn't keep records."

"You mean there may be a thousand false passbooks . . ."

"More than that," Vitaly said. "I didn't invent this idea. The morgue job just made it easier for me. Every time a drunk in the railroad station loses his papers you can bet they'll be in somebody else's pockets within a week. With a new photograph pasted in."

"We need to know the names," the girl said then, "the names of everyone you delivered false papers to."

"Like I said, I kept no records."

"Your only chance for leniency . . ."

"I'm not asking for leniency. I don't want it. I know all the punishments. I've already had most of them. And I don't expect to be shot because then my friends might send articles to the foreign papers and turn me into a martyr. The Kremlin is scared to death of martyrs. Very embarrassing."

Ornishchenco said, "You could certainly help your position if you told us even one name. The girl you were meeting in the Café Tambov, for instance."

"That means she got away from you," Vitaly said. "Good for her."

"What was her name?"

"I can't remember."

"That means you won't tell us?"

"Exactly."

Rita Talisheva took a cigarette out of her jacket pocket and lit it. "Since you've had so much experience with the police, I'm sure you remember that there are techniques of persuasion."

Vitaly smiled and said, "If you'd taken the time to read through my dossier you'd know that I have the worst memory in Moscow. *Nothing* can stimulate it."

64.

George Kincaid walked through the wide loading area that divided his lumberyard, Delaney beside him.

"He was a steady worker," Kincaid said. "That's about all I can tell you. Stuck on the job too. That's the big headache today. People work for a couple months, save a little money. Then they take off and go skiing. Girls too. The same thing. Can't keep a bookkeeper if she's younger than forty years old. But Chad worked for me right along from the time he started in seventy-seven."

"You must know him pretty well."

"Matter of fact, I don't. I like him but I don't know him. I got a policy. I don't mingle with the help. I'm fair-minded but I'm not chummy. If somebody screws up, I tell them what I think. If they keep it up, I shut off their water. Mistakes cost money. So I run a tight ship. Spic and span and strictly business."

"Do you have any storage space that the help can use?"

"No, I don't."

"Some of Chad's books and things are missing from his room. I thought he might have stashed them here."

"Not that I know of."

"What if he had done it, without mentioning it to you? Is there any particular place he might have used?"

"There's an old tool shed down the way here. Got a table and some chairs in there so the boys can eat their lunch inside when the weather's bad. I don't think he left anything there, but he could have. Let's take a look."

They went into the shed and Kincaid switched on the overhead light. A bank of fluorescent tubes flickered and buzzed, then flashed on, bright and blue-white.

Delaney looked around the room. It was a catchall. Broken furniture, pieces of machinery, and odd bits of lumber and plywood piled against the walls. Overhead, on sheets of marine plywood laid across the rafters, a shapeless mass of boxes and cartons and more machine parts.

"What's all that?" Delaney said, looking up.

"Junk. If you haul it out, I'll give it to you."

"You mind if I take a look at it?"

"What if I said no?" Kincaid said.

"I'd come back with a warrant."

"That's what I thought." He started for the door "Help yourself. I'll be in the office if there's anything else you need."

Up on a stepladder, standing precariously on top of it climbing down and moving it from time to time around the edges of the makeshift overhead platform, Delaney patiently examined the cartons of plumbing fixtures spark plugs, scraps of wood and wire and steel cable lamp bases, broken tools, saw blades, and miscellaneou impersonal junk, looking for something that seemed to have a personal stamp, something that might have bee stored there by Chad Norris.

After almost two hours, sweating through his shirt, grease and grime on his hands and forearms, he found what he was looking for. Under a paint-stained tarp were two fresh cartons, two feet square, thirty inches deep, sealed tight with plastic tape, tied and knotted with twine.

Delaney lifted the cartons off the platform one at a time, straining and struggling with their compact dead weight, and managed to horse them down the ladder to the floor.

Cutting the twine and the tape, he opened the cartons. Then he dragged a chair across the floor, sat down, and began examining the contents.

As soon as he'd seen the two boxes under the tarpaulin, Delaney had sensed they belonged to Norris. His investigator's instinct told him that something inside would prove it. But as he lifted out the contents, one article at a time, he found no shred of personal identification. In fact, any sign of ownership that had been there had been systematically eliminated. In every book or notebook, on every map or chart or folder or envelope where a name had been written, it had been neatly nipped off with a scissors. Or carefully blacked out with ink.

Still, in Delaney's mind, the cartons were a revelation. As he spread their contents around him on the floor, a pattern came clear at once. Every single item, every book, every map, involved one subject—Russia. It seemed that very facet of life in the Soviet Union was covered. Economics, agriculture, living conditions, religion, housing, prison reform, political trends, leaders' biographies, industry, art and culture, railroads and the highway system.

The pages showed that everything had been thoroughly read, passages underlined or checked, bookmarks still in place. Clear evidence that someone, for reasons of his own, had instructed himself thoroughly about life in Russia.

And in the bottom of the second carton were seven textbooks on the language itself, grammar and usage, regional words and slang, poetry and literature. In these books, too, the owner's name had been carefully excised.

One perforated page, however, had been overlooked. Holding it up to the light, Delaney read:

>United States Army
>Foreign Language Instruction
>University of Michigan

---

65. At a few minutes before midnight Chad sat watching Elena as she moved around her apartment. Cleaning, dusting, putting dishes and glasses away in cupboards, taking the sheets off the bed and putting them in the hamper, sweeping the floor, cleaning the sinks and the bathtub, mopping the small square of bare floor in the kitchen area, folding clothes, ironing blouses polishing the mirror on the door of the armoire. Finally he said, "What are you doing? Will you tell me what you're doing?"

"Just straightening up a little."

"A *little*? For the past two hours you haven't stopped You haven't sat down once."

"I always clean up like this when I go away."

"Come here," he said then.

"Am I making you nervous?"

"No. Come here."

She walked over to him, wearing a cotton apron over her skirt and blouse, still holding a damp sponge in her hand. He pulled her down on his lap.

"You'll get all dirty," she said.

"No, I won't. There's no dirt left in this place." He took the sponge out of her hand and sailed it across the room to the kitchen floor. He pulled her close to him and held her tight, both arms around her waist.

"What are you doing?" she said.

"I'm slowing you down."

"I'm all right."

"No, you're not. You're not fooling anybody. You're keeping yourself busy so you won't have time to think. Are you scared?"

"A little bit."

"Are you having second thoughts?"

"I don't know that expression," she said.

"It means maybe you've changed your mind, that you don't want to leave this apartment, that you don't want to leave Russia, that you don't want to go with me."

She was silent for a long time, her head resting on his shoulder.

"Hello?" he said finally. "Are you asleep?"

"No. I'm thinking about what you said."

"What do you think?"

"All kinds of things. But nothing neat and simple that I can explain the way I'd like to. I'm really not such an intellectual person, you know. Rational and well-organized. I mean all kinds of things are important to me. *Things. Objects.* I'm like a bird making a nest. I *collect* things. Nice things that I can look at and pick up and take care of. Like the things in this room. They have no real value, most of them. But to me . . . I mean if I ask myself, if somebody else asked me, what I'm really like, I'd have to say that if you look at the place I live in, you'll know the answer."

She looked around the room. "This is me . . . this place . . . what I've made of it. It's like a history of my life for the five years I've lived here."

"And the next place you live will be the next chapter."

"I know that. I'm not like a spoiled baby who can only sleep in one bed, covered with the same blanket always. But still, I can't help feeling strange when I realize that in a few minutes I'll lock that door behind me and never come back. In a few days somebody else will be sleeping in this bed and I'll be thousands of miles away."

"With me."

"That's the good part," she said. "And wherever we live I'll make it nice. I will speak American slang and chew gum all the time and never sing sad songs about the Volga."

Chad left first. By the building's rear exit. At twenty-five minutes past twelve.

He walked to Kropotkin Ulitsa, turned left to Zubov Boulevard, turned left again, and walked to the corner of Zubov and Metrostoyevsk across the street from the subway station. He sat on a bench there, in the shadows away from the street light, and waited.

The gears had meshed now. The switch had been thrown. No detours or turning back. Unless . . . unless he couldn't bring her to the final narrow channel, unless she backed off, turned away, refused to follow. Until now he had hypnotized her with half-truths. Now it had to be the full truth.

He was relieved. Even if it meant an abrupt end to the entire plan, he was relieved that he could tell her the truth now.

Her car turned off Metrostoyevsk and stopped at the curb on Zubov. He crossed the sidewalk, opened the car door, and got in.

Driving along the Garden Ring past Arbat Ulitsa and Kalinina Prospekt, she turned left on Zvenigorod Highway. Chad watched the road ahead, all the memorized turn-offs and destinations and highway numbers clear in his mind.

When she began easing right for the Leningrad Expressway, Chad said, "Don't turn off. Stay on this road."

"I can't. This road doesn't go to Leningrad."

"We're not going to Leningrad."

"What do you mean?"

"Stay in the center lane. We want the road to Rzhev."

"That's clear out of the way, Chad. I know what I'm doing."

"So do I."

She kept the car in the center lane. As they passed the Leningrad turnoff, she said, "I don't understand."

"We're going to Leningrad. Then we're going to Valdagersk. Just the way we planned it. But first we have to stop somewhere else."

66. Viktor Denishev stood at his office window look-ing out over the spires and highrise skyline of Moscow. When he turned back to Lepik, who was sitting on the couch facing Denishev's desk, he said, "It still doesn't make sense to me. Delaney in California. What could those people tell him that his agency doesn't already know?"

"Maybe Delaney's *not* connected with Norris. Maybe he's as much in the dark as we are."

Denishev walked back to his desk and sat down. "If that's true, then we're back to where we started. Has somebody kidnapped Norris, or is he involved in some private adventure that has nothing to do with the government? What about that woman in New York?"

"We have a new report on her. It's being assembled now. It should be on your desk in a few minutes."

"Did you read it?"

"Pousanov did. And he briefed me. He says Vera Wiberg's name before she was married was Vera Smaga. She's not Austrian. She's Ukrainian. Born in Zhitomir in 1912. She and her brother, *Tonu,* were leaders in the Ukrainian movement from the time they were in school in Kiev. He was convicted of treason in 1946, and just after he was executed, she disappeared. Her dossier says she probably escaped through Czechoslovakia. No word of her since then. Not till now."

"Any relatives here?"

"An aunt in Zhitomir, a cousin in Lugansk, and a son in a fishing village north of Leningrad."

"You said her husband is a Finn?"

"That's right. But this son is from an earlier marriage. Or maybe she wasn't married when she had him. He uses his mother's maiden name."

"What about him?"

"A party member, Pousanov says. Good worker. Single man. Never been in trouble. Clean record all the way."

"I don't trust clean records. Get an up-to-date report on him. Find out if he writes to his mama and if she writes to him. Let's see how far the leaves fell from the tree. We have a missing American who may know an old Ukrainian dissident who may have a son who fishes in the Gulf of Finland. Not a very good stew, but it's better than going hungry."

67. ■ Delaney came into his hotel room, threw his jacket on the bed, and turned on the television set. Walter Cronkite's face blurred and crackled into focus, full-screen.

"In Moscow the 1980 Olympic Games are going ahead smoothly. As expected, East Germany is dominant so far with strong contenders in every event. But the

United States team got a shot in the arm today when Dilly Upshaw won the two-hundred meter in world-record time. That makes two world records for Upshaw and his second gold medal. He had previously placed first in the one-hundred-meter dash when Hans Nidorf of West Germany pulled a thigh muscle and collapsed as he started the final heat.

"With all this first-rate competition, however, the lead story from Moscow continues to be the unexplained disappearance of the U.S. team's record-holding decathlon man. In a satellite interview with Milton Goodrich, who is conducting the Chad Norris investigation, here, in Moscow, is Roger Mudd."

Delaney turned away from the set and picked up the telephone. When the hotel operator came on, he said, "This is Bill Delaney in two-seventeen. What about my call to Virginia? . . . What? I told you it was urgent. Never mind. I'll place it myself."

He closed the connection with his finger, released it, checked the long-distance dialing instructions by the phone, and dialed. As the number locked in and began to ring, he watched Milton Goodrich on the television screen.

"We have no evidence that indicates any crime has been committed. No reason to believe that Norris has been kidnapped. So our investigation here, with the complete cooperation of the Soviet authorities and the Moscow police . . ."

Still watching the television screen, Delaney spoke into the telephone. "This is Bill Delaney. Urgent call. I have to speak with Lonny Perigo. . . . No, he can't call me back and I can't call him back. I'm leaving for the airport in twenty minutes . . . good . . . I'll hang on."

On television, Roger Mudd was questioning Goodrich.

"Your conclusion is that Chad Norris disappeared voluntarily?"

Goodrich, looking like a man with a broken egg in his hand, said,

"Since it's an ongoing investigation, we are still withholding final conclusions. But yes, that is one of the possibilities we're considering."

"Hello, Lonny. This is Bill. Just a second." Delaney flipped off the television set, then picked up the telephone receiver again. "What have we got?"

"Not much," Perigo said. "The military check on Norris's father didn't give us anything. There are people named Norris in every branch of the service. I sent the whole shebang along to Stabler. But none of the dates seem to work out right. And none of them show a dependent son named Chad. Or any other male Norris with the right birthdate."

"What about the boy himself? Still no military record?"

"Negative."

"No draft registration?"

"Nothing. We ran down Charles Norris, Chuck Norris, Clyde Norris, everything that was even close. We even found two Chad Norrises. One of them is forty years old. Drives a dump truck in Waco, Texas. The other one's a black kid from Washington who lost an arm in Vietnam."

"What about the Social Security application?"

"He gave May 2, 1953, as his birthdate. Place of birth, Cook County, Illinois."

"Does it check?"

"No. No record of a male Norris born on that date or any other date a month before or a month after. The only Chad Norris *ever* born in Cook County was a girl with a Filipino mother. She was born in 1970."

"So where does that leave us?" Delaney said.

"Nowhere."

"Can a man be twenty-seven years old and never have his name appear in any public records?"

"The answer is no. But it happens all the time. *If* somebody *makes* it happen."

"I've been trying to dodge that one."

"I know what you mean," Perigo said. "It's a pain in the ass to have to start all over again. From square one. But we have to face it. The only man who leaves no tracks is a made-up man. When a name doesn't show up in any records, it's because it's a *fake* name."

"In other words there *isn't* any Chad Norris."

"That's my guess," Perigo said.

"Then who the hell is he?"

"That's the rough one. If you've got the name it's easier to find the man. If you've got the man, it's a lot easier to find out his name. But when you don't have the name *or* the man . . ."

"You're making my day, you bastard."

"I'm not telling you anything you don't already know."

"Maybe not. But like I said, I've been trying to dodge it."

"The pattern's clear. Since 1976 he's out in the open. Paid his bills. Filed his tax returns. Before that, he didn't exist."

"Yes, he did. We just don't know who he was."

"Same thing."

"Keep digging. And add this to your list. University of Michigan. Military language training program. Russian section. Anytime from 1970 to 1976. Get me a list of all the names that were enrolled there during that period."

68.

On a dark street at the north edge of Volokolamsk, a city one hundred and thirty kilometers west of Moscow, Chad and Elena sat in her car, the motor off, the lights out.

Elena had been crying. Now she was pale and silent and angry, sitting stiff behind the steering wheel, looking straight ahead at the dark residential street.

"I admit I didn't tell you everything before," Chad said. "But I couldn't. I was afraid to. I didn't want you to misunderstand."

"But I *did* misunderstand. *Now* I understand. I know you were lying about everything."

"No, I wasn't. I didn't tell you everything but I didn't lie to you."

"Do you really think I'm such an idiot? Just because I love you do you think my head doesn't work anymore?"

"Damn it, I explained to you what I did and why I did it. If you can't understand that, if you won't accept it . . ."

"I understand it, all right. I understand *now*. But I certainly don't *accept* it. And if you were me you wouldn't accept it either. If you trust someone, if they trust you, you don't have to manipulate them . . ."

"Wait a minute," Chad said. "Are you saying that if I'd told you everything that first night we were together in your apartment, you'd have said, 'Fine. Perfect. That sounds like a great idea to me'?"

"I don't know. Probably not. I think I would have said what I'm saying now. That it's an insane idea. I would have tried to talk you out of it. But I wouldn't have felt used and lied to the way I feel now."

"God, you're impossible."

"When I think back on it, when I see how contrived everything was . . ."

"It *wasn't* contrived. I told you that."

"Then what would you call it? How do you think I feel when I think about those two weeks in Helsinki? We didn't just *find* each other. You were *looking* for me. Or somebody *like* me.

"First you went out with Alevtina. But she's divorced and has a two-year-old child living with her. Then you tried Lidia Tikhonov. But she lives with her parents and her uncle. So then you came to me, a girl with a car, an apartment of her own, and no family at all in Moscow. Someone to hide you and drive you around and give you a bed to sleep in."

"You don't believe that and you know it."

"Don't I? What else can I believe?"

"You can believe what I'm saying to you."

"I won't be a fool. I can't be a fool even for you."

"I *was* trying to get information," he said. "I *did* want to make friends with somebody who lived in Moscow. I admit that. I was like a bird making a nest. Picking up any twig or straw I could find. But you changed all that. You brought everything into focus for me. I grew up. I stopped feeling sorry for myself and started to make specific plans. And every plan I made had your name stamped on it."

There was a long silence. Finally he said, "All right, let's forget it. If you'll drive me to the railroad station, I'll get a train to Zubtsoy and you can go back to Moscow."

"Why are you so angry? I'm the one who should be angry."

"I'm tired of talking about it. If you don't want to take me to the station, I'll walk."

She started the car and drove south toward the center of the city. Neither of them spoke till they saw the station ahead of them, at the foot of the street they were driving on.

"I *want* to believe you," she said then. "You know that. When you told me you'd been planning some way you could get me out of Russia, when you told me all the details, all the arrangements you'd made, I *did* believe you. I was frightened but I tried not to show it. I thought if you were willing to give up so much, to take such risks for me . . . but now it turns out . . . now I don't know what to believe."

When she pulled in at the curb by the terminal entrance, he said, "I'll check the schedule." He got out of the car and walked into the station. In a few minutes he came outside again and stood by the open car window on the driver's side. "There's a train at five. I'll take that."

"That's almost two hours from now."

"It's all right. I'll wait in the station."

"Don't do that. I'll wait here with you."

He shook his head. "You might as well start toward home."

"Please," she said. "Get in the car."

When he got in, she said, "You can't do it, Chad. Do you really think you can do this by yourself?"

"I don't know."

Another silence. At last she said, "You *were* planning this before you met me, weren't you?"

"It doesn't matter now."

"It matters to me."

"Maybe it's hard to believe," he said then, "but I *didn't* plan it before. Not as anything real. I dreamed it maybe. I dreamed all kinds of things. I hoped for miracles. But I never thought there was anything I could *do*. Not really. No matter how much I wanted to.

"But after Helsinki, when I was going crazy thinking about you, all kinds of things started to come together in my head. Everything that was impossible before started to look possible. Even before I won the Oregon trials I was starting to plan how I could get you out.

"And afterwards, after I'd contacted those Ukrainian people in San Francisco and they'd steered me to that woman in New York, when I felt absolutely sure that I could pull it off and get you out, only then did it hit me that I could go even farther, that I could do this other thing that had never seemed possible before. And once it got into my head I couldn't get rid of it. I can't get rid of it now. I can't just say, 'To hell with it. Let's drive to Valdagersk, get on that fishing boat, and forget about everything else.' When I'm this close to Komenka, I couldn't live with myself if I didn't even *try*. When I was thousands of miles away, it looked impossible. It still looks impossible. I know that. But I have to try. I can't just walk away. In a way I'm relieved you're not going with me. That was the part I hated most. Putting *you* in a scary situation. I'd rather have you stay in Moscow and never see you again than to get you hurt or in some bad trouble."

"That's not what you said before."

"I know what I said. But I was wrong."

She sat half-turned in the seat looking at him. Then she said, "No, you weren't."

Turning herself square under the steering wheel, she started the engine, drove to the first intersection, and turned west.

"Where we going?" Chad said.

"West on the Rzhev Highway, then north along the Volga to a little town called Komenka."

"I thought you said . . ."

"I changed my mind. You can't go there by yourself."

"Yes, I can," he said. "If you think I'm lying to you . . . if you don't believe me . . ."

"I don't think you're lying. I believe you now."

69. When Delaney's Aeroflot jet landed at the Moscow airport, Stabler was waiting to meet him. As they drove north toward the city, Stabler looked into the rear-view mirror and said, "Follow the leader is the name of the game."

"What else is new?"

"Did they tail you in California?"

Delaney nodded. "I lost the first two but they must have guessed San Jose because all the time I was there somebody was hanging around. Denishev must be having luck recruiting American students. Either that or their intelligence office found a way to duplicate California kids."

Stabler grinned. "Maybe they caught one in the American Express office and cloned him."

"What's happening?" Delaney said then.

"Nothing new on Norris. They're still going through the motions, but the official strategy seems to be to bury the story. *Pravda* and *Izvestia* print only Olympic stuff. The glory of the Soviet Bloc. And interviews with visiting celebrities saying how adorable Moscow is. If they mention Norris it's hidden on a back page. The day after you left there was a story that Norris is hiding somewhere because he's afraid to compete with Klemenko, the Russian decathlon man."

"What about Sims and Goodrich?"

"The ambassador is spending all his time in the officials' box at Lenin Stadium, and Goodrich is pretending to supervise a manhunt from here to the Black Sea. Mostly they're silent. Very low profiles. They're stymied and don't want to admit it."

"What about our friend? Anything from him?"

"The word I get is that Denishev thinks Norris works for us."

"He's back where he started," Delaney said. Then, "Did we get some pictures of Norris?"

Stabler nodded. "Everything except the Helsinki stuff. Somebody blocked that."

"Denishev?"

"Who else? Buchanan used all the pressure he could, but the Helsinki people gave him a different story every hour or so. Finally they told him that most of the pictures and negatives we wanted had been accidentally shipped to a magazine in Australia."

"Boat mail, right?"

"That's right. The word is they're between Helsinki and Melbourne on some freighter."

"Pretty fancy story," Delaney said.

"Yeah. I'm sure Denishev furnished the story when they furnished him the pictures."

"What about the stuff from other sources?"

"Standard sports page junk. Action shots. Team shots. Beauty queens. I went over all of it. Nothing there."

"Did Perigo tell you I checked with him?"

"Yeah. He's striking out all over the place. Michigan's language school showed no Norris. They sent us the whole student list from seventy to seventy-six, and we triple-checked it. Zip."

They drove directly to the embassy building, through the gate, and into the basement garage. As soon as Delaney was behind his desk, he called Lyman Scruggs in Virginia.

"What do you think?" Delaney said.

"You tell me."

"It's a con. There is no Chad Norris. At least there wasn't till somebody made him up. He may be a clean-cut kid with an apple in his mouth, but he's done a snow job on a lot of people for four years. No finger-prints, no driver's license, no birth certificate. He's the only one who has the answers we need, and we can't find him to ask him the questions."

"Catch twenty-two."

"Right. So you've got the ball, Papa, and we're coming to the short strokes. Wake up a few of those teenage bubble-heads you've got over there and chain them to the computers. If I remember my freshman psychology, a guy who changes his name sometimes leaves in a clue to his real name, consciously or subconsciously."

"That's what they say."

"So let's take the name *Chad Norris* apart. Translate

it, decode it, and rearrange it. Have the computers do
every number they can on those ten letters, and shoot
the printouts to me as quick as you can."

70.

70. Denishev walked along a corridor from his
office to the screening room, Pavel Lepik beside him.

"Delaney went straight to his office from the airport.
We have surveillance teams at all the embassy entrances.
We'll have reports on his movements whenever he leaves."

"Good. What about those two people who were arrested in San Francisco?"

"They were taken to Washington."

"Any mention of it in the newspapers?"

"Not so far."

"Was our embassy in Washington notified?"

"No."

Denishev spent more than two hours in the screening
room, watching film of the events Chad had competed
in at Helsinki, watching television interviews and award
ceremonies, and seeing all the newspaper still photos of
him flashed one after another on the screen.

Among the last pictures was a long shot of Chad and
Elena walking across the infield of Helsinki stadium,
smiling and talking. Leaning across to Lepik, Denishev
said, "Who is the girl?"

"We don't know. Several of the still pictures have unidentified people in them. Only the athletes and officials are identified on the back."

When they walked out of the screening room, Denishev said, "I don't want any of this material returned to Finland. And I want to see big enlargements of all the photographs with unidentified people in them."

At lunch time Denishev went downstairs alone, walked to a park not far from his office building, and met Renart Ornishchenco. They bought sausage sandwiches and beer from a lunch cart and sat on a bench in the shade.

"What about Vitaly Lusis?" Denishev said.

"No surprises from that one. We know him well by now."

"No names at all?"

"Many names," Ornishchenco said. "He gave us long lists of names. All made up in his head. Detailed biographies of people who never existed. Addresses. Telephone numbers. Complete scenarios like a film. And all false. He gave us only two real names. One of them died six years ago, the other ten."

Denishev chuckled. "It's a pity we didn't recruit him when he was a student."

"I'm sure we could have. We could recruit him now. He's perfectly agreeable. He'll follow any stream he comes to. I'm certain he would love to work with us. At least he would go through the motions. He'll do anything that catches his fancy. But for us it would be like sleeping with a hand grenade. He's a truly dangerous man. And he will never change. When he's old and weak in his chair he will still be dangerous. Because he doesn't care if he's dead or alive."

"He was born too late."

Ornishchenco nodded. "We used to have a thousand friends like him."

In his office after lunch Denishev shuffled through the

photo enlargements while Lepik looked on. "We're checking with the Helsinki Sports Federation. All these individuals with Norris will be identified."

"Good." Denishev picked up the photograph of Chad and Elena, studied it closely. "This girl, too?"

"Yes. That's one of the pictures we're checking in Helsinki."

Denishev stood up and walked to the window with the enlargement, held it in the strong light from outside, and continued to stare at it. "Bring me that magnifying glass on my desk."

Lepik picked up the ivory and silver chartroom glass and carried it across the room to Denishev.

Holding the glass in one hand, the picture in the other, Denishev continued to study it. When he walked back to his desk, he said, "Did you notice that little button on the lapel of her jacket?"

"I saw it but I couldn't make it out."

"Neither could I till I looked at it under the glass." He handed the glass and the picture across the desk to Lepik. "If you look closely you'll see she's wearing an Intourist merit button."

As Lepik inspected the picture quickly, then looked up, Denishev said, "That pretty girl with a big smile is a Russian girl. I want her name and her dossier on my desk first thing tomorrow morning."

"I'll go to Intourist myself."

"Good."

On his way out of the building ten minutes later, Lepik stopped in Denishev's office again. "About that slip of paper they found in Vera Smaga's apartment in New York, the one word was erased and scribbled over so it can't be made out at all. Decoding just called me about it. The other word, they say, is *Klemenko*. Since it was on the same paper with Norris's name, Decoding thinks it must refer to Yury Klemenko. He's the decathlon man on the Soviet team."

"Too easy. Does that answer satisfy you, Pavel?"

"No."

"It doesn't satisfy me, either. I want Saneev to see that scrap of paper."

"Boris Saneev?"

"That's right. He'll tell us what's written on it."

"He's in prison. He's been in Lubyanka since . . ."

"All the more reason for him to be helpful."

---

71. Komenka, on the banks of the Volga between Zubtsoy and Staritsa, is one of the oldest towns in northwest Russia. In the ninth century, when Rurik, the Vasengian chieftain, swept down from Scandinavia and stayed on to rule Novgorod, the walls and ramparts of Komenka were already ancient and worn. Its gray stone buildings and narrow twisting streets were familiar sights to the traders and flax merchants who moved up and down the river between Kalinin and Nelidovo.

In 1036, when Vladimir's twelve sons were struggling for succession to the Kiev throne, Ludmila, the wife of Kochergin, fled to the Komenka convent on a cliff above the river and lived there for two years with her three daughters.

Ivan I built a castle near Komenka in 1332, and the

regent, Boris Godunov, kept secret headquarters there during Russia's 1590 war with Sweden. Peter II was born there in the castle in 1716 and died in the same room when he was fourteen years old.

After his father's murder in 1801, Alexander I took refuge there in the home of a merchant, and Pushkin, three weeks before his death in a duel in 1837, spent seven days in a Komenka inn and wrote a long poem about the splendor of the town and the beauty of the Volga there.

In the last century, however, Komenka, like Smolny Ulitsa in Moscow, has survived because it is small, and in the Kremlin planners' view, unimportant. The shipping has gone downstream to Zubtsoy or upstream to Kalinin. The mills have all gone to larger cities, and whatever small flax production is left is shipped direct from the fields to the mills by truck. The fields near the town, too small for major crops, grow mostly produce—potatoes, carrots, lettuce, leeks, and turnips.

Since the young people of Komenka go off to the city or to the army as soon as they are allowed to, the fields are tended, to a large degree, by the older people who still live in the town or on farms around its edge.

In a differently honed society, Komenka, because of its age and its medieval atmosphere and its truly remarkable situation beside the Volga, would be a Salzburg, a major lure for tourists.

In Russia, however, it is ignored and neglected, barely marked on maps and seldom referred to in guidebooks. Its three thousand inhabitants live in splendid isolation; they barter and bargain with each other and count time by the changing seasons.

It was early morning, just past six o'clock, when Elena turned north out of Zubtsoy and followed the river up to

Komenka. Coming into the town area, only the road along the Volga was wide enough for two lanes of traffic. All the streets leading uphill into the town were blocked by steel posts four feet high, two feet apart, anchored in concrete in the cobblestone streets, the passages too narrow for even the smallest cars.

"Now what?" Elena said.

"Stay on this road. It goes past the town, then up behind it. According to the map I had, it makes a complete circle. And right at the top, behind the town, there's a place where three roads branch off and go west. We take the center one. They told me there would be a sign."

Following the road, they moved up and around the walls of the village to the flat fields and birch forests behind it. Where the top gate opened in the wall, they turned and drove two kilometers west.

"There's the intersection," Elena said. "And there's the sign. It says the right-hand road, not the center one."

Stopping in the intersection, no other cars on the road since they'd turned uphill from the river, they looked at the enameled metal sign just ahead.

TRUCKERS: THE PEOPLE'S VEGETABLE PRODUCTION
UNIT FOR KALININ OBLAST STRAIGHT AHEAD.
EIGHT KILOMETERS.

Compared with the areas around Moscow, the countryside Chad saw as they drove along the narrow road was from another century. Long stretches of scraggly fields, flat and dreary and untended. Thickets and bramble patches and uneven clusters of birch and pine. And random stone piles here and there in the ragged fields.

It was ancient-looking terrain, much of it looking as though it had never been plowed or lived on, as though no one had loved or fought or struggled or raised food and animals there.

The few people he saw, scratching the ground with hoes in the early half-light or just standing dumb in front of crumbling stone and timber huts, seemed also from another age. Only the television antennas on the ruined buildings gave evidence of real present time.

The way was well-marked. They found the place they were looking for with no trouble. The road followed a two-kilometer stretch of ten-foot-high chain-link fence, topped by a multiple-strand tangle of barbed wire.

They slowed down at the entrance gate, wide enough for a large truck to pass through, with a two-story guard station on either side, then speeded up again and followed the fence to the next corner. A rough road turned off the main road there. They followed that. It ran with the fence line, all the way along the eight- or ten-kilometer perimeter of the big produce farm.

Elena drove carefully over the rutted road, her eyes fixed on the unpredictable surface, while Chad studied the open fields beyond the fence inside the barbed wire enclosure.

It was almost forty minutes before they completed the full circuit and came to the front entrance again. Elena stopped the car and turned off the engine. She turned to Chad and said, "There's no one here."

He looked out past her, beyond the wire fence and the guard stations, up the road to the long humpbacked knoll, to the stretched-out jumble of two-story concrete buildings, gray and isolated like some clumsy attempt at a new Stonehenge. No trees there. No grass or vegetation at all. Just a low, graveled hill, pushed together, it seemed, by earth-movers, and topped by those cruel and cubelike institutional buildings.

Not a sound or a movement. No puff of smoke or whiff of gasoline or frying food. No evidence whatsoever of human life. Nothing.

"I guess not," Chad said. "What does that mean?"

"I don't know. But I think we should move along. Just in case somebody we can't see can see us." She started the car, turned around, and drove back toward Komenka.

72.

Delaney leaned back in his chair, lit a cigarette, and looked at the pile of papers on his desk. Photographs, file folders, newspaper clippings, and two stacks of computer printout information decoded and transferred to $8\frac{1}{2}$-by-11-inch pages.

He leaned over and flipped the switch on his office intercom. When Stabler answered, Delaney said, "How you doing?"

"I've got a headache."

"Me, too. Come in and let's kick it around."

When Stabler walked in with a sheet of paper folded into an airplane, Delaney said, "You really *are* punchy."

"This is the last page from your printout stuff. It got into my folder by mistake when they collated." He sailed the airplane so it landed on Delaney's desk.

"Did you look at it?"

"I looked at *everything*. Half a dozen times. I need a white cane."

"Anything on it?"

"Sure. Fifty additional permutations of combinations of remote mathematical possibilities."

"So where are we?" Delaney said.

"I don't know about you, but I'm noplace. We asked a simple question, and Langley gave us a thousand very complicated answers."

"No word from our friend?"

"The word is that nobody trusts the reward that's being offered. The people think it's a trick. They're not used to being paid for giving information to the police. So they're laying back. Goodrich is making noises about a door-to-door search, but that's just a smoke screen. By the time they finished a door-to-door search of Moscow, it would be time for the 1984 Olympics."

"You think Norris is dead, don't you?"

"I don't know. But I'd hate to bet money against it. It doesn't make sense that some kid from the California boondocks can just go up in smoke, whether it was his idea or somebody else's."

"I know it doesn't," Delaney said, "but all the same something tells me he's not dead. It's too neat. And one thing I'm sure of: When we unravel this thing, it sure as hell won't be *neat*."

He picked up the paper airplane and unfolded it. "Let's see what I missed." He glanced down the page. "It's really mind-boggling what they can manage to do with one man's name. A thousand variations in a dozen languages. And ninety percent of them look like they came out of a Bulgarian telephone directory. Listen to this . . . Radon, Shindo, Ronda, Donar, Danish, Danro. With every kind of first name you can imagine, all of them dragged out of the ten letters in one name . . . Chad Norris.

"Here's a few that even sound like real people. Rich, Carson, Shorr, Richardson, Richards, Hardin. Take your pick. Which one is Chad Norris? His real name is probably Gus Jones or Stanley Smith or Jack Brown. Jesus, I'm tired."

He tossed the sheet of paper on his desk, pressed his intercom button, and said, "Helen, we're going under in here. We need a couple of serious drinks."

He lit a cigarette then, tossed the pack to Stabler, and leaned back in his chair. "I'm getting too old for this lasagna. Everything's petering out except my memory. All the things I want to forget crawl into bed with me every night. I look at a list of names and at least half of them ring a bell from sometime in the past.

"I played high school football with a big dumb kid named Rich. Two guys from Muscatine laid a block on him on a kick return, and he's been in a wheelchair ever since. Carson . . . I've known lots of guys named Carson. During the war there was an ensign on my ship named Floyd Carson. He went through the whole mess without a scratch, and two days before he was due to be shipped home some whore in Manila cut his throat."

The door opened and Helen Veach brought in two heavy glass tumblers, full to the edge.

"No tray?" Stabler said.

"It's not the Hotel Metropole," she said. "Just plain food here. And plenty of booze."

"Have a drink with us," Delaney said.

"Ask me in an hour," she said. "I'm up to my neck in yesterday's work."

As she went out and closed the door behind her, Delaney said, "I meant what I said before. Why is it all the crap keeps coming back? All your friends get rich or they move to Greenwich or they turn into drunks. And you're left with a few assorted dead men prowling around your room at night."

He picked up the sheet of paper again. "I could give

you a list of corpses and cripples and hard-luck assholes you wouldn't believe. Shorr. I had a buddy in Iowa named Ernie Shorr. As far as I knew nothing bad ever happened to him. His problem was that *nothing* happened to him. He was one of those golden boys. Good-looking as a poster, smart in school, top-notch basketball player. But the week after he finished high school, he started selling toasters and hair dryers in his uncle's store. Then he married some dimwit girl with big boobs and round heels and in seven years they had five kids. And like they say, that's all she wrote. Last time I saw Ernie, he was fifty years old and he looked seventy. Didn't know his ass from his elbow.

"Then there was Hardin. Cliff Hardin. He and I were in Naval Intelligence together. Two weeks before the great Cuban fuck-up invasion he was in Miami, going upstairs in the elevator at the Hotel Fontainebleau, and somebody blew his head off with a shotgun. Going right down the line here . . . Richardson. I've known lots of Richardsons, too. Half a dozen maybe." He took a drink and lit a fresh cigarette. "The last one was a guy here in Moscow. Must be nine or ten years ago. You remember Harlan Richardson?"

"I was still at Langley then. But I remember the case."

"He's another one of those spooks who parades around my bedroom at night, pointing his finger and saying, 'It's all your fault, you bastard.' "

"That was a trade-off, wasn't it?"

"Supposed to be. That's what Denishev was trying to set up. But we didn't buy it. *I* didn't buy it. So Richardson took the fall. He's still taking it."

"Somebody always gets shafted."

"That's right. I just like it better when it's not an innocent bystander. Most of the people we deal with know the name of the game. Whatever risks they take, they have a reason. Money or politics or pussy. I mean they know what they're getting into. But when somebody gets dumped on for no reason at all, when a nice straight guy with a wife and kid goes down just because he was standing there, *that's* a little hard to digest."

He pressed his intercom switch and said, "We're dry, Helen. Bring the bottle this time."

He leaned over to stub out his cigarette in the ashtray. "Remember that kid of his? He and his mother were ready to take on Congress and the Kremlin and anybody they could flush out. They were ready to declare war if they had to, to get Richardson out of jail."

Delaney took a pad of paper off his desk and doodled on it for a minute. When he looked up he said, "When you cross out the letters N-O-R-R-I-S from Richardson, you know what you're left with? C-H-A-D. How did the bloody fucking computers miss that?"

"They didn't. They just did it the other way around."

"How old was that kid of Richardson's?"

"In 1971 he was seventeen or eighteen, wasn't he? I guess he'd be about twenty-seven now."

"Chad Norris is twenty-seven."

"So are a lot of other people," Stabler said.

Delaney switched on his intercom again. "Forget the booze for a minute. Tell Morgan to unlock the 1971 box and bring me the file on Harlan Richardson. Tell him I'm in a hurry." He turned back to Stabler. "How about that retouched photograph of Norris, the one with the hair shortened and the beard cut off?"

"It's on my desk."

"Let's take a look at it. I want to match it with a picture of Richardson's kid if we've got one."

As Stabler started for the door, Delaney said, "And

bring that student list from the University of Michigan. I'll bet you a two-dollar bill they had a Richardson there."

As Stabler left the office, Helen came in with the drinks. She handed a glass to Delaney and said, "What kind of a look is that you've got on your face?"

"That's the look of a cat who's about to catch a mouse."

73.

When he was twenty-five years old, one foggy and cool afternoon in San Jose, Chad carried his army footlocker upstairs from Clara Kellogg's basement storage room, opened it, and stacked the contents in neat piles on the floor by his bed.

At the bottom of the locker, along with a thin packet of letters and half a dozen paperback books, he found the spiral-bound notebook he had bought and begun to write in six years before. He glanced at what he'd written, then tossed the notebook back into the footlocker.

Later, after he'd sorted through all the clothes and papers, after he'd kept out some shirts and a couple of books, he closed the locker and carried it downstairs again. But he left the notebook in his room, locked in a desk drawer.

He ignored it for more than a week. Then, late one night, he took it out and read over, slowly and carefully, what he had written in 1973. Some trick of time or sense-memory made it as painful to read at twenty-five as it had been to write at nineteen. His eyes kept returning to the final paragraph.

> I couldn't handle it. I couldn't deal with it at all. My mother couldn't either. We fell apart, each of us, in our own way.

Chad didn't sleep well that night. Every night he dreamed he was running, vaulting, competing. But this night he ran desperately, in the dark, with soft, sandy ground underfoot, loud voices and whistles, automobile horns, and brakes screeching.

At three in the morning he woke up, wet with sweat. He got up, took a shower, and put on clean pajamas. Then, like an act of exorcism, he sat down at his desk, took out the notebook, and finished the ugly story he had tried to write down six years before.

> In January 1971, two weeks after Christmas, my father had to make a trip to Europe. To Russia. That was normal for him. He traveled a lot. Whenever his company made a sale to an overseas manufacturer or to a European government, as soon as the equipment had been installed and tested, Dad always went to look things over, to make sure that everything was running smoothly. Mom and I were at the airport pretty often. To drop him off or pick him up.
>
> He always wrote or called as soon as he got to where he was going. That last time we had a letter from Kharkov. And he telephoned twice. Then, after a week when we had heard nothing from him, two sober young men came to the door one Sunday morning and told us Dad had been arrested in Kharkov and taken to Moscow.
>
> Next day the story was in *The New York Times*.

Front page. It said the trial would be held in ten days. The charge . . . conspiring to commit an act of espionage against the Soviet people.

We had no direct word from him. We were not allowed to call him or write him. But after his trial, the day before the story came out in the papers, a man from Washington came to see us, older than the first two, white hair, wearing a dark suit and a banker's gray tie. He told us Dad had been sentenced to life imprisonment.

I dropped out of high school the next day. For the next two years my mother and I spent more time in Washington and New York than we did at home in Stamford.

We talked and argued and pleaded; we wrote letters, sent telegrams, and tried to get the support of anyone we could, any reporter, any congressman, any public agency.

We circulated petitions, sent out hundreds of letters and appeals, held press conferences, and appeared on any radio or television show that would have us.

At first we had a lot of public sympathy and support. Both senators from Connecticut promised they would stick with us. And they did. For almost six months.

After that people began to lose interest. Every day there were new people with new problems. Ours was old hat.

But we kept at it. We spent all the money my folks had saved, borrowed what we could, and finally we sold the house in Stamford and spent that money, trying to keep the issue alive, hoping for some new interest or reassurance, any kind of help at all, but not getting it.

Finally my mother collapsed, and they took her to the hospital. Nervous exhaustion, the doctors said. But she said to me, "It's killing me, honey. I just can't hack it anymore. I can't get up *hoping* every day when I know I'll go to bed that night with no hope left. I just can't fight forever when there's no way to win. And you can't either. I won't let you.

"We're broke and I'm sick and it's time for you to go back to school and get on with your life. That's what your dad would want you to do. That's what he'd want us both to do."

Two months later she flew to Mexico and divorced my father. And not long after that she married John Wiswell, a lawyer from Darien who'd gone to school with Dad and who'd been helping Mother and me as much as he could.

"I'm not a solitary lady," Mom said to me. "I can't make it by myself. Your dad wouldn't want me to."

She wanted me to come to Darien and live with her and John, to finish up high school and then go on to college. I said, "Fine. That's what I'll do." But the next day I took the train up to Hartford and enlisted in the army.

As Chad walked back and forth in the narrow morning streets of Komenka, all those details, all that long-past frustration and heartbreak, spun through his head, tangled together with complex present equations that couldn't be solved or dismissed.

With his hands in his pockets and his hat low on his forehead, he passed and repassed, on the opposite side of the street, the tiny book and stationery shop where Elena had gone to ask dangerous questions.

When she came out at last and crossed the street to meet him, he said, "Any luck?" and she said, "I'll tell you when we're in the car."

As soon as they were on the road again, turned around and heading southwest toward Zubtsoy, Elena said, "She was a tough old lady. Didn't want to give up anything. Not at first. But after I listened to her attack Yevtushenko for half an hour, she asked me what I was doing in Komenka. I pretended it was something secret that I couldn't talk about. Then, finally, I let her wheedle it out of me. I showed her my Intourist credentials and said I was also a journalist working for *Izvestia,* that I'd been sent here to do some research on the big produce farm west of town."

"What did she say?"

"First she asked me if I knew that all the workers out there were political prisoners. I pretended that I didn't know it, and she said, 'I'll tell you something else. They moved them all out a month ago. Didn't tell a soul around here what they were doing, but I found out. It's because of the Olympic show in Moscow with thousands of strangers prowling around. The Kremlin doesn't want anybody looking through wire fences at prisoners. So till all the visitors go back to where they came from, every prisoner within three hundred kilometers of Moscow has been stuck away behind walls, all of them transferred to the big prisons.' "

"Did she know where?"

"*Tula,* she said. All the men here were taken to the prison in Tula."

"Tula?" Chad said. "That's south of Moscow."

"Straight south. Three hundred kilometers southeast of where we are now."

"Is the prison inside the city?"

"Dead center. It's a well-known place in Russia. There's an underground folk song about it. It says there are a thousand roads to Tula but no road out."

---

74. "It's beautiful," Delaney said. "Once that first olive pops out of the bottle, you know they'll keep on coming. *Dale Richardson*. Isn't that a bitch. Nothing on Chad Norris, but all the information we can handle on Dale Richardson. Now we know what he's up to. He's here to do something about his old man. God knows what he's got in his head, but whatever it is he's pointing for a head-on collision somewhere."

"We still don't know where he is, Bill."

"Maybe not. But we know where he's heading. At least we will know as soon as we get the call about his father. When we pinpoint where they've stuck Harlan Richardson, we'll know where to look for his kid. I guarantee it."

Stabler looked at the clipboard on his lap. "Dale Richardson got out of the army in August 1976. Five days later Chad Rossen enrolled in college in California. Do you think he was planning all this that far back?"

"I don't see how. But he must have been planning something. We won't know those answers till we find him. We won't know the beginning till we've seen the end. What about Dilly Upshaw?"

"Bardsman checked in half an hour ago. He'll talk to Upshaw as soon as he can shake him loose."

"Norris can't be alone on this thing. Somebody's been hiding him. And it has to be someone he knew before he got here. I wish I knew how much time we've got."

"We're at least one up on Goodrich. You can bet on that. And if Denishev's people are clued in, we'd know it by now, wouldn't we?"

"Maybe yes. Maybe no. Sometimes you get what you pay for. Sometimes you don't."

75.

Denishev and Lepik sat at a long table in the room adjoining Denishev's office, Lepik reading from an open file folder in front of him. "Her name is Elena Baklanova. Born October twenty-first, 1955. Her father was Valery Baklanova. Her grandfather was Gregory Baklanova. And her great-grandfather, on her mother's side, was Kunstantin Tsiolkovsky."

"Impressive bloodlines." Denishev picked up Elena's photograph and studied it. "Norris is either smart or lucky."

"She graduated Karl Marx University in 1975," Lepik went on. "Went to work at once for Intourist. She has a good record there and a top rating." Lepik looked up. "I talked with her supervisor. He says she's loyal and reliable. She's fluent in English, French, and German and half a dozen Russian dialects. She has been allowed to leave the Soviet Union with tour groups on several occasions."

"Politics?"

"Party member since she was eighteen. Active in young Communist activities since she was in lower school. Good with detail work. A good organizer. Made a thirty-minute speech at the Youth-for-Lenin Congress in Minsk in 1978, excerpts reprinted in *Izvestia*." He slid a photocopy of the article across the table to Denishev. "No political problems. No questionable activities."

"What about her friends?"

"People she knew in school mostly. Many of them work for Intourist or other state agencies. Their records are as clean as hers. A few of them were involved in student protests a few years ago but nothing serious."

"She's too good to be true," Denishev said. "My son should find a girl like this. On the other hand what would a girl like this want with my son?"

"When she was very young, fifteen or sixteen, she had a serious love affair. A young man named Sergei Kosyph, almost as young as she was. They were in school together and they went away on holidays together. But he fell behind in his school work and was taken into the army. He disappeared in North Vietnam in 1973. Presumed dead."

"Since then?"

"There are other names here, but more friends than lovers it seems. Most of her social life is with groups of people her own age. At her apartment or theirs."

"Where does she live?"

"Smolny Ulitsa. Number eighteen. She lives alone in a one-room apartment and has a 1978 car. A Zhigulis."

"How did she manage that?"

"The apartment came after she received a Soviet Youth

Plaque in 1975. She was allowed to buy the car after the speech she made in Minsk."

"So her only transgression is that she was photographed with an American athlete in Helsinki?"

"We're questioning the other Intourist girls who were in Finland with her. We'll see how well she knew Norris."

Denishev reached across the table and pulled the file over to him. He studied the pages carefully. Suddenly he looked up. "What about this? What's Zhabotinsky's name doing in here?"

"No real connection. Zhabotinsky's present wife, Larisa, was a childhood friend of Elena Baklanova."

Denishev flipped quickly to the last pages in the folder, read for a few moments, then looked up. "Not *just* a childhood friend. A grown-up friend. Larisa Zhabotinsky's in a Moscow hospital right now. Tried to kill herself. Baklanova visited that hospital. Before that she visited Shota Zhabotinsky's apartment, where Larisa is staying. And before that, Larisa and Shota and Baklanova all had a meal together at Hotel Rossiya."

"I didn't have time to go through the entire file," Lepik said.

"Maybe all those innocent social evenings weren't so innocent. Maybe she spent some time with Larisa and Leonid Zhabotinsky and their friends."

The telephone rang then and Denishev picked it up. When he replaced the receiver, he said to Lepik, "One of your people has a report from the Intourist girls who were in Helsinki. He's waiting in your office."

When Lepik left the room, Denishev picked up the file folder and walked through the connecting doorway to his office. Placing the folder on his desk, he sat down in his chair, leaned back, his hands clasped together in his lap, and closed his eyes.

In a few minutes Lepik was back. "Voronin talked with a girl named Lidia Tikhonov. She was with the Soviet group in Finland and she remembers Chad Norris. He took her to supper one evening. He asked her a lot of questions about Moscow. A lot of details about herself and her family. But they went out together just that one time. After that she saw Norris with Elena Baklanova. She believes they went to a hotel together, in the daytime, at least twice."

Denishev sat quietly, nodding his head. "And the report came back from Boris Saneev," Lepik went on. "On the piece of paper our people took from Vera Smaga's New York apartment, the one where she'd written down Chad Norris's name, Saneev says the other word is *Komenka*."

"Komenka? Is he sure?"

"No question about it, he says. You know Saneev."

Denishev picked up his phone then, pressed an intercom button, and said, "Ask Comrade Ornishchenco to come into my office." When he hung up he said to Lepik, "Do we know where to locate Elena Baklanova?"

"It's her summer holiday. Her supervisor said she left Moscow for two weeks."

"Of course she did. I'm not surprised. And I'm certain that no one knows exactly where she went."

"A driving tour, he said. No itinerary. Just going from one town to the next."

"And all by herself."

"That's what he told me. It's what she told him."

Ornishchenco came into the office then and Denishev, with no preliminaries, said, "When your man was following Vitaly Lusis the other morning, Vitaly was trying to make contact with a young woman. Isn't that correct?"

"Yes. He *did* make contact."

"If he saw the young woman again, could your man identify her?"

"I'm not sure. I know he wasn't able to get very close to her. After the contact he stayed with Vitaly. Those were his instructions."

Denishev handed him an enlarged photograph of Elena. "Show him this. I need to know if she's the woman Vitaly passed an envelope to."

After Ornishchenco left the office, Denishev leaned back in his chair again, turned on a recording device built into his desk, and said to Lepik, "All right. Let's see what we can stitch together."

He put his hands behind his head and looked up at the ceiling. "Vera Smaga is an old enemy of the Soviet state, a dissident who supports Ukrainian independence. But . . . as far as we know she has been inactive since she escaped from the Soviet Union and went to New York. But *has* she? What about her son in Valdagersk, a fisherman who takes his boat out to sea every morning? He seems to be a blameless man. What's his name again?"

"Muonio Smaga."

"Right. The name of a poet. So . . . in the mother's apartment we find a piece of paper with two things written on it. The name of an American athlete, Chad Norris, and the name of a Russian village, Komenka. Nothing peculiar about that. Just an old woman scribbling on a piece of paper. Looking at a sports story in the newspaper as she remembers a town in her native country.

"But then we get a complication. This Chad Norris comes to Moscow and disappears. No evidence that he was kidnapped or killed. So . . . as a theory, let's assume he disappeared deliberately.

"Why would he do that? And *could* he do it in

Moscow? Just drop out of sight and leave no trace? Not easily. He must eat. He must sleep somewhere. Difficult problem. Especially for a foreigner.

"Let's say he found a way to change his appearance. Shaved his beard maybe. He's still an American. He still has a language problem. He's still in a city he's never seen before. And he'd need a passbook if he wanted to move around. Even in the city. All big difficulties unless he has someone to help him.

"So who does he know in Moscow? We find that he has a friend, an acquaintance at least, perhaps an intimate companion. She is a lovely and intelligent Russian girl, an Intourist employee who knows the city very well. Knows the whole country well. Also, her best friend is the wife of a Soviet exile, a man whose only friends are dissidents and rebels. Could Elena Baklanova have met some of those people? She certainly must have been invited on some occasion to Leonid Zhabotinsky's apartment, drank some wine, ate some food, talked with the other guests.

"And since Vitaly Lusis was one of Zhabotinsky's close friends, she could have met him there. *If* she met him, and *if* she needed a Soviet passbook so her American friend, whatever his reasons, could move around freely pretending to be a Russian, then she might have known what we have just discovered—that Vitaly Lusis was the man to go to."

"Norris had an American passport. Why would he need Russian papers?"

"Maybe he intended to travel outside the approved tourist areas. Kirov maybe. Or Saransk. Maybe we'll find out he wanted to visit Komenka."

"Or maybe he wants to help his girl friend cross some border and go with him to America."

"That's possible," Denishev said. "But couldn't she get out without his coming in? Her dossier shows she's been outside the Soviet Union several times. What was to stop her from staying in Helsinki when she met Norris?"

"Remember, we're talking about a man who turned away from Olympic competition after preparing himself for years. If the girl's that important to him . . ."

"You're right. I'm not ruling that out. But I suspect there's something else involved. I keep coming back to Vera Smaga. *And* Komenka."

"Why Komenka? There's nothing there, is there?"

"No. That's what intrigues me. There's nothing at all in Komenka. But not far from there, eight or ten kilometers if I remember right, there's a prison, a minimum security work farm for low-risk prisoners."

Ornishchenco came back into the office then. "I showed the photograph to Caslavska. He can't be absolutely certain because he was never very close to the girl. But the face seems much the same, he says. He said she was wearing a yellow slicker."

"Not as definite as I'd like," Denishev said. "But not negative either." He turned to Lepik. "Find out if the Baklanova girl has a yellow raincoat. And order up the files on all the prisoners at the Komenka work farm. And send out a description of her car and the license plate numbers to all traffic control sections, especially between here and Leningrad. Do we have a good man in Valdagersk?"

"Yes," Ornishchenco said. "Pechenkina."

"Good. I want to talk to him. Also to the man in Rzhev. And I don't have to tell you, every move we make now is important. Time is important."

"You haven't forgotten," Ornishchenco said, "that all the prisoners at Komenka have been temporarily moved to Tula."

"No, I haven't. But one of those Komenka prisoners may be the lure. I want to know *which* one, whether he's there or not at the moment."

76.

At a roadside emergency turnoff area, black-topped and badly lighted, nine o'clock at night, just off the west-to-east highway between Smolensk and Serpukhov, Chad sat waiting in Elena's car, watching her through the glass of a telephone kiosk thirty feet away.

Two hours earlier, on the outskirts of Vyazma, in a parking lot clogged with cars, almost all of them Zhigulis, he had found a car that looked exactly like Elena's. He had removed the orange-on-black license plates and replaced them with Elena's Moscow plates, black with white numbers.

A few miles farther on, in a parking area outside a factory, he had traded plates again, put the stolen orange and black plates on an old gray Chaika and the Chaika plates, also orange and black, on Elena's Zhigulis sedan.

He saw Elena hang up the roadside telephone. When she walked back to the car and got in, he said, "Did you get him?"

"Yes. I just caught him. He was leaving for the airport. He has a flight to Vienna tonight."

"How is your friend?"

"Shota says she's not in danger now. She's had transfusions and vitamin shots and good hospital care. They will probably let her go home in a few days."

"That's good."

Elena shook her head. "She won't talk to anyone. Even to Shota. And she won't eat unless she's forced to. Her friends are worried about what will happen when she leaves the hospital. It's like I told you before. And it's no better now. Unless some miracle happens it won't *be* any better."

She shook her head again and gripped the steering wheel with both hands. "I can't let myself think about it. It makes me crazy. I would do anything to help her, but I know there's nothing to be done. She's the only one who can help herself, and she doesn't want to."

She started the car, pulled out on the dark highway, and headed east toward Obrinsk. "Shota told me about a safe house," she said. "It's just past Serpukhov between two villages, Dabki and Luzhki. There's an animal farm there where thousands of bison are bred and cared for. And just above it, in a forest on the hillside, a man named Pavlodak lives in a cabin by himself. He's very old and lives on his pension. We can stay with him tonight."

"Can you trust him?"

"Shota says yes. He survived a terrible work camp near Ayaguz. That's the code word. When anybody hands him a slip of paper with the word *Ayaguz* on it, he lets them stay in his house, no questions asked."

Except for the heavy trucks and vans driving fast with their lights dim and yellow, the highway was clear. Elena was able to make good time. Even so, it was nearly midnight when they found Pavlodak's house, following Shota's instructions. They hid the car behind a great wall of cord wood in the back and went inside the one-room fieldstone cabin.

The old man was almost deaf. He spoke in staccato

bursts with a thick Uzbek accent. He gave them dark bread and goat cheese and two stone mugs of chilled cider, then motioned them up the ladder to the loft. On the floor by the window under the eaves there was a straw mattress and a blanket.

When they were undressed and under the blanket, Chad lay on his stomach, propped up on his forearms, looking out the window. "God, it's beautiful out there. I've never seen anything like that."

The house was high on a slope, the downhill side resting on stilts. A quarter of a mile below was the Oka River, black and gleaming, a wide fenced meadow beyond that, and in the distance, a range of dark hills, birch trees in a white line at their base. The moon, coin-round and low, lighted everything blue and silver, and thick herds of bison moved slowly across the misty floor of the valley.

"They look fierce but they're very peaceful," Elena said.

"That's because they're vegetarians."

"No. It's because they have small brains. Inside that huge head is a brain the size of a grape. All they know is to eat, sleep, and make little bisons once a year."

"Not a bad life," Chad said.

"It's a fine life if you're a bison."

He blew out the candle and pulled her close to him under the blanket, his arms tight around her. "Are you all right?" he said.

"I don't know. I'm trying not to think about it. I'm trying not to think about anything."

"I made a mistake. I shouldn't have dragged you into this."

"You didn't force me."

"I persuaded you."

"I persuaded myself."

"I know you're scared," he said. "I can feel it. You're scared to death."

"More for you than I am for myself."

They lay still in the dark. They could hear tree limbs brushing the roof over their heads, and downstairs the old man moved around softly in his sock feet. "How far are we from Tula?" Chad said then.

"An hour's drive. Maybe a little more. We can be there very early in the morning."

"I don't want you to come with me."

"I *have* to come with you," she said.

"No, you don't. I'll drive the car in. Or if that's too risky, I'll go in on the bus. There'll be an early morning bus going there."

"Then what will you do?" she said.

"I'll look around. See what the situation is."

"And ask a few questions in your United States Army Russian?"

"I speak it well. You said so yourself."

"That's true," she said. "For someone who isn't Russian you do speak well. But that's exactly what you sound like . . . someone who *isn't* Russian. All you have to do is ask one question of the wrong person and you'll be locked up so fast you'll be dizzy."

"That doesn't matter. I have to take the chance. I don't want you with me. I don't want to get you in trouble."

"I'm in trouble already," she said.

"No, you're not. If you went back to Moscow tomorrow no one would know anything. You could pick up right where you left off."

"What about us then? What about the plans we were making before we left Moscow?"

"I was stupid. I thought I had things worked out. But

I found out different. Now I don't know what I'll run into at Tula."

"I already told you what you'll run into. A stone wall. You'll see the biggest, ugliest prison you've ever looked at. One look and you'll know it's hopeless."

"I still have to look. I have to see for myself. I can't just back off and say I'm licked until I'm sure I *am* licked."

She was silent again for a long moment. Then, "And what do *I* do? Shall I go home to Moscow and read the papers every day to see what's happened to you?"

"I know how you feel, but you're better off there than you would be with me."

"No, I'm not," she said. "Shota told me some other things on the telephone. I didn't want to tell you but now I have to. Vitaly, the man who gave me the passbook you're carrying, was arrested. He's in jail. The KGB broke into my apartment and searched it. And they've been questioning my friends. You see how it is? I'm a fugitive now. If we don't make it to Finland, I'll go to prison. And so will you."

part 5

77. At twenty minutes before midnight, Delaney
went upstairs from his office to the main floor of the
embassy building. He stopped in the lobby to make a
baseball bet with Levi Osterman, the Marine Corps
sergeant on guard duty there. Delaney took the Cincin-
nati Reds, and Osterman, from Gary, Indiana, bet on the
Chicago Cubs, the game to be played the following
Sunday in Chicago.

Outside, Delaney walked slowly across the walled-in
garden to the parking area, got into his car, and drove
to the main gate of the embassy grounds. After talking
for a few minutes with the guard there, he moved ahead
into the street, turned right, and headed toward Kalinina
Prospekt. In his rearview mirror he saw a car pull out
and follow him.

In eight minutes he arrived at his apartment building,
turned in to the underground garage, parked his car,
locked it, and went upstairs in the elevator. The Georgian
clock in his foyer chimed midnight as he unlocked his
apartment door.

Walking through the living room in the dark, he
switched on the bedroom light, took off all his clothes
down to his shorts, and got dressed again; his shirt, his
tie and socks and shoes, everything he put on, was made

in Moscow. The suit, dark and drab and ill-fitting, was instantly recognizable as Russian.

Going back into the living room, he turned on the light and read through *Pravda,* slowly and carefully, till just after twelve forty-five. He switched off the reading lamp then, went into the bedroom, and turned off the lights there.

Outside his apartment, he locked the door, walked through the corridor, passed the elevator, and went down the service stairs.

At street level he turned down a long dim-lit hall to an exit sign, opened the heavy service door, and stepped out on the sidewalk.

As he crossed to the curb, a black Chaika limousine rolled up and stopped there, a uniformed Soviet soldier behind the wheel. Delaney got into the backseat and the car pulled away from the curb.

Half a block away, on another side of Delaney's square-block apartment building, the two men who had followed him home from the embassy still sat in their car, smoking and talking, carefully watching the garage entrance.

78.

Lepik walked from his office to Denishev's, sat down in a leather chair, and said, "Delaney left the embassy and went home. Lights out."

"Why can't I do that?" Denishev said. He sat behind his littered desk with his jacket off, his tie loosened.

"All the files are here now," Lepik went on, "and the staff is going through them. I sent a man to the railway station for food and hot tea. At one thirty I'll give everybody a half-hour break."

"What about Baklanova's car? Any report?"

"A call just came in from the motor police in Vyazma. They found the car there in an apartment building parking lot. They're searching the building now to see if Norris and the girl are there."

"Vyazma?" Denishev said. "What are they doing there? That's not the way to Komenka."

"They've already been to Komenka. A bookstore woman there called the police in Rzhev. She said a girl with Intourist credentials was in her store this morning, asking a lot of questions about the produce farm west of town."

"That explains Vyazma. Now they must be on their way to Tula."

"But why would they stop? Why would they leave the car?"

"Are you sure about the automobile license plates?"

"No question."

"Maybe they stole a car. Americans are good at that." Denishev lit a cigarette. "Alert the highway police between Vyazma and Tula. Tell them to stop every car with a man and woman in it."

79. Chad and Elena got up before dawn, dressed in the dark, and climbed down the ladder from the loft. The old man was up already, in his pants and socks and undershirt, starting a fire in the cookstove.

"Can we leave our car here for a while?" Elena said to him. "We'll come back for it this afternoon."

"It's the same to me."

"We want to take the workers' bus into Tula."

"Two kilometers down this road," he said. "The way you came in. Where the road crosses the highway there's a place that the Tula bus stops."

It was still dark when they got on the bus. But all the seats were taken. They pushed their way back in the crowded aisle. Each time the bus stopped, the new passengers shoving and struggling to get on board pushed them back even farther.

At last they were wedged in so tight there was no need to hold on to the safety straps or to the backs of seats. However much the bus lurched and swerved and screeched to sudden stops, there was no room to fall.

Elena and Chad stood facing each other, locked together, unable to move or speak in the crush and the noise, the body smell and tobacco smoke, barely able to breathe.

Daylight had just begun to streak the sky when the

stumbled off the bus, stiff and twisted, at the central bus terminal in Tula. But the sidewalks were already crowded. Men and women in work clothes, carrying cloth sacks or dinner pails, bumping and bruising their way through the crowds on their way to one or the other of the city's giant iron works. The streets and buildings were gritty and stained. The air was thick and close, tasting of smoke and gas fumes.

On all sides, down all the intersecting streets, great metal towers and sawtooth industrial roofs and smoke-stacks and scaffolds and construction cranes framed and studded the city, the stacks belching flame and gas clouds, and thousands of whistles and bells and work sirens and vehicle horns blasting and wailing and thump-ing out a wave of ugly sounds to match the dirt and grime and deadly sulphurous stink in the cruel streets of Tula.

The prison, its walls painted a flaking bilious green, was dead center in the city, seven blocks from the bus terminal, a solid, windowless pile of stone and cement and twenty-foot walls three feet thick, the gates in its long, five-sided perimeter made of heavy gauge black-painted steel, no grates or openings in their rusting surfaces.

When they came to the last corner and saw the prison close-up for the first time, Chad and Elena stood across the street from it, their backs against a building wall, and stared, silent and stunned.

At last, barely audible, Chad said, "Jesus Christ."

Staying on the opposite side of the street, they walked the full circle of the prison, studying the harsh monu-mental sameness of it, the unending heavy mass of wall, no hint of life at the gates, no visible evidence of any life or movement whatsoever behind the walls.

When they came back, finally, to the corner where they

had begun, they stopped, like two wound-down toys, and stood there, slack and silent, still gazing at the prison walls across the street.

At last Elena said, "I'm sorry. It's even worse than I've heard."

Chad didn't answer. He kept staring at the green walls, his hands in his pockets, the worker's cap pulled low on his forehead.

All the years of speculation and study and imagining, all the efforts to pinpoint his father in some physical environment, had in no way prepared him for this cold absolute in front of him, this lifeless place with its atmosphere of gray and painful permanence.

They went into a café and sat in a back corner drinking hot tea and eating bread. Elena concentrated fiercely on the mechanics of her breakfast and tried not to look at Chad's eyes. He sat with both hands around his tea glass staring down at the table top.

Across the room, a thin, balding man wearing steel-rim spectacles read his paper, drank his tea, and glanced at them occasionally. But they didn't notice him. And when they paid their check and left the café, the bald man trailing along behind them, they didn't see the two men lounging outside, one on either side of the café entrance.

Chad and Elena were grabbed from behind suddenly, their arms pinned, and pushed across the sidewalk to the curb where an automobile was parked with its door swung open.

Chad wrenched himself free and threw one of the men down on the pavement. He had looped his arm around the neck of the other man, the one holding Elena, when the bald man stepped behind her suddenly, forced her against the side of the car, and held a snub-nosed automatic against her head. "Don't make a problem," he said in Russian. "Put yourselves into the car."

30.

Delaney stood at the window of a hundred-year-old farmhouse, tall with high angles, carefully mortised beams, and planks of hand-cut ancient wood, a waist-high fieldstone foundation, a steep-pitched roof, and a great expanse of meadow sloping down to the road half a mile away. A round pond with geese and ducks swimming on it was just below the barns, and cattle and sheep grazed free in the fields around the house.

Two young men in army uniforms were in the house with Delaney. One, a sergeant, was at another window across the room. As the black Chaika turned off the road and started up the lane toward the house, he said, "Ahh, they're coming now." He studied the car with his field glasses, turned to Delaney, and said, "Two people in the car with them."

Elena was in the front seat between the bald man and the driver. Chad was in back, between the other two men.

When they got out of the car, Delaney and the man in the sergeant's uniform came down from the house to meet them. "My name's Delaney. And if you're not Dale Richardson I've gone to a lot of trouble for nothing."

Chad looked at Elena. She shook her head almost imperceptibly. Chad turned back to Delaney and said nothing.

"You don't have to tighten up," Delaney said. "Nobody's going to hurt you. I'm sorry we had to grab you off the street, but there wasn't any other way. Unless I'm mistaken we're only an hour or so ahead of the Russian police."

Chad looked at Delaney's clothes, then at the sergeant's uniform. "Don't believe everything you see," Delaney said. I'm a card-carrying American. I work for the United States government. These men work with me."

"You don't look American," Chad said.

"You don't either. No wonder nobody recognized you."

"How'd you find us?"

"A lot of work, a little luck, and some guesswork. Once we figured out you were Dale Richardson I decided you were trying to make contact with your father. And when we found out he'd been transferred to Tula, I figured you'd show up in Tula, too." He nodded toward Elena. "Dilly Upshaw clued us in about your friend here."

The bald man stepped forward and handed Delaney two blue passbooks. "Her name's Elena Baklanova."

Delaney glanced at Elena's passbook, then handed it back to her. "Upshaw couldn't remember your name. But he remembered what you look like. Gave us a very accurate description. So we staked out Tula Prison last night and waited for you to show up."

"Now what?" Chad said.

"That's up to you."

"I'll bet it is. You'll have me back in the Olympic Village before I can . . ."

"Not me," Delaney said. "I'm not a truant officer. Matter of fact you can go straight back to Tula if you want to. We can drop you off there within a half-hour."

"I don't follow you. Aren't you with the FBI?"

"Nope."

"Then I don't know what's going on."

"It's not that complicated. First I was trying to find you. Now I'm trying to wise you up. If you make any dumb move to contact your father, if you have any crazy idea that you can get him out of that concrete box they've got him in, forget it. You're walking on eggs and you have been ever since you hit Moscow. I'd guess you've broken a dozen Soviet laws so far. *Serious* laws. If you want to spend twenty years in a carpet factory in Bukhara you're off to a good start."

"If you're not with the FBI, who do you work for?"

"The government. Like I said. I had the same orders everybody else had. Find Chad Norris. Just another missing person. But when I found out your real name, it changed the whole picture. I started to take a personal interest."

Chad stood there in the thin early sunlight looking at Delaney, studying his face, his clothes, all the details about him. Finally he said, "You could be Russian for all I know. How do I know you're what you say you are?"

"You don't. I could show you credentials, but I'm not going to. Besides, my papers could be as phony as yours are." He tossed Chad's Soviet passbook back to him.

"Did you know my father?" Chad said then. "Is that what you're trying to tell me?"

"I didn't *know* him exactly. Let's say I knew a lot *about* him."

"What does that mean?"

"It means I had a lot to do with him. It's my fault your father's in prison."

81. "It's a horseshit business," Delaney said. "Nobody ever said it wasn't."

It was half an hour later. Elena was inside the house. Chad and Delaney were standing beside a cattle pen down below the barns.

"The choices are always crap," Delaney went on. "And the toughest part of all is when you don't *have* a choice. When the choice is made for you. When all you can do is bite your lip and suck in your gut and wish you were selling shoes in Chicago."

He offered Chad a cigarette, then lit one for himself. "I'd never heard the name *Harlan Richardson* till he was arrested. Currency violations, they said at first. Then later they accused him of being a foreign agent. Our embassy saw to it that he had good legal representation. They stayed on top of it as much as they could. But the evidence was staggering. They'd found twenty thousand rubles in your dad's hotel room and partial designs for a new Soviet antitank weapon.

"Those things would have been more than enough to cook his goose. But they also came up with an Air Force officer who testified that Richardson had offered him ten thousand rubles to turn over military secrets."

"He was set up," Chad said.

"Sure he was. We all knew it. But it's hard to prove.

They can plant evidence on anybody. Or they don't even *have* to plant it. They just show the evidence in court and somebody testifies where he found it and nobody gets to contradict him. It was obvious that they'd done a number on your father, but nobody knew why. Not till after the trial, several months after, when he'd already been sent off to prison.

"I'd been working here in Moscow for nine or ten years by then. My business depends on local people. Recruiting. Regular Russian people with regular jobs who work for me on the side. Some of them do it for money and some of them because they're sore at the Kremlin or sore at their wives. But whatever their reasons, the store can't open without them.

"Anyway, I'd built up a good group through the years. Twenty or thirty first-rate people. Real sources. I had a man in the Politburo, a colonel in military planning, and one of the top economists in their Department of Production. We had a pipeline into every corner. The KGB knew we were getting hot reports but they couldn't figure out how. So they tried to use muscle. The word came floating in that for every one of my people I turned over to them, one American prisoner would be released from a Soviet jail and sent home. The first man they offered to let go was your dad."

"When was this?" Chad said.

"Two months, three months maybe, after his trial. They knew what they were doing. They timed it right. All hell was breaking loose in Washington then about your father. You remember. You and your mother were in the middle of it. So when the word came through to the State Department that we could shake Richardson loose just by handing over one Soviet citizen who happened to be working for me, they made up their minds in a hurry. The order came down to make the swap. There was only one catch. Nobody knew any names. Nobody knew who we had to trade. Nobody but me."

"And you killed it."

"Not just like that. Not easy like that. I hated what they'd done to your dad. I thought it was the worst kind of crap. But they were leaning on me to do the same thing to somebody else."

"Not exactly. They were asking you to turn over an agent so a man could be released who *wasn't* an agent."

"That's one way of looking at it. The other way is this: I figured your father had a good shot at getting released sometime later. He was locked up but he wasn't dead." He dropped his cigarette on the ground and stepped on it. "But anybody *I* blew the whistle on wouldn't be that lucky. They'd have a big noisy trial and within two months they'd be standing against a wall with a dozen bullets ripping into them."

"There are all kinds of ways of being dead."

"Wrong." Delaney shook his head. "There's only one way."

"Let me put it this way," Chad said then. "Your reasons may work for you, but they're lousy for me. My mother's dead and my dad's been locked up like an animal for nine years, and all that time I've been stumbling around like a blind man in a mine field. I used to lie awake at night planning what I'd do if I ever stood face-to-face with whoever caused all that."

"Get it straight. I didn't *cause* it."

"Maybe not. But you could have *fixed* it. It all adds up to the same thing."

Chad turned and walked away, up the slope toward the house. Delaney stood watching him. Then he slowly fished in his pocket and took out another cigarette.

82.

"*Richardson*," Denishev said. He looked up from the folder on his desk. "It makes sense. And Richardson's son. The crazy young boy who wanted to fight the world is now a crazy young man. If Chad Norris is really Dale Richardson it answers a lot of questions."

A secretary came into the office and handed a slip of paper to Pavel Lepik, who sat beside Denishev's desk.

"What is it?" Denishev said.

"The car in Vyazma does not belong to Elena Baklanova."

"But the license plates . . ."

"Her license plates but *not* her car."

"Then that car's plates must be on her car."

"No. The stolen plates were found fifteen kilometers away on a third car."

Denishev looked at his watch. "So Baklanova and her friend may be in Tula by now. We've lost track of Delaney, so he could be there too. And I'm back at the beginning point. Back where I began. I say Norris and Delaney are connected. I say they have some plan to get Harlan Richardson out of prison and out of the country."

"Maybe at Komenka there could have been a problem," Lepik said. "But Tula is a fortress . . ."

"All the same I want Richardson out of there. I want him here in Moscow. In Lubyanka. And I want him there by noon. Contact Novikov in Tula and tell him to go to the prison with two men. Pick up Richardson and bring him direct to Moscow. I don't want any surprises."

"He'll need transfer papers."

"No, he won't. There's no time for that. Tell him to use my name. If there's any difficulty the prison supervisor can call me here."

83.
As Lepik went to his own office to call Ramauld Novikov in Tula, a black Chaika limousine driven by a Soviet army sergeant pulled through the south gateway of the prison. Delaney, in the backseat, rolled down his window, held up a bright red KGB passbook, and said in Russian to the prison guard, "Andrei Kranskoi to see Supervisor Ugrumov."

As the car rolled ahead to the parking area outside the Administration Building, Delaney put the passbook back in his pocket and muttered to himself, "You're crazy, Delaney. And the older you get, the crazier you get."

Inside Supervisor Ugrumov's office, Delaney, scowling and pacing, began the conversation in impatient anger and worked up quickly to a full shout.

"I am not here to discuss procedures and formalities. There is no time for that. I came in person so there would be no senseless delays." He looked at his watch.

"The prisoner, Richardson, must be outside in my car in five minutes, or I will not be responsible for the consequences."

Ugrumov, looking uncomfortable, muttered something about authorization. "I think I must consult with my superior."

Delaney held up his red passbook. "*This* is your authorization. *I* am your authorization. *Andrei Kranskoi.* Special Section. Moscow."

When Ugrumov seemed to hesitate still, Delaney said, "Never mind *your* superior. Let's call *my* superior, the man who sent me here. Viktor Denishev. Does that name mean anything in Tula?"

"Yes, of course, but . . ."

"Let's call him in Moscow. Let's wake him up at home and tell him you need his personal guarantee . . ."

"No, I don't think . . . I mean I'm sure my own superior . . ." He reached for the telephone receiver.

"I insist," Delaney said. He took the telephone receiver away from Ugrumov and said, "Operator. Get me Viktor Denishev in Moscow. The number is four-four-six–two-three-two-three." Turning back to Ugrumov, he said, "You are causing a serious delay. I hope you have a good explanation ready."

Ugrumov, visibly shaken now, moved to his office door, opened it, and said to an assistant, "Prisoner Harlan Richardson, the American. I need to know exactly where he is at this moment. Locate him for me."

Delaney, scowling, the phone held to his ear, heard the number he'd asked for begin to ring.

In his basement office, Pete Stabler picked up the phone. A thin, gray-haired man was sitting beside him. Stabler said nothing, made no sound in the receiver till Delaney said, "This is Kranskoi, Comrade Denishev."

Stabler quickly handed the phone to the man beside him. In a heavy, surly voice the man said, "Yes, Kranskoi."

"Supervisor Ugrumov at the Tula prison questions my authority. He is causing a delay."

Ugrumov, beginning to turn red, moved closer to Delaney and said, "No, I didn't say that. I didn't mean to . . ."

Delaney, still speaking into the receiver, cut him off. "He says he cannot release the prisoner even with *your* authority. Without the proper papers . . ."

"No. Please . . ." Ugrumov began. Delaney turned to him abruptly, said, "Here is Viktor Denishev to speak to you," and handed him the receiver.

His face very red now. Ugrumov found his authority voice for an instant and said, "This is Supervisor Yevgeny Ugrumov . . ."

He got no further. Standing five feet away, Delaney could hear a storm of angry and profane Russian coming through the receiver. Ugrumov stood motionless, staring straight ahead. When the line went dead suddenly, the connection broken at the other end, he lowered the receiver slowly into its cradle. "Please," he said to Delaney. "Please intercede for me. I had no intention . . ."

"It's a question of time," Delaney said. "If there's no further delay I'm sure Comrade Denishev will be understanding."

Six minutes later the black Chaika rolled out through the prison gate. Sitting beside Delaney in the backseat, dressed in prison work clothes, was Harlan Richardson, a solid man in his fifties, his skin weathered from outdoor work, his hair thick and white.

As the Chaika turned right at the first corner and headed toward the highway running north out of Tula, it met and passed a gray Zil sedan, two dead-serious young men in the front seat, Ramauld Novikov in the back.

As the gray car neared the prison gate, all three of the men inside it took out their red passbooks.

84.

Delaney hung up the telephone receiver in the farmhouse, then walked outside where Elena stood watching his men load an army truck. The Chaika was parked behind the house, and a third vehicle, a small brown sedan with damaged paint, sat just in front of the truck.

Down the slope, beyond the barn area, Delaney could see Chad and his father walking back and forth, talking, stopping from time to time, then starting to walk again.

Standing beside Elena, Delaney said, "You've heard about Homer Barnett, haven't you?"

"I think so. He's Chad's coach, isn't he?"

Delaney nodded. "But you've never seen him?"

"No. Maybe I saw him sometime in Helsinki, but if I did I don't remember."

"If you had seen him, you would remember, I think. He looks a little like Chad's father. Same build. Same white hair."

The man in the sergeant's uniform came up to Delaney then and said, "We're ready for you."

Eight four-by-four-by-five wooden packing boxes sat on the ground behind the truck, military identification and routing numbers stenciled on each one. Four of them had new industrial-strength washing machines inside; four of them were empty.

Chad and his father and Elena and Delaney each got into one of the empty boxes. The sergeant and the other four men nailed the lids in place, then loaded the boxes forward in the truck; the other four boxes with machines inside went behind them, closer to the tailgate.

The Chaika limousine left first, followed by the brown car with three men inside. Ten minutes later the sergeant started the truck's engine and followed them down the dirt road that would lead to the Moscow–Tula highway.

When the limousine was only fifty yards from the highway, it pulled off the road and parked in a sparse grove of trees. The driver walked back to the road and got into the backseat of the brown car. At the highway they turned south toward Tula. But when they came to the first intersection they turned west toward Smolensk.

The army truck, heading north toward Moscow, was stopped at a roadblock every ten or fifteen miles. At the third one, after he'd shown his papers and his load of washing machines, the sergeant said, "This is the third time I've been stopped. What's going on?"

"We're looking for a black limousine. A Chaika. It's supposed to be someplace between here and Tula."

"I don't know if it was a Chaika or not," the sergeant said. "But I saw a big black car parked west of the highway fifteen or twenty kilometers north of Tula."

"When was that?"

"An hour ago. A little more maybe."

He told the officer specifically where he'd seen the car, and the man said, "Pull over there and wait. I'll call this in to helicopter control. They might need more directions."

The sergeant pulled the truck over and parked it at the edge of the road. He got down from his cab and leaned against the front fender, smoking a cigarette. When he was halfway through his second cigarette, the officer walked across the road from the radio car and said, "We located it. Looks like it might be what we're looking for. Thanks for the help."

As he started his engine and pulled away from the roadblock, the sergeant tapped three times on the back wall of the cab. Delaney, listening for that signal, made four return taps on the side of the box he was hiding in.

85.

"I don't give a damn what you say. I'm not going to leave him," Chad said. "I'm not going off in one direction while he goes off in another one. I waited too long. Besides, I don't trust this place and these people. I'm still not sure I trust you."

"I don't care if you trust me," Delaney said. "But if you want this thing to end right, you have to do it by the numbers."

They were standing in a thick, ragged woods, half a mile off the main road, twelve kilometers south of Moscow. A laundry truck and a nondescript green sedan were parked just behind the army truck. The sergeant and the other two drivers were opening the last two packing boxes, the ones with Richardson and Elena inside.

"*You* do it by the numbers," Chad said. "You do anything you want to. Just don't try to send my dad off someplace and me someplace else. I won't let you. You screwed him up once. You're not going to do it again. I'm going to stay right with him and we're going to get out of this bughouse country. And we're going to do it together."

"That's the one thing you *can't* do. You try to stick with him and you'll be hanging a bell around his neck. What do you think you can do . . . waltz him into the embassy? Forget it. They'd be on the phone to the police in five minutes."

"Like hell they would."

"Your father's a prisoner. There's no loophole in the embassy code that lets them give refuge to a convict. He'd be back in jail before . . ."

"He's not a convict. Don't call him a convict."

"That's what he *is*. And that's what he'll be . . . as long as he stays in Russia."

"You can talk till you're blue in the face," Chad said. "If he gets in that car, *I* get in. I'm not gonna leave him."

"If you want him out of here, you will. I told you what you have to do. You have to go to the embassy and do your act. You have to clean up the mess you made. If you do that, if you make enough faces and tell enough lies, I'll get your father out of Moscow. But if you try to hang on to him like some snot-nose kid . . ."

"Don't call me a kid."

"Why not? I'll call you any damn thing I want to. I'm getting tired of changing your diapers."

Chad swung at Delaney's head. But Delaney stepped

inside the punch, spun him around, pressured him sharply just behind the ear, and caught him as his legs buckled and he started to slump to the ground.

He carried him to the laundry truck and loaded him into the back, locking the door from the outside. To the driver he said, "He'll raise all kinds of hell when he comes to. But don't let him out till you're inside the embassy grounds."

86.

At eleven fifteen in the morning Homer Barnett walked out through the gate of the Olympic Village carrying a blue canvas gym bag. He got into a taxi and gave the driver a slip of paper with the words *Ukraina Hotel* written on it. The taxi pulled away from the curb and turned toward Komsomolsky Prospekt.

Five minutes later Pete Stabler walked out through the same gate, got into his car, and headed back toward the embassy. The car that had followed him everywhere for the past two days was following him still. Stabler grinned as he glanced into the rearview mirror. "You're chasing the wrong fox, boys."

Barnett's taxi turned off Komsomolsky and headed north along the Garden circle, through Zubov, Smolensky, and Chaikovskova Ulitsa to Kalinina. When they turned off Kutuzovsky, pulled into the driveway of Hotel Ukraina, and stopped at the curb, Delaney was waiting there, wearing his own clothes again, the Russian suit and shoes he'd worn to Tula back in the closet in his apartment.

Delaney opened the taxi door and got in beside Barnett. He closed the sliding-glass partition between the front and back seats, put his hand on the canvas bag, and said, "Is everything here?"

Barnett nodded. "I even put in a pair of specs. I had my reading glasses on when they took the passport picture."

"Good. How about the reservation?"

"Stabler says it's all set. British Airways. Flight Two-sixteen. Leaves at twelve thirty. Ticket's at the desk."

Delaney checked his watch. "We're on the money."

When Barnett got out of the taxi, Delaney said to the driver, "Gorky Street. The southeast corner of the Ul Raskovoi intersection. Take Gruzinskaya."

Ten minutes later they were curbside at the corner of Raskovoi and Gorky, the engine running, the driver smoking a cigarette, Delaney looking out the back window at the approaching traffic.

Suddenly Delaney turned to the driver and said, "There's a blue limousine coming up behind us. An American Lincoln. When it stops for the intersection, pull in behind and follow it."

When the light changed, the two cars sped north on Gorky into Leningradsky Prospekt, the blue Lincoln with an official Olympic Seal on its rear window, the taxi staying close behind it.

In the long dark tunnel at Boltusk Ulitsa, just before the Leningradskoye interchange, there was a four-minute traffic stall, horns bleating and angry shouts in the dark, the cars bumper-to-bumper, their engines filling the tunnel with a fog of carbon monoxide.

THE LAST DECATHLON 253

Coming out of the tunnel finally, the taxi driver saw that his backseat was empty. Delaney was gone. A twenty-ruble bill was tucked between the sliding panes of the glass partition.

In the blue limousine, the man who had driven the brown sedan earlier that day was behind the wheel, Delaney beside him, Harlan Richardson in the backseat.

Delaney passed the bag back to Richardson. "Here are some clothes to put on. I think they'll fit. Put on the glasses too."

As they turned onto the Leningrad Highway, heading for Sheremetyevo Airport, Delaney said to the driver, "Don't push too hard. I don't want to play games with the traffic police."

At five minutes past noon, when Delaney and Richardson walked into the British Airways section of the international terminal, Hugh Coker, ginger-haired and portly, senior passenger agent for B.A. in Moscow for eleven years, came forward to meet them. Shaking hands with Delaney, he said, "Stabler rang up and asked me to keep an eye out for you. I've got Mr. Barnett's ticket here."

"Good," Delaney said. "Hang on to it." Turning to Richardson, he said, "This is Mr. Coker, Mr. Barnett. I'm going to ask him to walk you through passport control and get you settled on the plane."

"Thank you," Richardson said.

Turning back to Coker, Delaney said, "Mr. Barnett's been under the weather. A bad bug of some kind. So he's a little weak. Not quite himself."

"We'll take care of him, don't worry. Just let me nip over here to the desk and get his boarding pass stamped, and I'll have him on board in no time."

As soon as Coker walked away, Delaney said to Richardson, "If you can act sick, do it. Keep your head down, keep those glasses on, and blow your nose a lot. Coker's an old hand. He'll get you through."

"It won't be hard to act sick. I *feel* sick."

"Good. So much the better."

"I don't even know . . ." Richardson began. "Everything's too fast for me. I want to thank you but I don't know how."

"Don't worry about it. Let's just get you on that plane and out of here."

"What about Dale?"

"He'll be all right. He has no problems now. He'll meet you in London in three or four days." Then, "Just don't forget that envelope I gave you. It's important. You know what to do?"

"Yes"

Coker came back then and Delaney said, "I'll wait for you in the bar. After the plane takes off I'll buy you a glass of Irish."

Bent over, coughing, a handkerchief held up to his mouth, with Coker explaining, nudging, maneuvering the immigration and passport-control people, Richardson made his way, stage by frustrating stage, to the boarding area, the officials seeing the photograph of a white-haired man with glasses carried by a white-haired man with glasses and hearing Coker's flood of explanation, "Olympic official . . . very ill . . . not himself . . . going to London for medical treatment . . ." and trying, with their faces averted, not to catch whatever Russian germ was causing Mr. Barnett to cough so hard.

On the plane at last, Coker found Richardson's seat, settled him into it, said good-bye, and went off to alert the chief steward that the gentleman in seat number M–18 might need special attention.

Just as Coker started to leave the plane, Richardson came forward, up the aisle, and caught him, handed him a small square envelope, and said, "I forgot to give this to Mr. Delaney. Would you please see that he gets it?"

"Be happy to. And enjoy your flight."

Sitting by the tinted plate glass window in the bar, Delaney watched the British Airways jet back slowly away from the telescoping passenger tunnel, then taxi heavily forward to its takeoff point. Following its path all the way along the runway, he watched it pick up speed, its wing and taillights blinking, till it lifted off, climbed steeply, and disappeared in the summer cloud cover at three thousand feet.

Later, having a drink with Coker, the picture of that climbing, turning plane stayed in his mind, burned in there, like a talisman of his life pattern. Half good, half bad. Half triumph, half failure. Failure after triumph sometimes. Triumph after failure almost never. An unpleasant copper aftertaste almost always.

After Coker left, Delaney stayed in the bar, had another drink and a sandwich, and opened the envelope that Richardson, as ordered, had sent to him. Inside was Barnett's passport. Delaney slipped it into his jacket pocket, crumpled the envelope, and dropped it into an ashtray.

Just before he left the terminal, he stepped into a phone booth and called Stabler. "The bird flew," he said. "They're out of Soviet air space by now. I gave him fifty bucks but he has no passport. No I.D. at all. Be sure Carpenter meets him at Heathrow or those British immigration guys will ship him to Guernsey on the next flight out. Did Norris show up?"

"I didn't see him but he's here. Shut up in an office with Sims and Goodrich."

"Good. Sit tight there. I've still got some loose ends. I'll be in touch with you."

When he hung up, he stayed in the telephone booth, smoking a cigarette. Then he called Denishev's office, spoke to his secretary, and left a message.

87. "We still don't know where Delaney is?" Denishev said.

"No," Lepik said.

"How about Norris?"

"He's been at the American Embassy since half-past eleven."

"How about the girl?"

"No sign of her."

Denishev's secretary buzzed him on the intercom then. He picked up the receiver, listened intently, grunted something unintelligible, and hung up.

Slumping back in his chair, he said, "Somebody just called on my private line. Told my secretary that Richardson left Moscow on a commercial flight an hour ago."

"Do you believe that?"

Denishev nodded. "It's Delaney. That's a Delaney touch. The description of the man at Tula Prison fits Delaney. And now this. This fits him too."

"I don't see how . . ."

"It doesn't matter *how*. The question now is, how do

we cover ourselves?" He lit a cigarette. "How can we cook the fish before it starts to smell?"

"If Richardson's out of the country, if he talks to the press, we can't pretend he's still in prison."

"That's true." Denishev sat up slowly. "But I think there's something we *can* do. Call Timoriev in the President's office. Tell him I'm on my way to see him on urgent business." Denishev stood up, took his jacket from the back of his chair, and put it on. "And Vrubel, from the Propaganda Ministry, tell him to meet me in Timoriev's office."

"I'll pick him up and bring him there myself," Lepik said.

He followed Denishev out of the office and along the hall toward the elevators.

"No. I need you for something else. I want you to leave for Valdagersk right away."

"Valdagersk? Pechenkina can . . ."

"Not Pechenkina. *You*. I want to make sure we don't get humiliated twice in one day. This is too important for Pechenkina. I will stay in the office tonight. Contact me as soon as you get there, as soon as you've talked with Muonio Smaga."

Denishev stepped into the elevator and the doors closed behind him. Lepik turned and walked quickly back to his office.

88. The telephone in Bill Delaney's bedroom rang twice, then stopped. Elena came into the room but did not pick up the receiver. It rang again. Three times. Then it stopped. The next time it rang she picked it up at once. Delaney's voice said, "Chad will be on television in five minutes."

Ambassador Sims came on the screen first, speaking English, a simultaneous Russian translation droning along with him.

> "I am delighted to announce to all the concerned people in the Soviet Union, in the United States, and around the world, that Chad Norris has been found. He is here with me in the Embassy of the United States in Moscow, and in a few minutes he will have something to say.
>
> "But first I want to introduce Milton Goodrich, a senior officer in the U.S. Department of Justice. More than any other individual we have Goodrich to thank for the safe return of this fine young American athlete."

Goodrich, looking starched and ill at ease, described in detail the spirit of cooperation that had existed between his men and the Moscow police organization. He praised a number of individuals, especially Ambassador Sims, bu he neglected to mention that Chad had not, in fact, been found. He had, in fact, simply wandered into the embassy and asked to be taken upstairs to the ambassador's office. Goodrich didn't mention that detail at all. And neither did Chad when he began to speak into the camera, humility in his voice, a look of innocence and fresh milk on his face.

"I just want to say that I'm very glad to be back here, and I'm sorry for all the worry and trouble I caused. Most of all I'm sorry if I let down my friends on the Olympic team, the coaches and the officials, and the other athletes who were counting on me. I know it's too late now for me to compete, and that's one of the biggest disappointments of my life.

"Ambassador Sims told me that a lot of people thought maybe I'd been kidnapped or that I was being held as a hostage for some reason. I just want to assure everybody that nothing like that happened.

"Naturally, everybody wants to know what *did* happen. I wish I could tell you, but I can't. As near as I can tell, it was a case of amnesia. It's never happened to me before, but it's the only explanation I can think of for what happened this time.

"All I can say is that when I went running that morning, the day the Olympics opened, I started along the Moskva River the same as I did every morning. And that's all I remember. From then till today.

"Today I found myself walking around the Moscow bus terminal with short hair and my beard shaved off, and wearing these Russian clothes. In my pocket there was a return bus ticket from Moscow to Orsk. I don't remember ever being in a place called Orsk, but it looks like that's where I was.

"I still have most of the money I was carrying the day I left the Olympic Village. I don't have any bruises, and my weight's the same as it was. Looks as if I've been eating, and I haven't been mistreated.

"So that's it. It's a mystery to me what happened. And I guess it always will be. Just amnesia is all I can figure out. My memory must have faded out on me, and I wandered around till it came back."

Ambassador Sims came on the screen again then, smiling and shaking Chad's hand. Elena got up to turn off the set when suddenly a Russian announcer's voice came on.

"From Tass here is a news bulletin: President Brezhnev this afternoon made an important anouncement. To symbolize the spirit of international friendship the Moscow Olympics have begun here, a historic step has been taken by the Soviet government

"Starting today, five citizens from other countrie who have committed serious crimes in Russia will b pardoned, released from prison, and sent home. Th first man on the list, Harlan Richardson, is from th United States. He was released today, and left Mos cow on a flight to the West this afternoon."

89.

"I felt like a jackass," Chad said. "I wanted to tell the truth, but I remembered what you said and I knew I couldn't. I felt like some dimwit kid caught in the garage with a bottle of beer."

"The important thing is your dad was in jail yesterday at this time and today he's on his way to London."

"That's what I mean. That's what I'd like to tell everybody. If I'd known that when I was on television . . ."

"You knew it when you heard about that announcement from the Kremlin."

"I didn't trust that. I didn't know what to make of it," Chad said. "I wasn't sure what had happened to him till you told me ten minutes ago."

They were walking through a sculpture garden four blocks from the American Embassy, midafternoon, forty minutes after Chad's television statement.

"I don't see why we can't tell the truth now," Chad said. "Why can't we?"

"Because we got what we wanted. We won. And winner-take-all never works. Not in my book it doesn't. When you win, it's a good idea to leave the other guy with something. Especially when you're in somebody else's country. And twice as important when that country is Russia."

"Why?"

"Because they're just like everybody else. They don't like to be laughed at."

"Does that mean nobody's ever gonna know how Dad got out of here?"

"The official story is that Brezhnev pardoned him and sent him home."

"I'm talking about the real story."

"Not many people know that. And the ones who know won't tell."

"Why not? I'd love to tell the truth about it."

"Then go ahead. But nobody will believe you."

"Maybe not. But they'd believe *you*," Chad said.

"I've got nothing to say. I wouldn't back you up. I don't even know you."

"You don't know *anybody*. You're like a rogue elephant."

"Where'd you pick that up?" Delaney said. "You wouldn't know a rogue elephant if he fell on you."

"Maybe not. But I know a cop-out when I see one."

"What is that supposed to mean?"

"I'm not knocking it. I just don't know how you do it. How do you tune out from everybody? How do you live with yourself?"

"How do *you* live with *your*self? Don't talk to me about cop-outs. You'll be flying back to California in a few days. You've got your father back. You've got the world by the ass. But what about your Russian girl friend? What happens to her? Or don't you give a damn?"

Chad stopped walking suddenly, his face pale, his fists clenched at his sides. "What are you gonna do, swing on me?" Delaney said. "You tried that once before . . . remember?" They stood face to face on the path. Finally Delaney said, "Answer my question. Do you give a damn or don't you?"

"I give a damn all right. It's driving me nuts."

Delaney walked away then and sat down on a bench. Finally Chad came and sat down beside him.

"What did you think was going to happen?" Delaney said. "How did you expect it to work out for her?"

"I was going to take her with me: That was the whole idea. That was what triggered everything. I mean I'd always had it in my head to try to do something about Dad. I never stopped thinking about it. That's why I learned all I could about Russia. I even learned the language. But I'm not crazy. I wasn't kidding myself. All the time I knew it was a million-to-one shot that I'd ever be able to *visit* him even let alone find some way to get him out, to bring him home. I mean I'm not Superman, for Christ's sake. I'm just a regular guy. My head told me I was nuts from the beginning, but something inside me said I was his only chance. If *I* gave up he was really finished. So that's how it was. I didn't know *what* I could do or *how* I could do it, but I kept trying to get myself ready anyway. Just in case.

"Then I met Elena in Finland and the next thing I knew I'd qualified for the Olympics and my head went crazy. Scheming and planning and trying to tie everything together. By the time I hit Moscow, before that even, that last night in New York, I'd convinced myself I could get her out. And I'd started to think there was a good chance I could take Dad too. Now I know different. Now I can see I was crazy. Even if he'd been at Komenka . . . I mean I had some half-assed idea about how I could make contact with him and get him out, but I know now it never would have worked. I mean from Valdagersk on it might have been all right, but getting him there . . . I don't know how in hell I could have done it."

"What's Valdagersk have to do with it?"

Chad told him the escape plan in detail, the way he'd

explained it to Elena. When he finished, he said, "So that's it. At least that *was* it. Now everything's shot. Dad's home free, thanks to you, but Elena . . ."

They walked to the nearest cabstand and took a taxi to Delaney's apartment building on Kalinina. When they pulled up at the entrance, Delaney took his keys out of his pocket and held them out to Chad. "There's food in the icebox and booze in the cabinet. I'll check in with you tomorrow morning sometime."

"Wait a minute. That wasn't the deal. We don't want to push you out of your apartment."

"Why not? It's the only offer you've got. I'll find an all-night poker game. Or some nice middle-aged hooker who'll put me up."

He held the keys out again. This time Chad took them. "The big one's for the downstairs door. The smaller one unlocks the apartment."

"What about the shiny one?"

"That's my extra car key. I've got a Porsche sitting in the underground garage. But that's not part of the offer. I don't want to see you joy-riding around town in my car. And just in case you've still got Valdagersk in your head . . . forget it."

When Chad got out of the taxi and went into the apartment building, Delaney said to the driver, "Pull up to the corner and turn right. I'll tell you where to stop."

He directed the driver to an empty parking space thirty yards down the street from the garage entrance to his building. "Turn off the engine and read the paper if you've got one. We may be here for a while."

Delaney slouched back in the seat then and lit a cigarette, his legs crossed, his eyes on the garage entrance.

After almost forty minutes, he decided he'd guessed wrong. He sat up in the seat, stubbed out his fifth cigarette, and was ready to leave when suddenly he saw his

black Porsche nose up the steep driveway from the underground garage, ease across the sidewalk, turn left on
Chaikovskova, and head northeast toward Gorky Street.

Delaney's taxi followed the Porsche all the way along
Leningradsky Prospekt till it angled right to the Leningrad Expressway, Chad driving, Elena sitting beside him,
the car heading northwest out of Moscow.

As his taxi turned back toward the city, Delaney
grinned and said to himself, "Maybe he's gonna amount
to something after all."

90.

"What about our friend?" Delaney said to
Stabler.

"Like I said, he reported in an hour or so ago. And I
expect to hear from him tonight."

"What are the odds?"

"Even money, I guess. He delivers when he can."

"I don't know," Delaney said.

"If we can't trust him, we can't trust anybody."

"You said it. I didn't."

"You hatched him, Bill. You should know the answer."

"I know I should but I don't. Can we trust him a
hundred percent?"

"About ninety, I'd say."

"This time that's not good enough," Delaney said. He
looked at his watch. "I'm going to Valdagersk. We got
a driver hanging around?"

"We've got Akinov."

"Good. Tell him we need a high-powered car that looks like a junker. He can pick me up in front of the Pushkin Museum in thirty minutes."

"You don't want to jockey this thing yourself, do you?"

"I sure don't. But I want to make sure our friend gives us a hundred percent instead of ninety."

"He won't do it, Bill. He won't go all the way. He can't afford to."

"Yes, he can," Delaney said. "He can't afford not to. I've got him by the short hair."

An hour later Delaney was thirty-five miles west of Moscow on the Leningrad Expressway, sitting in the backseat of a weathered gray Zhigulis, a brown leather satchel on the floor by his feet.

91. It was past one o'clock in the morning when Chad and Elena drove through Vyborg. They turned southwest along the coast, passed through Primorsk, and arrived at last in Valdagersk. By then it was nearly two o'clock.

Parking the car in the town lot, they walked south on the badly lighted road that followed the easy curve of Valdagersk Bay.

At twenty-five past two they found Muonio Smaga's boat tied up at his dock, the name *Vera* painted on the bow. And up the slope away from the water they saw the house Chad had described to Elena, the house Vera Smaga had described to him.

As they walked toward the house, Elena said, "I'm so scared I'm shaking."

"It's all right," Chad said. "Everything is just the way they said it would be."

"*That* scares me too."

"Don't worry. It's going to work."

"I don't know what to say to him," she said then.

"You don't have to say anything. I'll do it."

The shades were drawn at all the windows, but as they walked up the outside steps to the porch, they could see dim light from inside bleeding out around the edges of the shades.

At the door they froze for a moment, looking at each other in the dark, Elena trying not to tremble, Chad with his hand on her arm. At last he lifted his hand and knocked on the door.

Muonio Smaga was short and thick, a flat round face with raisin eyes, thin strands of hair half-covering his pale skull. He wore a heavy fisherman's sweater and stained pants shoved into rubber boots. He stood in the doorway, wedged there, it seemed, like a heavy section of tree trunk, studying Elena's face, and Chad's, and saying nothing.

After a long moment Chad said, "Tompkins Square."

Muonio stepped back from the doorway and motioned them inside.

As soon as the door was closed, he said in Russian, "Do you have the money?" Chad took a folded packet of rubles out of his pants pocket and handed it over. In his other pocket he had five hundred rubles for the Finn who would pick them up from Muonio's boat and carry them in another boat to the harbor at Hamina.

Muonio walked to the lamp and counted the rubles quickly in the yellow light. Then he said, "I have work to do to get my boat ready. We'll leave in an hour. There's vodka and bread on the table and a bed in the corner if you want it." Putting on a cap and jacket, he opened the door and clomped outside, across the wooden deck of his house, and down the steps to the sand.

"You shouldn't have given him the money," Elena said.

"Why not? That was the agreement."

"You should have waited till we were on the boat. He could go without us and leave us sitting here."

"We could burn his house down too, but we're not going to."

Chad sat by the window then, looking out around the edge of the shade. The dock light burned orange in the dark, and Muonio had turned on the running lights on his launch so he could see to wrestle the nets and fishing gear around on the afterdeck.

"It's a good-sized boat," Chad said to Elena. "A flying bridge and a cabin that must sleep two or three."

"Good," she said. "The bigger the better. The faster the better."

"It's not a cowboy movie. Nobody's going to chase us."

"I hope you're right."

At three thirty Muonio came back to the house and led them down to the boat. As soon as they were on board, he said, "There's a tarpaulin there on the fantail. Get under it and lie down."

"Can't we go down in the cabin?" Elena said.

"No. Under the canvas. Hurry up."

92. Delaney thought often of the last time he'd seen Mira Diomidov, the last hour they'd spent together in the hospital, when the doctors had allowed her to go home for five weeks and had then, on an hour's notice, rushed her back to the intensive care unit.

Through the months of her illness, the fire, the beauty, the famous energy, had all drained slowly out of her. Her skin tightened across her cheekbones, her eyes dulled and sank gradually deeper in their sockets, and the auburn hair lost its color and sheen. Even the long-fingered ivory hands, which could shatter an audience with a slow gesture, became only armatures for hands, fragile and translucent.

But the rare cello voice stayed pure and strong, defying the disease and deterioration, retaining its range and all its tones, whispering and fluting with warmth and humor and variety.

"I've wrecked you, Delaney," she said that last time they were together as he sat by the bed holding her cool hand. "I stole your soul like a Zulu who's had his picture taken.

"Remember the play I did two seasons ago? By the wild Romanian who wore lavender socks. Remember what that character said . . . Natalia was her name, wasn't it? It must have been. It's always *Natalia* when Romanians write about a Russian woman.

"She said, 'When I take you into my bed, when you sleep through the night with me, when you make love to a Russian woman, you *are* a Russian. You *become* a Russian.' Remember that speech, Delaney? That's what I've done to you. I crept inside you in the night and gave you a Russian heart.

"You'll go home to America some day and get old and white-haired and beautiful. And at last they'll bury you out there in those corn fields you showed me pictures of. But you will still be a Russian with Russian memories. I promise you that. With your Russian soul floating around somewhere in the American night."

Sitting in the gray Zhigulis at three thirty in the morning, parked on an empty hill above Valdagersk, looking across the dark town at the black expanse of sea stretching out to the south and the west, the lights of twenty or thirty fishing boats moving out of the harbor, one boat moving fast and powerful ahead of the others, Delaney thought of it again, that final time with Mira, the way her voice had sounded, the things she'd said to him, rough and warm and loving, stubbornly unsentimental. "You're Russian now, you bastard. I invented you. You're my homemade peasant. Dreamy and drunk and sweet and strong. And warm in the bed."

He had denied what she'd said through all the years since, denied it to himself. But all the while, like fluid taking the shape of its container, he knew that the man from Iowa and Washington, D.C., the lean and reckless drinking companion of Jack Kennedy and a hundred other people, had gradually worn away and vanished, leaving something neither fish nor fowl, neither young nor old, neither American nor Russian, but more Russian, much more, as Mira had promised him, than anything else.

93.

Making no effort to deceive, not slowing down or rigging nets or changing course, Muonio pushed the launch full ahead toward a point some twenty-five nautical miles southwest of Valdagersk and perhaps thirty nautical miles southeast of the port of Hamina in Finland.

It was Muonio's pattern. He followed the same course every day. Proceeded at the same speed. His launch was more powerful than the boats of the other Valdagersk fishermen. He fished farther out. The Soviet patrol boats knew him, knew his boat, and stopped him for inspection only on the scheduled inspection days.

An hour and twenty minutes out from Valdagersk, Muonio shut off his engine, dropped anchor, and began to feed out the close-corded nets he used, deep nets to pull in the fish his competitors didn't come out for, but small in dimension, those nets, so they could be lowered, winched, and gathered by one strong man working alone on a side-slipping boat in all weather.

As soon as the engines were quiet, Muonio walked to the afterdeck, to the tarpaulin that Chad and Elena were hiding under, and said, "Don't show yourselves yet. Helicopters fly over sometimes. I'll tell you when it's time to come out."

He worked with his nets then for almost a half-hour.

The dark had begun to break up in the east when he heard the sound of Erkko's boat coming down from the north, from Hamina.

When the stubby blue boat, two-thirds the length of Muonio's, eased alongside, Erkko tossed two lines across and Muonio lashed the launches loosely together. They stood prow to stern, side by side, on the glass-smooth early morning sea.

Elias Erkko came out of the below-decks galley of his boat with two mugs of coffee. He handed one across to Muonio and they stood wide-legged, each at the rail of his own launch, drinking coffee and talking their fisherman's language, an angular mix of Russian-tinged Finnish and Finnish-polluted Russian.

Erkko glanced toward the tarpaulin on Muonio's afterdeck, and Muonio nodded his head. He walked over then, lifted one corner of the canvas, and said, "Now. You can come out now."

When they came to the rail of the launch, Erkko, switching to schoolbook English, said, "Do you carry my money?"

Chad took out the packet of rubles and handed it to him. He flipped through the bills quickly and said, "Come. We leave now." He reached out and took Elena's arm as she climbed from one launch to the other with Chad just behind her.

Erkko had begun to pull up his anchor and Muonio was freeing the lines that held the two launches together when Pavel Lepik appeared suddenly behind him, just at the top of the gangway coming up from Muonio's cabin.

He had an automatic weapon in one hand and a brown leather satchel in the other. Pointing the gun at Muonio, he said, "You're going, too. Climb across to the other launch."

"What do you mean? You said . . ."

"Do it," Lepik said. "Right now."

"But it's not what you told me . . ."

"I know what I told you. Now I'm telling you something else."

Lepik came forward two steps and Muonio backed up, moved over to the railing, and climbed awkwardly across into the other boat. Lepik moved to the railing, then pointed the weapon at Erkko and said, "Start your engine. The rest of you sit down on the deck where I can see you."

Lepik waited till Erkko's engines were throbbing, the rush of water at the stern causing the restraining lines to creak, the two launches scraping and thumping against each other. Then he stepped up on the rail of the *Vera* and jumped across to the afterdeck of Erkko's launch. Still carrying the heavy bag in one hand, he said to Muonio, "Free the lines."

He threw the brown leather satchel across the railing then. It hit the afterdeck of Muonio's launch and slid almost to the gangway leading down to the cabin.

As Erkko's launch pulled away from the other boat, Lepik came close to him and shouted above the sound of the engine, "The faster you get away from here, the better off we'll be."

They were almost a mile away, the whole structure of the blue launch vibrating from the strain Erkko was putting on the engine, when Muonio's launch exploded behind them, a blinding white flash, a cloud of purple smoke, then a high-burning tower of red and orange flame against the early morning half-light.

94. From where Delaney stood, still on the ground-rise above Valdagersk, powerful binoculars up to his eyes, the east light behind him, the sea to the west was still wide and dark. When the launch exploded out beyond the horizon, it showed gold and scarlet against the blackness for just an instant, like a fire jewel.

Delaney took the glasses down from his eyes then, got into the backseat of the car, and said to the driver, "Let's go to Vyborg."

Thirty-five minutes later, in the Vyborg post office and telephone center, he gave the supervising operator the number of a pay phone on the docks in Hamina, Finland. She directed him to a booth and when she signaled with her hand he picked up the receiver. On the third ring Wes Buchanan answered.

"Is that you, Wes?"

"I think so. Why am I up so early?"

"You're lucky. I haven't been to bed yet."

"Where are we? All I know is Stabler told me to wait by this phone booth starting at three."

"We've got four orphans coming your way. Stabler's cleared everything with the Finns and the State Department, but I wanted you there to keep the pieces together. There's a Soviet citizen named Muonio Smaga. Looks like he'll be going to New York to live with his mama. And there's another Soviet citizen named Lepik. I *know*

he'll be going to the States because I promised him he
would. He's heard about San Diego. Thinks he'd like
to live there. You get him to Washington and Scruggs
will take over from there."

"You said four people. That's only two."

"Yeah . . . well, there's a couple of kids you don't have
to worry about. They've got the world by the tail. They
can go wherever they want to."

95. The following afternoon Delaney stood by a
sausage cart in an almost deserted park south of Pavelet-
sky Stadium in Moscow. He bought two sausages on sticks
and carried them down the winding path to a bench in
the shade surrounded by flowering bushes and dwarfed
trees. Viktor Denishev sat there on the bench holding a
plastic cup filled with red wine.

Delaney handed him one of the sausages. "It's not the
Praga," he said.

"*Nothing* is."

Delaney sat on the end of the bench, picked up his cup
of wine from the ground where he'd left it, and took
a sip.

"Do you like the Bulgarian wine?" he said.

"I prefer the Georgian."

"Have you tasted the wines from California?"

Denishev nodded. "Last year. When your secretary of
state visited the Kremlin."

"Some people say they're as good as any wines in the world."

"What do you say?"

"I disagree."

"So do I."

Denishev ate his sausage carefully, then tossed the stick into a trash container. Coming back to the bench, he sat down and said, "I don't think you asked me here to discuss California wines."

"Of course not," Delaney said. "The fact is I wanted to commend you."

"What have I done?"

"Not you so much as your government. The decision to release the prisoners. It was a fine gesture, I thought. Humane. A good example for other countries to see."

Denishev sipped his wine. Then he said, "Are you speaking for your government or for yourself?"

"I am never authorized to speak for the government. I'm speaking for myself."

"Then I will speak for myself," Denishev said. "I disapproved of that decision. I believe that convicted criminals must serve their sentences. Those people should not be released. Richardson should not have been released." He drank down the rest of his wine and wiped his mouth carefully with a blue handkerchief. Then he said, "Last time we talked we discussed the Chad Norris disappearance. I thought perhaps you wanted to talk about that again."

Delaney shook his head. "I don't know much about it. As it turned out I had nothing to do with that investigation. But I did hear his story when he spoke on television."

"So did I. Amnesia is a tragic thing. More common than most of us realize. And still we know very little about it."

"Did you believe his story?"

"Didn't you?"

"I'm not sure. Some people in our embassy found it hard to believe."

"Some people are frightened by the truth."

"You believed him then?" Delaney said.

Denishev nodded. "I believe that your investigators from Washington and the Moscow police would certainly have known if his story was *not* true. Although I was not personally involved any more than you were, I am told the investigation was thorough and complete. Hundreds of people were questioned. There was even a suspicion that Norris was involved in an adventure with a girl, a Soviet citizen."

Denishev took out a cigarette, offered one to Delaney, and lighted them both. "But that suspicion, I understand, was incorrect. They tell me the girl in question was killed in an accident the night before last. Trying to emigrate illegally to another country."

"What kind of accident?"

"A boat explosion in the Gulf of Finland."

They got up then and walked toward the park exit. Delaney said, "It must be an odd feeling for Chad Norris. Waiting to go back to America and realizing he's accomplished nothing he came over here to do."

Denishev gave him a sharp, quick look. Something flashed behind his eyes; he stopped walking suddenly, and it seemed he was about to speak. But he caught himself, buttoned his jacket carefully, and said very deliberately, "As I said, I believe his story. But even if I didn't it wouldn't matter. He was never my responsibility."

96.

Curt Gowdy, full-face on the television screen, said, "So the decathlon is over, the results are in, and Valderrama, the Cuban, has won. Mittag of East Germany takes the silver, and Klemenko, the favorite, has to settle for a bronze medal. A disappointing event, this 1980 decathlon. No new record and no answer to the question we were all asking, 'Just how good is Chad Norris?' "

"What's the answer?" Elena said. She and Chad were sitting in the lobby of the Hotel Stenvall in Helsinki, slouched down on a long couch, their feet up on a coffee table, watching the Olympic wind-up on television.

"The answer is . . . let's take a walk."

They stood up, crossed the lobby to the entrance, and strolled out into the street. The sun was bright, the day was clear and beginning to feel cool, some mid-August hint of autumn in the air.

"You didn't answer my question," she said.

"I missed it."

"No, you didn't. The man said, 'How good is Chad Norris?' "

"Abraham Lincoln said, 'A man's legs should be long enough to reach the ground.' George Bernard Shaw said, 'A man who sees the world as it is, is called a cynic by all the people who don't.' "

"What does that have to do with . . ."

"William Butler Yeats said, 'Cast a cold eye on life, on death. Horseman, pass by.' And some strange freak whose name I don't remember said, 'Here lies the major work of a minor artist . . . himself.' "

"I don't know what you're talking about."

"I'm saying I'm tired of Chad Norris. I've used him up. I'm putting him back in the box where I found him. It's a fake name and I always felt fake with it. I never felt at home. I wasn't living in my own skin."

"Then why . . ."

"Very simple. Your best question yet. I couldn't face being Dale Richardson. There were a lot of things I didn't want to be reminded of. And I didn't want anybody else to be reminded either. I want to crawl in a hole and disappear. And I almost did."

"Now what?"

"Who knows? First of all I'd like to stop running and walk a little. Or sit down. Or lie down maybe. I think I'll drink a few beers, take long naps, and go to the movies a lot. Stuff like that. Mostly I don't feel like pushing myself. No more training and sweating and running and jumping." He looked down at her. "Are you getting nervous? We may end up poor and hungry. Dale Richardson may turn out to be a hobo."

They turned the corner into a narrow twisting street and stopped. Each of them saw the same thing at the same instant. Just ahead of them was the old stone-and-timber hotel they'd found when they were in Helsinki in April. Elena started to laugh.

"Did you steer me here?"

"No," he said. "Did you steer me?"

"No. I could never have found it."

"What's so funny?"

"Nothing. It makes me happy just to look at it."

"One thing we don't need is another hotel," he said.

"That's true."

"I mean they've got us living in the fanciest hotel in Helsinki."

"No question about it."

"Who needs a run-down relic on a side street when you can stay in the . . . what's the name of it?"

"The Stenvall."

"Right. Who would pick this crummy place when they could sleep in the Stenvall?"

She looked up at him and said, "*I* would."

They crossed the street, went into the dark lobby, and filled out registration cards. As they walked up the narrow stairs to the top floor, Elena said, "What is a hobo? I don't know that word."

"A hobo is a bum, a dropout, a nonachiever. Hoboes go barefoot in the summer and sleep under bridges a lot."

"I like to go barefoot," she said. As they walked down the hall toward their room, she put her arm around his waist. "And I think I might like to sleep under a bridge."